T0354784

SAY YES

SAY YES

SIMONA SHARA

ARCHWAY
PUBLISHING

Archway Publishing books may be ordered through booksellers or by contacting:

Archway Publishing
1663 Liberty Drive
Bloomington, IN 47403
www.archwaypublishing.com
844-669-3957

ISBN: 978-1-6657-3977-1 (sc)
ISBN: 978-1-6657-3978-8 (hc)
ISBN: 978-1-6657-3979-5 (e)

Library of Congress Control Number: 2023904092

Print information available on the last page.

Archway Publishing rev. date: 03/30/2023

If I speak in the tongues of men or angels, but do not have love, I am only a resounding gong or a clanging cymbal
—1 Corinthians 1:13

JULY 28, 2018
LAS VEGAS, NEVADA

Tick ... tock ... tick ... tock ... tick ... Second by second. Tick ... tock ... tick ... Time appears to have slowed or even halted ... I can feel my breathing, hear my heartbeat, and see the blood flowing through my veins. And that sound is stuck in my head: tick ... tock ... tick ... It's a clock, I realize through the fog.

His voice echoes off the walls.

It's as if I have my eyes open, but I can't see anything. Am I closing them? Extremely uncomfortable, hard, and cold. Is that me on the floor? I put my hand on the surface and think I'm lying on the tiles. Tick ... tock ... tick ... tock ...

I want to say something, but all I can do is gargle or imagine I'm gargling. I'm tired, and my eyelids are heavy. Maybe it's one of those realistic dreams I have when I sleep and dream. Tick ... tock ... tick ...

God, why are you so loud? And the darkness returns, floating, nauseous, and aching. Something is going on around me. I try to turn my head and move my arms. I'm not sure why I can't, but it appears that my body is rising in the air and moving. Yes, it appears that I am flying. The darkness returns. I hear nothing, and everything flows out.

I open my eyes and look around at the movement. Do you talk

to me? I see the outlines of a person, but the image is very faint. I take off again in the air and land on a stray cloud. It was so simple to leave. I close my eyes, desperate to sleep.

As the temperature drops, the sensations worsen. I touch the other person's hot body. Oh my goodness, he's naked. I try to move, but I'm immobile, like a stone. I finally open my eyes and see white teeth, dark, red eyes, and a collarbone tattoo. That solemn expression splits me in half. I want to cry and scream as if I'm tearing myself and humanity apart, but I can't move.

I hear him sniffing and saying, "Beauty, do you like that?" He kisses my lips, my body, my breasts, and I lie helpless, crying silently. One stroke, two strokes, three strokes …

With a sniff in my ear, the rhythm accelerates steadily. There is a lot of pain, stinging, and burning there. *No, no, no, no!* I exclaim in my head. I cry and scream, "Please, help, someone!" My crotch hurts a lot, and I'm about to be overwhelmed by the horror I witnessed. And then there is darkness …

Again, that vexing tick … tock …

Let's take a look. It's bright outside. I'm half-dressed in a bed in a luxurious room. A strange man is lying on my stomach next to me. I stare at his features for a long time before returning to thoughts from the night before. We went out to have fun with my coworkers for the first time in three months. It was my birthday party, and I put on the most beautiful dress I'd ever worn. It was great fun. One club changed to another, and we danced to insanity. I drank another cosmopolitan and danced some more. Later, the bartender brought me another cocktail, but I said I didn't order it. He pointed to a group of men and stated that it was their gift. My mind was disconnected after drinking that cocktail. I have no recollection of how I got here or where I am. The only memory I have is of being unable to move and being raped by this man. The resurrected memories make me shudder. I roll out of bed quietly, my crotch and thighs covered in dried blood, my panties ripped in half. In that place, I feel even more ashamed. I realize that my virginity is no longer with me—but not in the way I had hoped.

She is guilty herself.

I gather the last of my self-esteem, tidy up the dress, grab my shoes, and walk quietly to the door. I find myself in the hallway, which is just as luxurious as the room. I dash into the elevator and see how horrible I look. My big green eyes are even bigger and red, my pupils have widened, my mascara has run away, and my long, dark brown hair were plucked out from hair bun. My lips have been bitten, but the outline of my red lipstick is still visible. In places, my short silver gown is smeared with blood. I shake off the view and think, *Luka, you are fantastic. What would Grandma have to say? "What did you expect if you dressed like a whore? You fall asleep as you lie down." My father would probably kill me if he found out what disgrace I have brought upon our family.*

The elevator enters the lobby. I stretch quietly. There are still some party lions and late casino visitors walking around. I'm still at Caesar's Palace. We went the club to have some fun with the girls. I shudder as I approached the front door in the warm mist of dawn.

Yes, this is me: a raped young woman. I am Luka Ilgauskaitė, a fourth-year business management student from Vilnius University, and I have just turned twenty-three years old. Through the Erasmus program, I have been given an incredible opportunity to travel to America to continue my studies. Yeah, all that sounds pretty bad to me—and it doesn't appear to be for me either.

CHAPTER ONE

LUKA

"Luka, wake up. Some minutes after seven. You will be late for the first lecture!" Elle said.

Elle's annoying voice drives me insane.

Eleonora, my best friend since kindergarten, is a green-eyed, red-haired, freckled, and very slender girl who flutters nonstop. My polar opposite. We'll be together for the rest of our lives. My sister Agnes is sometimes envious of our friendship. We grew up together, went to kindergarten and school together, sat on the same bench, and lamented Elle's never-ending first loves. At Vilnius University, I majored in business management, and Elle majored in in interior design. Elle's parents are very wealthy, so she doesn't have to study hard, but I am constantly worried about losing my scholarship. We applied for the Erasmus program at Elle's urging, and we found ourselves in America. Elle traveled around the country for three months after we arrived, and I got a job in Las Vegas with other exchange students. We worked at the Bellagio, cleaning the hotel rooms after their frantic parties. I had to clean the sunken floor several times, but I was pleased with my efforts and the reward I received. Everything changed *that night*, but I kept quiet about it.

After that heinous incident, I no longer loved Las Vegas or my job. I no longer wanted to look at those happy and intoxicated faces. That morning, I decided to quit my job at the hotel and return to Chicago, and I found work at Old Vilnius, a Lithuanian restaurant. "Elle, give me five minutes. My shift at the restaurant only ended four hours ago." I was comforted despite the fact that I am mortally tired.

"Don't be concerned. After all, I stated that you would have to give up overtime, and now you work nonstop. After all, we live in a dorm, you have a scholarship, and can afford to unwind."

"OK, Eleonora. I'm getting up. You can be a lot like my mother at times."

I really miss my mom. I long for Lithuania. I haven't seen my parents, sister, or brother in more than six months. I'm not sure when I'll see them again. I don't have enough money to fly home whenever I want.

My parents, who are from the middle class, live in a small town in Western Lithuania. Living in a small town has its advantages and disadvantages. Everyone quickly finds out if someone dies, marries, makes trouble, or does something else. The local shops, the beauty salon where the same hairdresser has been working since I started walking, the post office, and the municipal building are the main tongue centers in the small town. Everyone knows each other well, friends and foes alike. In the event of a disaster, the entire town comes together and helps one another, but after a few weeks, everyone is alienated again. My parents own a small horse farm and spin in the same manner as the squirrels. They make every effort to ensure that nothing is missing for their kids.

When my dad found out I was going to America to further my education, he was overjoyed. My sister Agnes, three years older me, relocated to the coast with her husband and twin daughters. I realize that I am jealous of my loneliness and the opportunity to achieve my goal at times, but she has chosen an early family life for herself. Nobody cares about the firstborn son, Arn; sometimes he returns home to see our parents, and sometimes he vanishes for a month or more. I have no idea what he does, where he is, or how makes money. My father does not speak to Arn at all, claiming that he is embarrassed to have raised such nonsense. When I am in the family room, I always avoid annoying my parents; after all, I am proud of them right now.

"Luka, are you here? Hello? Did you hear what I say?" Elle asked, returning me to reality.

"No ... what? Yes, forgive me. I was thinking about my family. What did you say?"

"I said you look really bad. When was the last time you ate or slept normally?" asked Elle.

"I do eat normally, and lack of sleep is only this week because I'm working double shifts. Rodriguez got sick, and I have to replace him."

Rodriguez is an excellent work partner. He is a dark-eyed, black-haired, broad-shouldered guy who is always in a good mood and has a good sense of humor. He is not afraid of poking fun at himself or others. A short beard and a bun tied at the top of his head make him look more like an Italian mafia member than a University of Chicago photography student. Rodriguez immigrated to the United States from Chile after his father won a green card in a lottery. I met him as soon as I arrived in Chicago, and I am grateful to have made another wonderful friend with whom I can discuss anything: art, work, family, politics, and so on. We usually work one shift together in the restaurant.

"I think you like Rodriguez more than I do," Elle said as she pushed me with her elbow.

"I'm not even thinking. You know I'm not looking for a relationship. I want to finish my studies, get a diploma, and find a job that I enjoy. I don't want to be a waitress or a maid for the rest of my life."

"Your truth, indeed. This beautiful body is too lovely to be enslaved." My red-haired friend lifted me up as usual.

I gazed out the subway window at the passing images. Chicago is a windy city that never sleeps or is silent. The sensation of landing at Chicago O'Hare International Airport was unrivaled: the crowds, the hustle and bustle, and the hundreds of different nationalities and races. I remember getting off the plane, squeezing the backpack firmly against me, and keeping Elle in sight; my first steps on American soil were so tentative. It was terrifying and thrilling; for the first time in my life, I felt completely free and independent. For a moment, I thought I, Luka Ilgauskaitė, would conquer America. But I didn't conquer it, and America forced me to do so on that fateful night of July 28. Forty-four days have passed since that event, and I still have trouble falling asleep at night, and when I do, I have nightmares. The sound of an old clock ticking and the smell of that man linger in my mind. It was the scariest experience of my life, but I can't blame anyone but myself for it.

Every night, I remember crying as I packed my suitcase and drove to Chicago. I resurrect all of the feelings that surrounded that moment: hatred for myself, hatred for him, and hatred for the rest of the world. It took a week for me to lick my wounds and get my hands on it, allowing me to walk down the street alone and call my family or Elle. Elle was still on the East Coast, and she had no idea what had happened to me. I got a new job and pretended everything was fine until she returned to the dorm. I still live with great shame and mystery. I can't even tell Elle because she'll start blaming herself for abandoning me.

I looked up at the passing skyscrapers and rejoiced in Chicago's grandeur.

"We've arrived at our destination. When will the lectures end?" Elle, as usual, twisted her red hair carelessly and chewed her gum loudly.

"At five today. I'll then go to the restaurant because I have an evening shift. I'll be late and may not be able to wait."

"Lu, I said this the morning that you look tired. I'm very concerned about you. When you returned from Vegas, you started working like a bull. You need to take a vacation." Elle resembled of a four-year-old girl when her mother asked for something.

"Don't look at me that way. Rodriguez is still ill, and the burden is great," I said.

The only way to forget is to work.

SEPTEMBER 14, 2018
CHICAGO

Finally, it's Friday. I finished the shift at work and started dreaming about stretching my legs in bed because I don't have to work this weekend. I need to write one piece and call my parents, but I'm still avoiding them. On the way home, I headed to Walmart and grabbed chips, candy, Oreos, popcorn, orange juice, and frozen pizza. I got back to the dorm at nine o'clock.

Elle and Martin, a guy from Latvia, went to the jazz festival in Millennium Park. No matter how much I love this style of music, fatigue has taken over. Maybe I will be rested enough tomorrow to listen to jazz, but right now, I will fall into bed, join the third season of *Teen Wolf*, and disconnect from the outside world.

Tick … tock … tick … tock … Hot breathing and turning to me … "Mari!"

"Oh my God, let me go, save me, someone, please!" I'm trying to push, but his body is not moving.

"Mari … Mari … beautiful Mari …"

I shout, "I'm not Mari. I'm Luka. Let me go please."

I open my eyes, and his eyes look like charcoal. His long, dense lashes tickle my cheek, my chin, and my jaw. He has a sleek, Greek-shaped nose and rough, pale eyes. I don't understand why I was shaken by that pain. I shed tears.

■ ■ ■

"Luka, wake up. Luka, wake up. You're dreaming."

I hear Elle's voice through the fog, open my eyes, and try to adjust to the lighting in the room. I still hear the clock in that room at Caesar's Palace.

"You scared me!" I said.

"And why did you sleep in your clothes? And with that trash?" A bunch of chips and candy wrappers are around me.

"And who is Mari? You kept repeating her name."

"I probably fell asleep watching the series. I don't know who she is ... maybe an actress in the series. What time is it?" It was still dark outside.

"Half past four in the morning, and I'm offended like a dog. Why did I wear these high heels?" She dropped her dirty heels on the floor.

"I did say the Converses were the best option for going to the festival." I collected all the items from the bed and placed them under the blanket.

"Yes, I understand this lesson. Don't lecture me." Elle collapsed on the bed.

"Elle, how was your date?" I asked.

"I laid a solid international foundation," Elle said with a smile. The guy most likely made a good impression.

Elle fell asleep within seconds. Her makeup will look charming when she wakes up.

■ ■ ■

A bright and dim light starts filtering through the dormitory window. I stare at the wall until the sun comes up. I am being driven insane by self-pity. I can't deal with my feelings about that night and that beast. It's strange, but a part of me wishes I could see that man again and ask him why he did what he did. I roll from side to side, trying to recall what happened. Why didn't I remember half the night. These thoughts do not make me feel better. Were there drugs in that drink? Who could have placed them on me? No, it was enough to live through that horrible day. Perhaps today will be better than yesterday.

I stayed in bed until nine o'clock in the morning.

Elle slept with her mouth open, and saliva was running down her lips. I couldn't control myself, and I took a few photos and a few selfies of us. I made one of the amusing photos the cover of her phone and giggled on my way to the cafe for breakfast. The beautiful weather was ideal for a long walk. It reminded me of summer in Lithuania.

I missed my homeland, but I was really enjoying the opportunity to live and study abroad. I knew it was an opportunity to achieve something more in my life than I would have achieved in Lithuania. Every day boosted my self-confidence. I knew I was lucky, and the people around me would be proud of me—despite the shameful event that I hoped would never come to light.

As usual, I ordered pancakes with maple syrup and a cup of strong coffee. I ate every piece of the pancakes and drank my coffee without rushing. The rich flavor of Lithuanian coffee could never be replicated in America, but you have to be content with what you have, right?

After an hour, I decided to pay a visit to Rodriguez and bring him some hot broth. I stood at his door for forty-five minutes with a bag of goodies, knocking as loudly as I could.

Rodriguez answered the door with a blanket and tangled hair. His eyes were red and teary, and he almost passed out at my feet.

"You look awful, mate," I said. "You must love me a lot because I brought warm chicken broth and delicious buns." I smiled as I picked up the shopping bags.

"You're amazing." He opened the door and invited me inside.

I tidied up his house while he was eating the broth. The room had been a mess for at least a week, and the dirty dishes no longer fit in the kitchen sink. Although it was unnecessary to speculate on the peculiarities of Rodriguez's lonely life, he was a guy. Elle flips our dorm room five times faster than Rodriguez does.

"Lu, I owe you my life." He chewed his food. "I haven't eaten normal food for days. You are so understanding."

"You forgot to mention that I cleaned your house. Rodriguez, your house only needs snakes." I laughed.

"Chica, you're a real angel. My parents will come over tonight." He sighed. "This morning, I thought about how to tidy the room, but it turned out to be a mission impossible."

"What about the turkey that thought—but then he got into the pot because he thought for too long?"

"Very funny." He sat down on the couch and tied his blanket tighter. "How are things at work? Very tired of working for yourself and me?"

"No, everything is fine," I said. "You'd help me if I had to, right?"

He covered his eyes with the blanket, showing that he would not sacrifice as much for me.

"Besides a very good tip, I'm not really complaining." I smiled and threw my pillow at him.

"I think I'll be back at work after the weekend. Let's watch football." He tapped his hand on the cushion.

We watched a football game and some movies, ordered a pizza, and waited for Elle. She had decided to spend time with friends that night. When his parents arrived, Elle, and I went to the jazz festival. We took an Uber to the park. We visited the Chicago Bean for the hundred time and took some good shots in its reflection. A small child splashed in the fountains, and we rushed over to the sorbet vendor. After eating our ice cream, we rolled closer to the stage, fell on the grass, and listened to good modern jazz.

I dedicated Sunday to communicating with my relatives. Mom kept telling me how the household was doing. A teacher had gotten pregnant by some bad-looking guy, and there was no hotter topic in the town. My mother was so interested in the mistakes of others, but only the devil knew what her own son was doing. She kept saying that her daughter—her pride—would never ever end up in such a shameful situation, and my father agreed with her. I listened and blushed. I had always thanked God for not getting pregnant my first time, which I didn't even remember. I didn't know if it was safe or not.

A good hour later, my mom told a story about her mother-in-law. Her grandson was going astray because she had recovered from her mother's family. My mom splashed coffee on the table and threw her cup. If I agreed with my mother, my father would say that I would have to go home to the village! My mother was angry that I valued her father's kinship more than hers. I finally went to bed. I had a headache for two hours and thought it was enough to be a good daughter who absorbs everything like a sponge. At twenty-three years old, I was still scared of my parents.

When Arn grew up, he never listened to our parents. He was not afraid of his father, and he did everything contrary to what he was told. Agnes married as soon as the opportunity arose, barely finishing twelfth grade, and she drove to a city that was far away from our parents. I was the good daughter who was always around. I always shrugged when my parents scolded me. I humbly and obediently carried out all their commands. I only went out to dance with my classmates when I was eighteen years old. My parents never had a problem with me or my behavior.

I always wanted my sister and brother to love me. Arn was always angry with me. I sometimes felt like a leper. I cried so many times that he didn't love me. Agnes was older and more beautiful than I was, and she cared more about her social life, her friends, and going out and having fun. She still found time for me. While I was growing up, I was plump, crooked, and scary. For many years, I wore braces. Most of the classmates made fun of me, but Agnes and Elle always protected me.

Everything changed when I started to mature. I became more feminine. I had a beautiful figure from my hard work on my parents' farm,, and I had long legs. My big green eyes fit perfectly on my small face, and my lips were naturally plump. My classmates began to show more attention, but I was focused on my studies and becoming an independent woman. I would be led by my parents, friends, and husband—if I had one—in the future. Dreams sometimes remain dreams. I had succumbed to the influence of people around me and was very angry about not being able to say no.

When I was a child, I wanted to dance. I was taken to a dance school. I was angry that my parents wouldn't let me go to a foreign star's concert because the tickets were very expensive. My dad wouldn't let me go to dance lessons because they cost fifty-five litas per month. I cried so much, but what else could I have done? When I was sixteen, my parents didn't allow me to go on a tour with the class that had been planned for six months.

We were supposed to go to Latvia to visit Rundale Castle and the seaside, but Arn disappeared for the whole summer. I had to take over my brother's work on the farm. That was how my life was. My only consolation was Elle and the horses. I'd been riding since childhood. Whether the horse had been ridden or not, it gave in to my desire to ride. I had my secret place near the house, by the lake. When I was sad, I went there wrote or read a book. My childhood was lonely.

When I arrived in Chicago, I saw a different life. People were spinning in their routines and walking down the streets with smiles on their faces. Everyone was in a hurry, but they were happy. They were not hiding in their shells. I began to realize that I didn't love myself, and I found myself being pushed like a chess piece. I began to grow spiritually. I made new friends and became an observer of the world around me. Coming to America broadened my horizons and inspired a desire to be different.

These reflections usually visited me when I was writing in my diary, and when I finished reading the last words in it, my enthusiasm for living was hidden deep in the drawer. I stayed in bed and dreamed that things would change someday. After doing some writing, I watched the series again. I am an endless girl from Lithuania, believing in a better future.

CHAPTER TWO

SEPTEMBER 17, 2018

Fall flows easily into the streets of Chicago without asking anyone. It's still warm outside, cicadas are chirping in the evenings, and it's already dark at seven o'clock in the evening. Such weather in Lithuania would be more reminiscent of summer, but here, instead of four seasons, there are only two seasons left—although everyone says that the weather will change a lot in November. Rodriguez, and I walk easily from the subway to the restaurant. We'll both be working the same evening shift today, so it's going to be a fun and cozy evening.

"Have you written the English essay you talked about last week?" Rodriguez was photographing the illuminated street as we walked. Lately, he has rarely parted with the camera.

"Yes," I answered. "I hope the evaluation will be satisfactory. English grammar is definitely not my forte." I half smiled and watched the cars rolling down the streets. Those stop signs at intersections instead of traffic lights and wide streets still seem strange to me. Here, one part of the road is equal to an entire Lithuanian road.

"Everything will be fine, chica. You are a diligent student. By the way, have you already thought about your future internship?"

Rodriguez suddenly turned and took a picture of my stupid facial expression.

"Stop! Don't take pictures of me when I'm not ready!" I always look three times fatter than I really am in photos. Although I fully understand that I have a rather slender figure at seventy-two centimeters tall, my childhood complexes took a toll. "I don't know about practice yet. I have written several inquiries to well-known fashion companies and fashion magazines, and I hope that some of them will accept me as an intern. How about you?" I happily ate the last bite of the chocolate bar.

"I will do an internship at the Filterphoto Gallery. Remember when we visited that gallery in August? The owner of the gallery is very friendly with students and willingly agreed to accept interns."

"Yes, I remember." About a dozen cars were parked near the restaurant. People crowded the restaurant, waiting to be served, and the staff barely had time to rotate between the tables. I nudged Rodriguez with my shoulder. "Well, the shift is starting. It's time for dinner, my friend."

"Of course it is, chica." Rodriguez's tinny laugh was drowned out by the commotion in the street.

SEPTEMBER 19, 2018

I put on a happy expression and hit the video call button. One beep. The second beep. The third beep.

"Hello, Mom. How are you?" I blurted out the words in the thinnest possible voice.

"Well, finally the little girl has appeared." That accusing tone again. "We finished the farmwork. The horses are provided with fodder for the winter. Your father is as angry as ever, like a hundred devils, everything is wrong with him, so I move around corners just to disagree." That sigh again. It seems that I am the only one who can save my mother from my father's psychological terror. "And how are you doing?"

"I'm fine." If you can call this stage of regret good. "I am studying, working, looking for a place to practice. So far, I have not received any response to the letters I have written regarding the practice. How is Agnes? I saw on Facebook that she and her family were on an excursion around Trakai?" Lithuania in the autumn is enchanting. The castle of Trakai and the golden leaves of the trees captivate my eye and soothe my heart. I miss that view and the autumn nights when the yard smells of apples.

"It was there that they brought the *kibins*. Agnes started a family early and now lives happily in Lithuania, not wandering around the world. Maybe it's time for you to squat, find a normal man, start a family, and give birth to some beautiful children." My mother looked into my eyes and continued her tirade about the importance of family and marriage. "You don't even have to look far. Remember my friend Adele's son Tom? He grew up a serious man, opened a car service in Klaipėda, and is still single. Think carefully. And now you have gone somewhere far away. We miss you. And your father is calmer when you are home."

Of course, it doesn't get any quieter when there's another head to yell at. I can't say I don't love my dad—I really do—but his constant yelling drives me crazy. I remember how I was waiting to go study in Vilnius—where peace would surround me. I wouldn't go home for several weekends in a row just to take a break from the endless conflicts at home. Of course, it was a pity for my mother. She alone had to listen to my father's ramblings about neighbors, friends, and non-friends. He raged about us, how ungrateful children we are, about me, and how I am a good-for-nothing woman. In my twenty-three years of life, I have heard everything. There may have been a period in childhood when my father was a happy person, but it was very short and blurry.

"Mom, don't start preaching about the family again. I'm still young. I want to finish my studies, establish myself at work, and achieve something. Only then will I think about a husband and children." It's the same topic every time. I understand my parents are worried about my studies. No matter how hard they try, they transfer money to me every month. "Anyway, I don't know if I want to start a relationship."

"Luka, don't make us sad with such words. And that's enough trouble with Arn." My mom sighed.

And again Arn? How different! He is the main topic of conversation between my mother and me. "What did Arn do now?"

"Arn inherited your grandfather's ways. He's hot-tempered. He hasn't grown out of adolescence in any way." Mother moved closer to the camera and whispered, "Do you remember Arn's friend Paul?"

"Yes, of course, I remember. What happened?" I was curious.

"Paul offered Arn a kind of business plan to transport luxury cars from abroad through Lithuania to farther abroad. In the beginning, it was really good. They earned a nice amount of money, as Arn says, *babkies*." Mother laughed. "Even your father was in a better mood, and he started talking to Arn. But where are you? The men ran to some club in Vilnius. What is his name there?" Mother closed her eyes and tried to remember his name. "Well, where is it often shown on TV?"

"*Metelica?*" I guessed.

"Yes, that's it. In other words, both of them got drunk and sat down to drink at the wheel. It's good that Arn wasn't driving." My mother sighed. "He wrecked a car—some kind of expensive sports car. That one burned, and only a pile of metal remained. Paul is now at Santaros Hospital with broken pelvic bones, and Arn paid for it with a head injury. He now walks like he has sold the Earth."

"The car wasn't theirs?"

"Of course not." My mother looked at me as if I were completely naive. "They took it from some mobster. They are now in such debt." Mother burst into tears.

I was heartbroken too.

"The most important thing is that they are alive. Just don't tell your father that I told you. This topic is taboo at home—and so he is angry with his son."

"Well, it's understandable that he's angry. Arn always wants to slide through life without doing anything hard. And he doesn't think at all that by acting so irresponsibly, he is causing trouble for himself and for all of us." I was very angry.

"I wish I didn't hear such talk. Shame! The brother tried, but he made a mistake." My mother blushed with anger. Arn was her firstborn, her beloved, and I had never heard her say anything is my brother's fault when he earns money. According to my mother, her son never does anything wrong. It is always someone else's fault.

"OK, Mom, I don't have time to talk. I have to go to my lecture. Send wishes to the housemates. Bye." I turned off the Skype app and slumped into my chair. *And why isn't my family like everyone else? We're the real Addams Family.*

The lectures flew by. During my lunch break, I ran to Starbucks for a cup of hot black coffee. I wouldn't call it coffee by any means, but habits take a toll.

Not coffee, but shit. I frowned when the phone in my backpack started ringing.

Strange number. American.

Well, American of course, you fool. You're in America after all.

Even my conscience mocked me. I was such a naive and gullible country girl. I hit the reply button and said, "Luka is listening."

"Good afternoon, Miss Luka. You have submitted a request for an internship opportunity at Fashion Icon. I am Anna Moss, head of the HR Department. Still interested in doing an internship with us?"

"Yes, really interested." I didn't even feel how hard I squeezed the coffee cup, but the coffee started pouring over the edges.

"That's very nice to hear, Miss Luka. Can you come to our office tomorrow at three in the afternoon?"

"Of course I can. And when I arrive, where do I go next?"

"Enter the lobby and introduce yourself to the building

supervisor. He will direct you to the right floor. Please have your personal documents and study program with you."

"Got it. Thank you for calling," I said.

"Have a good rest and see you tomorrow, Miss Luka."

Yes, yes, yes, at least one problem is solved. I started jumping in the middle of the street. I was overcome with euphoria. *I practically have the internship in my hand—if I don't mess up the interview. And what should I wear? I need a friend's advice.*

I quickly texted Elle:

> *Luka: Elle, can you believe what a good day today is?*
> *Elle: What happened? Tell me xoxo.*
> *Luka: I got an internship offer—not just anywhere, but guess where?*
> *Elle: Luka, I swear, if you don't tell me yourself, I'll beat you!*
> *Luka:* ☺ ☺ ☺
> *Elle: Lu, I'm taking you off my besties list* ☺.
> *Luka: All right, all right. I'm going to interview for an internship at Fashion Icon tomorrow. I really didn't expect them to answer. I have nothing to wear!*
> *Elle: Seriously? Cool. Do you still have lectures? Xoxo.*
> *Luka: One more lecture, and that's it. Why do you ask?*
> *Elle: How? Why? Meet me at TJ Maxx on Michigan Avenue in an hour?*
> *Luka: By the old pier?*
> *Elle: Yes, there. In an hour—and don't be late xoxo.*

OK, a wardrobe update is long overdue. Anyway, I don't really care what I wear. I never followed fashion because I didn't have money to buy new clothes. I usually dress in Elle's old clothes because we are very similar. I also buy things in thrift stores. I came to America with one suitcase, and it was packed with what I needed every day. I definitely can't go to a job interview in ripped jeans and sneakers.

After the lecture, I rushed to the subway, and fifteen minutes later, I was walking along Lake Michigan, toward the old pier.

"Luka, wait!"

"Where are you going in such a hurry?"

"To you, you fool." Elle hugged me and started jumping like a little child.

"OK, that's enough. Are you in a good mood today?" I pushed my friend away and looked at her from head to toe. She glowed strangely.

"Yes. Today is a good day for me too." Elle smiled stupidly and looked hopeful.

"Eleonora Gedvilaite, are you in love?" I pushed my friend to the side, and we walked toward the pier.

We visited three stores and finally went to Macy's. After much searching, I bought a peach business dress, a beautiful emerald skirt, black pants, and a few blouses. Elle also convinced me that I definitely need new shoes with a small heel or a platform. I had to buy several pairs of shoes that I could adapt to all styles. I spent $570 on my new wardrobe. It still hurts my heart that I spent the money I was saving for the car on such unnecessary purchases.

Well, I still have to go for a walk.

To celebrate my first interview, Elle suggested drinking wine and pampering myself with girly procedures. For the rest of the evening, Elle, and I made each other beautiful, had fun spouting nonsense, and tasted cheap wine from a box. When I ran out of words, I fell into a restless sleep. That night, I dreamed of that man from the hotel room.

SEPTEMBER 20, 2018

This morning started as usual: Elle did not respond to my call to get up, she slept through her first lecture, and she woke up running from corner to corner, cursing everyone around her, except herself. While searching for her notes, she fell over twice, tripped over her bag, and ended up kicking the bag into a corner. Her notes fell out. She shouted, "Done, I'm running my bean," and she left for her lecture. If I didn't know Elle, I would be really worried about her mental state.

I allowed myself to miss lectures today because:

a. I am a diligent student, and I turn in all my work on time.
b. I have additional points for active postgraduate activities.
c. I informed the curator of my program that I will have an interview, and she wrote an excuse note for me.

What can I say? Well done. I feel practically an adult.

Luka, pull yourself together. You are an independent adult. You are about to graduate and start a full adult life. Pull yourself together!

I looked at my reflection in the mirror: dark brown hair falling in loose curls over my shoulders, big green eyes, and plump lips. I add another coat of mascara, a peachy dress that perfectly accentuates my brown skin, and heels that elongate my legs. I spritzed on my favorite Victoria's Secret amber and honey body mist, threw on my jacket, applied lip gloss, and took a deep breath. Well, here it is: the first serious step toward the job I want.

The Fashion Icon's main office was located in the heart of Chicago, in the Willis Tower. Rodriguez, and I once went up to the glass observation decks on the 104th floor. Looking through the building's wide glass balconies, the entire skyline of Chicago opened up: skyscrapers, Lake Michigan, the Chicago Eye, and planes taking off and landing. Being up there, I felt so powerful, but here on the ground, I felt more like a simple ant.

I entered the lobby, which looked impressive: dark marble floors and gray-hued walls, light furniture of nonstandard shapes, and modern works of art. It all caught the eye.

A tall, gray-haired man with soft features and rosy cheeks greeted me with a big smile. "Good afternoon, miss. How can I help you?"

"Good day. Can you tell me which floor the Fashion Icon office is on? I got a call yesterday from Ms. Anna Moss from human resources, and she invited me for an interview." I blurted it all out in one breath and with such an eerie accent that the look on that sweet gentleman's face made me think he didn't understand anything.

"Oh yes, Miss Luka with a very strange last name. Mrs. Moss left you a visitor's card. Please take it." He handed me a beautiful visitor card. "Please, miss, follow me. You will need to go up to the 101st floor."

I was escorted to the elevator. We exchanged a few pleasantries about the weather and traffic before the elevator doors opened, and before I could catch myself, the elevator stopped on the 101st floor. The lobby was even more chic. A massive wooden receptionist's desk faced the elevator. Behind the table was a beautiful blonde in a perfect black suit. Behind her was a stone-decorated wall; water was cascading from the ceiling, creating the illusion of a waterfall. The walls were light, making the rooms seem three times larger than they actually were.

I approached the table, and the girl sitting there didn't even pay attention to me.

"Good day. I have an appointment with Mrs. Anna Moss at three o'clock."

The blonde raised her carefully powdered face and looked at me indifferently. For the first time in my life, I regretted not wearing name-brand clothes.

"Good day. Sit down. You will be invited soon." She did not even bother to show me where to sit, and she continued to read her gossip magazine.

OK, blondie. I'll sit down. Thanks.

I found a U-shaped couch and sat on it. Perfectly beautiful girls, wearing chic suits or dresses, walked past me. All their shoes had pointed toes and thin heels. The whole office echoed as their heels hit the marble floor. I started to feel sick because I realized that I didn't fit in there—and I never would. My place was definitely not in a company that cares about the winds of fashion, promotes the latest clothing collections of the most famous designers, and organizes spectacular fashion shows. *What was I thinking when I applied for an internship at such a famous company?*

"Miss Luka Ilgauskaitė? It is very nice to see you here."

I flinched when I heard my name.

A beautiful middle-aged lady approached me. She was at least ten centimeters taller than me, was slimmer, and had flawlessly smooth skin and bleached, short, tousled hair. Her blue eyes shone with tenderness. She wore white wide-leg pants, a loose linen blouse, and Louboutin shoes.

"Go-o-od mor-ning." I started stuttering at the right time and right on the spot.

"I'm Anna Moss." She held out her graceful hand with a perfect French manicure. My nails had never looked so perfect. "Please, let's go to my office." She turned to the receptionist and said, "Serafina, enough reading gossip. Bring a couple of cups of black coffee. Thank you."

I hastily followed Mrs. Anna into her office. It was white and spotlessly clean—and my eyes hurt from the cleanliness. Through the glass wall behind Anna's desk, I could see the skyline of Chicago. I was impressed.

Anna motioned to the white modern chair in front of her desk. "So, Luka, tell me about yourself." Anna looked me over from head to toe.

And that appraising look again? *Don't pass out, Luka.* "About myself? I am twenty-three years old, and I came here from Lithuania. I am in my final year as a business management student—"

"Stop, stop, Luka. I already read all this in your application. Tell me about your hobbies, friends, and family. Everything is interesting to me." Anna made herself more comfortable in her chair.

The receptionist walked through the door and almost hissed, setting down a tray with a couple of cups of black coffee and cream.

"Thanks, Serafina. You can go ahead and blow your brains out in the gossip section."

Serafina's complexion turned from an excess of matte to purple.

I thought, *I'm going to start stomping around like a little kid and squealing in displeasure.* At that moment, I realized I might fit in there after all.

"I am the third child in my family. I have an older brother, Arn, who is thirty-two years old, and a sister, Agnes, who is twenty-six years old. Arn still can't find a place under the sun. He gets involved in all kinds of fights and serious business matters. Agnes has already created her own family. She is raising twins at the moment." I smiled as I remembered her little girls. "My parents are simple small farmers. They worked hard all their lives, and we also had to taste hard work. I am the first in my family to graduate with honors and continue my studies. My mother loves her children and wishes them well, but she sometimes takes care of them too much, damaging the health of herself and her children."

I sighed and wondered how much more to tell Mrs. Anna about my boring life.

"My dad is a real soldier, so everything at home, like in the army, is based on strict rules. From an early age, we knew what was possible and what was not. I will probably be afraid of my father's wrath for the rest of my life." I paused. "I also have a grandmother, my father's mother. She hates my mother, and when she comes to visit my parents on the farm, there are always fights. It sounds comical from the outside, but sometimes I want to break free." I shrugged.

Mrs. Moss listened with interest.

"My biggest hobby and way of relaxing is riding horses. My parents have a small horse farm, cherish Lithuanian traditions, and breed Žemaitukai—little Samogitian—horses. I don't have many friends. My best friend, Elle, came with me to America. She is studying interior design, and when I came here, I met Rodriguez, a promising photographer." I suddenly realized that I must have told her too much. "Sorry. When I get nervous, I tend to talk too much. I'm usually a better listener than a speaker." I felt my face turning red.

"Everything is fine, Luka. I like open and communicative people." Anna seemed sincere. "Are you ready to dive into the world of fashion?"

"Are you asking me?" I looked around the office with wide-open eyes.

Anna started laughing. "Of course I am. Do you have your lecture schedule with you? You mentioned on your resume that you work at Old Vilnius restaurant? Will you be able to combine practice and work?"

"It will work. I have almost no lectures for the next two months—maybe only a couple a week because I accumulated extra points, and I work mostly on the evening shift at a restaurant. I'll adjust my work schedule if necessary."

"Good. We just need young interns with fresh ideas. The internship is unpaid, but after two months, if you work well, we will consider other possibilities. You will start work on Monday—if it suits you." Anna looked straight into my eyes as she spoke.

I could only nod my head. "Yes, well, that's fine," I said with a trembling voice.

"And now about work. You will be an assistant secretary to a Fashion Icon manager. The work day will start at eight o'clock in the morning. Mrs. Black likes punctuality. Got it?"

I nodded again.

"OK honey, go home—and see you on Monday. Now go to the administration office and collect the practice card. I will show you your workplace on Monday."

My legs stood up by themselves, my body moved toward the door, my hand shook Anna's hand by itself, my lips were smiling, and bees were buzzing in my brain. I blushed all over and could not hide my joy. I quickly went to the administration office, picked up my practice card, and got a work cell phone that did most of the computer functions perfectly. I left the skyscraper with a big smile. It was well after six o'clock. I quickly walked to the nearest subway station. I had to be at the restaurant in half an hour.

Rodriguez was waiting in the lounge, ready for work, wearing a black shirt and an apron. "Hello, chica. Wow, you look hot." Rodriguez looked me over from head to toe and looked really stunned.

I bowed theatrically. "Well, you look at me like that again, I swear, I'll crush you like a mouse." I poked my little fist against Rodriguez's nose.

"Stop it, chica. You look really wonderful. How did your interview go?"

"I was accepted!" Overwhelmed with joy, I ran into Rodriguez's arms. We spun around like tow trucks and giggled in blissful euphoria. Rodriguez was always happy with even the smallest success of mine.

"I'm so happy for you, chica. Such great news should be celebrated. Maybe we can go to a bar this weekend?"

"When you look at me like that, I really can't refuse. I'll let Elle know about the weekend plans."

I looked for my mobile phone in my bag. I wasn't ready to go partying yet, but the mood was perfect today. *I can't let my friends down, can I? I have to forget that night finally and start living a normal life.*

"Of course, Elle. How about without Elle?" Rodriguez didn't look very pleased, but I let it pass and texted Elle: *I got the internship! This weekend, we'll go to the bar. I'll cook.* I immediately got the answer: *Holy shit! We're going to beat ourselves up over the weekend—and don't try to argue.* Elle always knew how to draw everything vividly.

The door to the lounge area opened, and the bartender entered. Adam's broad shoulders barely fit through the doorway, and his slightly wavy hair was disheveled in back. "Don't be lazy. The restaurant is bursting with visitors. Get to work quickly." He whistled and slapped his tongue. "Luka, you look amazing."

Rodriguez looked at Adam and said, "We'll be right back. Don't yell, honey. And stop drooling—she's already busy."

We began the long evening shift.

CHAPTER THREE

The weekend went by so fast. Weekend plans and going to the bar had to be postponed for another time because the restaurant needed extra hands. Without hesitating, I agreed to work extra shifts. This option was more acceptable than going to a bar. I still didn't want to tell Elle about the horrific experience in Las Vegas and reveal the reason why I don't want to have fun. Of course, Elle was angry, but I pretended to be very sorry and promised that we would celebrate in the near future.

On Monday, I got up at seven o'clock in the morning, carefully combed my hair, and tied it in a tight ponytail on the top of my head. I highlighted my eyelids with soft shadows and a sharp black line, applied several coats of mascara, and put blush on my cheeks. *Wow, I look no worse than that stony blonde.*

It was quite chilly outside, and I wore a pink silk long-sleeved blouse that I bought from the bargain section of *TJ Maxx*, a black pencil skirt, and a coat.

Elle opened her eyes and said, "Girl, you look cool."

"And you are lying all tangled up with mascara on the pillow. When did you come back yesterday?"

"Late. Martin, and I were at a Latin club, and we danced until dawn." Elle's face was distorted by a silly smile.

"Ooh, Miss Eleonora is smiling. Is the end of the world coming?" I smiled at Elle.

"Shut up!" Elle threw a pillow at me.

I couldn't stop laughing. "OK, sleeping beauty. I'm on my way to the office, and you should clean yourself and the room." I smiled. "Something is creaking under your bed. I'm not kidding—it's really creaking." I waved my hand and thought that all kinds of parasites were breeding under Elle's bed because she put all her things and her garbage there. Her mother cleans so much that you won't find even the slightest bit of trash or dust in the house, but Elle is the complete opposite. Sometimes I suspect that Elle was adopted.

"Yeah, maybe someday." Elle sent an air kiss and rolled over.

The trip to the office didn't take long, and I was at the office half an hour earlier than I needed to be. In the lobby, I greeted the supervisor, Tony Richmond. He had been working there for half his life. He and his wonderful wife, Adelain, had three sons and seven grandchildren. After a pleasant conversation with Tony, I went up to the 101st floor. It was still twenty minutes to nine, and the office was half empty. After taking off my coat, I sat down on the U-shaped sofa.

Ten minutes later, Anna appeared. She wore a red pencil dress and black Louboutin shoes. "Good morning, Luka. I hope you had a restful weekend."

"Good morning, Mrs. Anna. Yes, I am rested. Thanks. How about you?"

"Oh, call me just Anna. After all, we are already friends, right?" She smiled. "My weekend was stormy." She winked. "Let's go. I'll lead you to your workplace."

I rushed after Anna into the unknown. *God, how does she walk so fast in those high heels?* In my office, two desks were facing each other, and between them was a wide passage to the manager's office, which was behind a glass wall. The manager's office also featured light colors and a glass wall overlooking Lake Michigan.

"Luka, this table and everything on it is yours now. Get comfortable and feel well. Mrs. Black will appear in a few minutes. Her secretary, Isabela, is sick, and you will replace her today."

Oh my God, I'm going to replace the secretary on my first day? Don't faint, Luka. Don't faint.

I didn't even feel that I was pinching my thigh.

"OK, Mrs. … OK, Anna." I collapsed into my office chair like a sack of potatoes as soon as Anna left the office.

Less than five minutes later, a stretched-out lady swam through the door like a swan. She was dressed head to toe in black, and she had bright red lips and sunglasses and flawlessly styled, streaked, shoulder-length hair. She was say no more than sixty years old.

I got up from my chair and said, "Good morning, Mrs. Black."

She didn't even turn around. After a few seconds, she stopped at the door to her office, slowly turned around, pushed down her glasses with one perfectly manicured hand, and looked at me.

I immediately felt the hairs on my arms and back stand up. I didn't know whether to sit down or keep standing. *Do I need to say something?* I just stood there with my eyes wide-open, waiting to see what would happen next.

"To my office. Immediately." Her commanding tone rang out from the high ceiling of the office. I shuddered and thought, *Oh my God, I'm going to be kicked out before I even start work.* I panicked for maybe the fifteenth time and followed the manager to her office.

She stood against the glass wall, grasped the hump of her straight nose with her fingertips, exhaled loudly, and turned to me with a sudden movement.

I jumped out of my seat.

She gave me one more look of appreciation, let out a loud sigh, and sat down in the leather chair.

I remained standing like a madman.

"Today is not the best day because my right hand decided to get sick. Imagine, she thinks she can get sick whenever she wants. She just started and got sick—and now I have to mess with an inexperienced intern. What's your name?"

"Mrs. Luka ... Mrs. Black ... my name is Luka Ilgauskaitė."

Oh my God, did I just call myself Mrs. Luka? I will die of shame.

Mrs. Black stared at me with her gray eyes, her expression not promising anything good. "OK, Luka, if Anna accepted you, then she likes you. Don't make Anna regret her choice." She glared at me again.

I felt like I was suffocating. *Oh my God, I am really out of breath. Stay calm, you're not going to come off like some little girl.* I tried to control myself. "No, Mrs. Black, I'll really try to keep Mrs. Anna from regretting." *Luka, can't you even talk anymore?*

"Well ... answer all calls. I hope you understand English better than you speak it! What's the accent here? Russian?" She was about to poke a hole in her notebook with her pen.

"No, I'm Lithuanian." *There's a lot of talk going on. Am I speaking to the head of the company?*

"What? It doesn't matter, Lulu. Just answer all calls and forward them to me if I show that I can talk. If I can't speak, then write down who called. Also, my son Iden is coming back from Turkey today. Book a table at the Hilton restaurant for two at eight this evening. Don't step here—you can go." She waved her pen toward the door and blew her lips.

"Understood, ma'am." As I walked toward the door, I realized that if I could survive the day, I would continue to live.

I typed "Hilton restaurant in Chicago" into a Google search. At least a dozen of them showed up. *And where should I call to book a table? God, I'm going to get kicked out, and I won't get my degree. I'll also be kicked out of America. I will never be able to work for a decent company in my life, and I will be completely ground with flour. My previous adventure in Las Vegas was not honorable, and now it smells like a total disaster.*

My hands started to sweat. I'd been sitting there for half an hour, and I was afraid to look into the boss's office.

Anna's friendly voice woke me up from my deep thoughts. "And how was the first meeting with our prima donna?"

"It's OK." I gave her a fake smile. "I just don't think she likes me. And she's going to kick me out of here because I don't know which Hilton restaurant I have to book a table at tonight." I almost started sobbing.

"There is a restaurant in Old Town, near the pier."

"Anna, you are my guardian angel." I almost hugged her.

"Everything is fine. How do you feel on your first day at work? I'm going to see Rose, and you are going to book the table." Anna winked at me and went to the manager's office.

The rest of the day was very intense. I realized that if you work at a company considered the favorite of the fashion world, you can't leave your desk—not even to go to the toilet—because you will miss fifteen calls. You also can't double-check who's calling and ask them to dictate their name to a letter. It turns out that's unethical. Mrs. Black has to be brought coffee regularly—every two hours without asking—and if you don't do it on time because you were on a call, she just waves her hands and snorts like my parents' mare, Zara. As far as I understand, snoring is not a good sign. If she closes her eyes and takes a deep breath so that her eyes pop out like a carousel, it's better to get my feet wet before there's a Hiroshima-like explosion.

That's how the first day went. I trudged home with a headache and was damn hungry. I only had a cup of cold coffee at work, which I brought to Mrs. Black too late. On the way home, I stopped at McDonald's and had a delicious Big Mac with a double portion of fries. I got back to the dorm well after seven o'clock and fell straight into bed.

Tomorrow is a new day with new challenges, and Mrs. Black can't stand me. That's really worrying, but I have to make the most of this opportunity and squeeze everything I can out of this practice. I can't give up. I have no right to lose. I know I'm going to want to give up tomorrow or the day after because I probably won't be able to push that hard, but I'll try.

Overwhelmed by restless thoughts, I finally dozed off. It was the first night I fell asleep without waking up to an alarm.

SEPTEMBER 24, 2018
IDEN

Liam is quietly humming Tupac's latest hit, and I can't focus. "Liam, can you be quiet?" *Of course you can't, specially so.*

"Of course, man." He turned the radio louder.

Liam is mad at me for breaking all the rules yesterday and tipping the stick with the alcohol. My nerves have been on edge lately, and I got us into a fight at the bar last night. We are both by nature fighters, but I am always the first to get into situations where we have to lick our wounds in the morning. Liam is my employee, and he is the only friend I can talk to about my problems. Liam, and I met while serving in the French Foreign Legion. He is from Norway or Sweden—who cares—but through my acquaintances, we arranged all the permits for him to live in America. After Mari's betrayal, he was the only one who helped her recover.

I sat in my SUV besides the Willis Tower and waited for Rose to arrive. Rose is my mother. I haven't had a warm relationship with her for a while now, but from time to time, I have to agree to have dinner together. I was flipping through the *Times Weekly*, wondering what had happened in America while I was in Turkey, when a girl coming out of a skyscraper caught my eye. She came quite close to my car and looked at the tinted windows to fix her tangled hair. Then she took out her phone and began to look around the street. It took me five seconds to recognize her. It was the same girl from Las Vegas—the same big green eyes, plump lips, and long legs.

I cannot believe it.

She kept looking down the street and tried to catch a cab.

You are so beautiful.

She saw my mother coming, got confused, and didn't know where to go. She bowed her head and started walking down the street.

What a coward you are.

"Iden, dear, it's so good to see you," Mom cooed as Liam held the car door open.

"Hello, Mother."

"I'm so glad you agreed to have dinner."

"And I'm glad too." *But definitely not because I will have dinner with you—but because of her.*

"How did you do in Turkey?"

After a few minutes, her chatter gave me a headache. "Who did you greet when you came to the car?" I tried to turn the conversation in the right direction.

"I don't remember." Rose's eyes widened.

"The girl who scared you so much." *Although I don't think anyone has warm feelings.*

"Oh, the intern?" *Like I should know she's an intern.* "It's Lulu or Leia, or maybe Luka. She is the new intern. Anna accepted her."

Wow. I need to text Anna: "Hello. What is the name of the new intern? Where does she study?" I sent it, and before we reached the Hilton, I got a reply: "Hello, dear. She is Luka Ilgauskaitė. She is a student from Lithuania. She came here on an exchange program, and she studies at the University of Chicago. Why are you asking?"

Why? Good question. There's something about her that I really like.

While Rose babbled on about her snobbish friends and corporate affairs, I just sat there and emailed a detective to find out more information about the lady I was interested in. *God, does that woman ever stop drooling? This evening will be so long for me. Damn Chicago traffic, Mother's babbling, yesterday's alcohol, and righteous Liam. Someone, shoot me please.*

NOVEMBER 26, 2018
LUKA

The alarm went off, I opened my eyes and realized that it was Monday again. I pulled the blanket over my head to hide from this realization. I was already used to the new rhythm.

I do my internship all week, and I work evening shifts at the restaurant. I go to lectures if necessary, and I call my family once a week. Isabela has recovered, and everything is clearer. We share our work. Going to work is more fun because Isabela turned out to be very friendly. She's a few years older than me. In our spare time, we click our tongues or make fun of Mrs. Black's grimaces. It's pouring outside today. Elle has not returned to sleep at the dormitory for the third night. She is very serious with Martin. Rodriguez went to his parents' house for Thanksgiving, and it's going to be very sad at the restaurant this week. I'll probably be alone for Thanksgiving.

I put on a warm knitted dress that fell lightly from the waist and long leather boots. I decided that it wasn't worth straightening my hair in this humidity, and I went out with naturally curly, loose hair. By the time I got to the place, I was curled up like a sheep. The supervisor, as always, politely bowed and complimented my hairstyle. I found the office empty, calmly looked through the press, and checked Mrs. Black's agenda.

Mrs. Black burst into the office like a hurricane. "Laura, get ready. You're going to the meeting with me." She pointed at me.

"Me?" I jumped up so suddenly that my chair fell over.

"Do you see Lily standing around anymore?"

What's up, Lily? My name is Luka. "Well, Mrs. Black, where's Isabel?" I asked.

"She has some urgent matters again. Ask fewer questions and be ready in five minutes." She stormed off to her office.

I stomped around the lobby for twenty minutes, waiting for Mrs. Black. Anna mentioned that she does not tolerate being late.

I was tense, and the stony blonde was killing everyone who passed by, especially me.

When Mrs. Black finally appeared, she gave me a look of displeasure—as if she had been waiting twenty minutes for me. She snorted like a mare and hurried toward the elevator.

Good thing she didn't start digging like a horse, I thought and smiled. I stood still, not knowing whether to go with her to the elevator or stay put.

"Did you fall asleep, Leia?" Mrs. Black said.

On my way to the elevator, I heard Serafina crying, which sounded like the buzzing of an annoying mosquito.

A black Bentley limousine was waiting for us at the sidewalk. The driver opened the door and held the umbrella while we got in. I had never been in such a luxury vehicle before, and for a moment, I felt like a movie star. The interior of the car was luxurious, the leather smelled like the car was fresh from the factory, and tinted windows protected us from prying eyes.

"Prepare a notebook and listen carefully. If I mention something important, make a note. We are going to a meeting with a new talent: Alvaro Rivera. He released his first clothing collection in September, which had an impressive demand, and he now plans to launch a winter season. I would love to take him under my management wing."

"Yes, Mrs. Black." I nodded, but my mind was already on the meeting. *I will finally get a chance to see behind the scenes of the negotiations.*

"Also, in the car, before we get to the meeting place, order four tickets to New York for this weekend. There will be a celebration of the opening of new fashion houses in Manhattan, which is teeming with potential talent." She marked something on his tablet. "You will fly too."

"Me?" I asked. "I cannot. I work a full shift at the restaurant on weekends."

Mrs. Black slid down her sunglasses, even though it was pouring outside, and gave me a head-to-toe look. "If you want to be signed to the practice report, you'll fly with me to the damn event." She started a phone conversation that continued all the way to the Hilton.

I curled up in the leather seat and tried everything I could to resolve the situation, but I couldn't figure out how to do it. Finally, I thought, *If Isabel is back at work tomorrow, I won't have to fly anywhere.*

The Bentley stopped just outside the front of the Hilton. The driver quickly opened the door and helped Mrs. Black out of the car. I got out of it by myself and practically ran after my boss.

The restaurant staff greeted Mrs. Black with smiles on their faces and escorted us to a secluded table set for five. My boss dropped her purse and coat on the table.

For a moment, my eyes and the waiter's eyes met. We both looked questioningly at her things and wondered who should pick them up. The waiter picked up the coat and disappeared into the restaurant.

Thank you, man, I thought.

"How long will you be standing at the table?" Mrs. Black asked.

My face turned red again. "Excuse me, but where should I sit?"

"Sit wherever you want." She lowered her eyes to her phone screen.

Ten minutes later, Alvaro Rivera, the culprit of the meeting, appeared. He was as bright as a peacock and gracefully elegant. I couldn't keep laughing at how furiously he and Mrs. Black were hugging each other, and their facial expressions were changing like New Year's fireworks. We sat down at the table and listened to Mr. Alvaro's talking about the absence of modern fashion in fashion.

I was so engrossed in listening to the discussion that I didn't notice Mrs. Black getting up from the table and introducing her son, Iden Black, to everyone. With a smile on my face, after Rivera's retort about French fashion, I turned to say hello to Mrs. Black's son—and my body froze. The same cold, dark eyes were looking at me. I will never forget those eyes or that look. A familiar smell reached my nostrils: forest and wood mixed with his body odor. My heart began to beat like crazy, my mouth began to salivate, and my body became heavy as a stone. Those eyes looked right through me. I started breathing more heavily and gripped the table.

"This is my son, Iden." Mrs. Black turned to her son. "Iden, you already know Mr. Alvaro Rivera, as well as his entourage. And here is Luka Ilgauskaitė, an intern at my company."

I forced myself to give him my hand. My trembling fingers were cold as ice, and the blood froze in my veins. When his firm hand gently took mine, I shuddered and pulled back. Nodding my head, I lowered my eyes to the table. I didn't understand who was saying what—I just sat and squeezed the edges of my dress. My head was ringing, I couldn't control myself, and my heart was beating faster and faster. I could hear my own heartbeat in my ears. It was as if I had gone back in time to that night in the hotel room in Las Vegas. My heartbeat was so fast and so loud. I was afraid to move or raise my eyes. I could not move at all because my body was frozen. Time seemed to stand still, and the space around me became sticky and solid. Every sound was harsh and deafening. I was practically hysterical.

"Miss Luka, do you like this coat pattern?" Rivera held up a sketch.

I finally raised my eyes, and Rivera shifted in his chair and caught my dull gaze. I really didn't want to give him a bad impression, but I didn't want to chat about coats or other fashionable rags. "Very interesting."

Finally, after an hour of suffering and not being able to hear what was going on around me, I jumped up from my chair and looked at Mrs. Black. She seemed startled by the sound of the chair, but she quickly caught on and went ice cold.

"Excuse me for bothering you, but I really need to go," I said as humbly as I could. "Please."

"OK, Lulu, go."

I said goodbye to everyone—or almost everyone because I didn't even dare to look in that man's direction. I quickly turned on my heel and ran outside. It didn't matter that it was raining. I just walked along Lake Michigan and silently cried. No one saw my tears because they were perfectly masked by the rain. The long-simmering abscess that had poisoned my body and mind had finally burst.

After a while, I sat down on a bench. All the memories flooded back, and it seemed like everything had happened yesterday: the room, the ticking of the clock, the cold, the voice, the look, the smell, and the violence. I remembered every touch and penetration. The fog covering my memories cleared, and I managed to remember that when I tried to resist, he tightened his grip on my hands and took my virginity without any introduction or caress. All the memories of that evening came back in a haze: the club, gossiping with coworkers, one cosmopolitan, another cocktail, and then the bartender serving me another cocktail, which, as far as I remember, was sent to me as a gift by some guy. After that third cocktail, I could barely stand. A coworker dragged us into the VIP area to meet some older guys. I was seated next to a very nice young man—or a Greek god. He had dark, stylishly cut and coiffed hair, dark, piercing eyes, white, straight teeth, plump lips, and designer clothes that emphasized his fit body and tanned skin. It was Iden. I remember having fun and feeling sick, and then everything started to spin. I asked my friend to take me home, and then I headed to the bathroom. Someone helped me, and then everything went offline. I woke up in that hotel room and ran away, but the memories caught up with me. *How can I continue to live? Did that man recognize me? Probably not. He seemed more intoxicated than I was that night.*

I sat on the bench until it got dark. Cold and soaking wet, I returned to the dorm, curled up under the covers, and cried. I didn't put on blush that night. I just looked out the window and wondered what to do next. *Should I stay as an intern since there is so little time*

*left before final exams or pack my suitcase and head home to my parents?
How disappointed they will be in me—but I am even more disappointed
in myself.* I spent half the night fighting with myself and all the
feelings that gripped my body. Maybe my mother was right—being
born a sparrow does not make you a swan. Had my vast ambitions
condemned me to eternal fear and misery? Maybe I could blame fate
for all my failures, but aren't we the makers of our own destinies?

In the morning, I could not lift my head from the pillow because it was torn in half. I was shaking. Even a couple of painkillers
didn't help.

Elle, returning to our room in the morning, was frightened to
see such a scene and called Anna. She explained that I had a bad cold
and couldn't even get out of bed. The real reason for my condition
was completely different: Iden Black. His image appeared every
time I closed my eyes. I couldn't believe that all the horrors from
Las Vegas had followed me to Chicago. I didn't know how to cope.
I was too weak to pretend that nothing had happened—that I didn't
know him—but what if he didn't recognize me?

I thought about the meeting and how he acted reserved and
businesslike. He showed no excitement or any sign that he knew me.
He was as cold as Mrs. Black. *Is it all in my head? Was it not the same
guy?* I was completely lost in my thoughts, and I didn't understand
what was reality and what was fiction. Two worlds had collided,
and I just had to wait for the thunderous explosion to wake me
from a deep sleep. With a little patience, would everything be fine?
Patience, however, was not my strongest attribute, and it usually
ran out quickly, leaving me halfway through the work in progress.

I stared at the ceiling. *God, give me strength and show me the right
path. Please don't abandon me at this stage of my life.*

CHAPTER FOUR

LUKA

I didn't get out of bed all week. I didn't want to eat or drink. Elle brought food to the dormitory, but as soon as I put a few bites in my mouth, I immediately got sick. Nobody was interested. I was apathetic even to myself. Elle ditched her weekend plans with Martin and spent Thanksgiving weekend with me. Anna called several times a day and asked how I was feeling. According to what she said, Mrs. Black was very unhappy that I didn't fly to New York with her. Anna and Isabel covered for me, and Isabel went instead of me. The weekend was over, and I had to confront myself—whether I wanted to or not.

I didn't feel any better on Monday. A week later, I took a shower and forced myself to eat half a cereal bar. I put on simple black pants and a warm sweater. I put my hair in a ponytail. I didn't even wear makeup. I looked in the mirror, and I was scared of myself. My eyes were blackened, and my face was pale. I brushed my cheeks with blush and my lashes with mascara. I gathered my things and headed to the subway.

I showed up at work at nine o'clock. Serafina reported that I look terrible, and I gave her the middle finger.

When I entered the office, Isabel said, "Luka, you look terribly pale. Are you feeling well?"

"Yes. I'm fine. I just slept very poorly. A few days will pass, and I will look better." I managed to squeeze out a smile.

I squirmed in my chair and turned on my computer. On the table, I found a pile of papers with my tasks for the week. My mind was wandering. "Isabel, I'm sorry I ruined your weekend plans and you had to go to New York."

She waved her hand. "Never mind. Everything's all right. I am very glad that I went." Isabel's face twisted into a smile. "Listen, Mrs. Black's son, Iden, was with us. Have you seen him. Handsome! What a six-foot-tall magazine-cover-worthy candy."

My guts immediately tightened, and I curled up into a ball. I couldn't believe he was so close to me, and that closeness made me feel awful.

"Luka, what's wrong?" Isabel asked.

"Nothing, everything is fine. I didn't eat anything in the morning, and my stomach hurts."

"Very wrong," Isabel said.

Mrs. Black invited us to her office.

A couple of hours passed, and I was still staring at the computer screen and trying to line up the guest list for an upcoming fashion show. All around me, there was action, but I couldn't see or hear anything. I was indifferent to everything. At one point, it became very cold. I shivered and kept looking at the computer screen. I tried to concentrate on work and not think about my personal problems. I felt a hand on my shoulder, and I jumped up and shouted, "Don't touch me!"

Isabel backed away from me in fear, and I wrapped my arms around myself.

"I'm sorry, Lu. Did I scare you? I just wanted to ask if you are going to lunch." Isabel had the gentlest voice.

"Forgive me." I covered my face with my hands. "I was scared. Everything's all right. I'm OK." *Everything will be fine.*

Isabel looked into my eyes for a long time and said, "Go wash your face and have lunch. I think you scared Mrs. Black. They're looking at you."

I turned my head to the manager's office and shuddered again. Mrs. Black and her son were looking at me. He was bent forward—with his legs wide apart and both hands clasped together—and was looking straight into my eyes. His black suit and white shirt showed his arrogance and power. I couldn't escape that look. I felt my pulse and the taste of metal in my mouth—I must have bitten my lip—but then I felt calm.

I smell cut grass and the smell of a freshly washed road. It smells like earth. I hear swallows chirping. I can feel the summer sun kissing my face, and the flies are buzzing around me. I can feel the grass with my hands. I open my eyes and see blue sky and fluffy clouds overhead. I look around at the meadow and the lake. I sit down and look into the distance. Everything is so green and beautiful. It's a Lithuanian summer. That fresh sweet smell, probably the July blossoms, but how did I get here? I don't understand anything. I just hear someone calling my name, but it echoes from afar. Luka, Luka, wake up, Luka. Why should I wake up if I'm not asleep? Everything went dark again.

I smell disinfectant, blood, and bandages. I open my eyes. It takes time to adjust to the artificial light. I try to sit up, but my head spins again.

"Don't get up, Luka. You're still very weak." Anna got up from the couch and came closer. It took me a while to realize I was in a ward. An IV was connected to my hand, and a strange device showed strange curves on a screen. Colored bracelets were on my other hand. I looked at Anna and said, "Where am I? What happened?"

"I don't know for sure because I wasn't around you, but Isabel told me that you looked very bad all day. You didn't see anything or hear what was being said to you. Then you got really scared, and you fainted. When you fell, you broke a glass vase with your hand, and the wound had to be stitched. The doctor said that there were no serious injuries."

My left arm was bound from wrist to shoulder. I didn't understand what was going on. "But how?"

"According to the blood tests, you are practically anemic. Luka, you experience a lot of stress, but you have to take care of your health. Do you have any personal problems? Maybe you need help?" There was excitement in Anna's voice.

"I'm very sorry to trouble you. I will pay for the damage." I didn't know where to go anymore. "I'm fine. I'm just tired."

"Everything is fine. You just scared us a lot. It's a good thing Mr. Iden didn't freak out and cover the wound like in an action movie and bring you here."

Oh my God. Oh my God. Oh my God. Just not him. Not that. And all this shit is just for him? My head began to spin again, and I felt nauseous. I closed my eyes.

"Luka, are you in a lot of pain? Maybe call a doctor?" Anna looked worried.

"No, everything is fine, Anna. Thanks for caring. It doesn't hurt." I turned to the window and realized it was dark outside. "By the way, what time is it?"

"It's almost eight o'clock. You have been offline for a long time."

"My roommate is probably very worried about me. I should call her. Is my phone here?"

"Yes, I'll give it to you." Anna went to my purse and took out my phone.

I found Elle's message: "Dear, I won't be coming home tonight and probably for the next few days. Martin and I came up with a spontaneous plan to fly to Florida. We are already boarding the plane. Don't be sad, love you xoxo."

One less problem—no need to explain what happened. With numb fingers, I wrote, "Everything is fine. Have fun." I turned to Anna. "Why are you here? Go home. I'm fine." I squeezed out a smile.

"Really, Luka? I feel really bad. We have overloaded you with work and your job at the restaurant." Anna's lower lip trembled.

"You really shouldn't blame yourself. It's my own fault. I rest little, and I eat even less." I smiled again.

"OK, if you need anything, you can call me or Isabel." Anna touched my hand and left.

I was finally alone with my thoughts. And my thoughts were black. I thought I might as well call my mom since I hadn't talked to her all week. I picked up my phone and dialed my mother's number. "Hello, Mom, how are you?"

"OK, honey. How are you? No word from you all week. I called you on Skype over the weekend, but you didn't answer. Did something happen?"

"Nothing, Mom. Everything is fine. I was just working a lot and then forgot to call back." You're lying. Luka, you're lying.

"And why are you calling on the phone and not Skype? Phone calls are expensive. Save your money."

"My phone was broken, and I had to do a factory reset. I didn't have time to reinstall the apps."

Silence.

My mother probably knows I'm lying. "Well, how are things with Arn? Has Paul returned from the spa?"

"Honey, this is not a phone conversation," she whispered. "Your father kicked Arn out of the house. Jesus, I can't, I feel sorry for the child. As far as I know, he is hiding with Paul."

There was another long pause.

"And I don't know where they will get the money for the broken car."

"How much money do you need?"

"Don't ask, daughter. Don't ask. We don't have such money. Father said not to interfere, and we are not allowed to interfere. Arn said he would never set foot in this house again."

"Not for the first time, Mom."

"Oh, lady, you're lucky to have a head and not a cabbage on your neck. You're studying and not doing menial work. How am I supposed to deal with all of you? How can I calm your father so that he does not refuse to see his son?"

"Father will get angry and stop. After all, they always communicate like this. Enemies one day—and friends the next. Can I call Dad?"

"Don't call him yet. He will think that he has to go home. Don't mess with it."

We talked about my sister and her twins, the never-ending farm work, and Grandma's eyes. *I'll have a few days of peace, and I won't have to keep explaining why we don't Skype.* After such a long talks my head and arm hurt. I asked the nurse for painkillers and fell asleep.

IDEN

I hate hospitals.

Liam is aware of the feelings that come over me whenever I have to visit such places, and he gave me a supportive pat on the shoulder and pushed me into the ward.

It was dusk inside, and a weak light by the bed was on. Luka was sleeping with her face turned toward me. I examined her better.

"Liam, she thinks I'm a monster," I whispered.

"From today's reaction, yes." He shrugged.

"In the restaurant, I understood that it would not be easy. She recognized me right away, but I didn't think it was that bad." *Did I expect her to jump into my arms?*

"She needs time." Liam looked at Luka. "I think she is an understanding girl. Explain everything to her and tell her the truth."

The truth? The truth is not very pleasant. "OK, Liam, you can go rest. I will be here." I tried to make myself comfortable.

"Hold on, man." Liam slapped my shoulder again and walked out the door.

And what the hell am I sitting here for? I walked over to the bed, took her warm hand, and stroked her palm with my thumb. *She is so fragile and innocent. I'm a real beast.* "Forgive me. I didn't want this. I'll find out who's to blame for the drugging that night." I sighed and kissed her little hand.

I really wanted you that night. I realize what I did, but do I dare to say it to your face?

I sat back down on the couch and stared at her until I fell asleep.

LUKA

When I woke up, it was completely dark outside. I turned my head to the other side and was stunned. Mr. Black was sitting on the sofa. His head was on the back of the sofa, the top button of his white shirt was unbuttoned, his tie was loose, his jacket was unbuttoned, and his eyes were closed. He was sleeping. My heart started pounding again. I considered running away from the ward or calling for help. *Either way, what would I say to everyone else? My rapist is sitting next to me? How would I prove it? Maybe it's not even him. Maybe I'm imagining it.*

While I was formulating an escape plan, his eyes opened. He stared at me with his dark eyes, and I was afraid to even breathe. He stretched and rubbed his eyes, but he didn't look away from me. Finally, after thinking about something, he said, "Good evening, Luka."

There was a long pause. Maybe he expected me to answer the same.

"How are you feeling?"

I still didn't answer. I just looked up at the ceiling.

"OK, you're not talking, but can I say a few words?"

"No! Get out!" I felt a sharp pain in my hand.

"Maybe you can stop jumping like that? Your hand is stitched." His calm voice drove me crazy.

"Please leave now," I said as calmly as I could.

"I'm not going anywhere until I tell you what I'm here for." Iden moved closer to the edge of the bed.

I automatically pulled my legs closer and curled up.

"Luka, I want to talk about that incident in Las Vegas."

Gathering all my strength, I looked up at him. His face looked calm, but his jaw was tightly clenched. *He is a man of great beauty, but his soul is rotten.*

"What happened that evening should not have happened. I was as intoxicated as you were." His words were thoughtful, and he pronounced the syllables slowly. "When we went to the hotel room, I thought you were like everyone else, that you liked to act, that you were unavailable. When I talked to you at the toilet, you said you wanted to get out of here. I realized that you wanted the same thing as me." Again a long pause, he said, "Afterward, everything was a blur. I have never uttered such stupidity before." He went to the window and put his hands in his pockets. "But that does not justify what happened."

Iden walked back to the couch, sat down, and ran his fingers through his hair.

"I listened—and please leave now." My voice sounded foreign. There was no life or humanity. I looked out the window and waited for the bastard to leave me alone.

"Luka—"

"No! Never say my name again." I turned to him, and for the first time, I dared to look him straight in the eyes.

Iden looked confused or tired.

I don't care. "From now on, I don't want to see or hear from you anymore. Get out of my life—just like you came in." I took a deep breath and tried to control myself so I wouldn't start crying. "I didn't ask you or anyone else to stun me and then abuse me animalistically." My voice dropped from a command to a barely audible whisper. *I lost my dream of love that night.* I couldn't control my inner trembling and started grinding my teeth. "You won't get back what you took from me. Go away!"

Iden got up from the couch and took a couple of steps toward the door. He stopped, turned to me, and looked me straight in the eyes. His gaze was different. It was not as animalistic as I remembered. It was empty and maybe even repentant.

Am I making things up again? "Don't be afraid. No one knows, and no one will ever find out. Your reputation will remain clean, Mr. Black." I looked at him one last time, turned to the window, and pulled the blanket up to my neck. Tears welled up in my eyes, and I tried not to move or give away that I was feeling bad.

Iden stood there for a few moments and then left.

The rest of the night was spent in self-pity and tears absorbed by the hard hospital pillow.

At half past two, the nurse came in and injected me with sedatives. I disconnected and slept until the morning.

After two days in the hospital, I was discharged. *I'm not sure if I can call a dorm room a home. I miss my home and my family very much.* I texted Arn and was pleasantly surprised when he wrote back. *Apparently, life is not all roses for him either if he is happy to communicate with me when our relationship is not very good.*

I went to the office on Thursday, and despite the insistence of Anna and Mrs. Black, I worked until the evening. I offered to pay for the broken vase, but Mrs. Black wouldn't let me. I haven't seen Elle for almost a week. She stayed with Martin after returning from Florida. Their relationship had reached a higher level.

It was cold outside, and I put on a warmer coat. The holidays were approaching, and Chicago was shining with all kinds of colors. I could feel the holiday spirit. The shop windows were full of Christmas decorations, and the streets were full of people who were looking for Christmas presents. On my first day back at the restaurant, it was nice to see my colleagues. Rodriguez told that he spent the week with his relatives, and he showed me a bunch of photographs. He enjoyed the time with his family, but he couldn't understand why I didn't call him to tell him I was in the hospital. I pretended that it was nothing serious because I didn't want him to worry.

We were halfway through our shift, and the restaurant was flooded with patrons. The manager was running around like crazy and telling everyone that the eighth table must be served especially carefully because the Chicago elite were visiting. Of course, I was lucky enough to serve the eighth table by lottery. I rushed to the table with my order book and smilingly approached the eighth table. A young, light-skinned guy, a small, brown-eyed girl with a short, curly nose, and a long-haired blonde were sitting at the table.

"Good afternoon. Have you decided?"

The young guy smiled and placed an order for himself and his girlfriend. They both chose the tuna steak. The blonde girl ordered a Caesar salad, and her friend, who was running late, ordered a medium steak with grilled vegetables.

"What drinks can I offer?"

"I think we'll have a 1966 Cristal, if you have it?"

"We have, but we don't sell this type of champagne in glasses— only in bottles."

"That works." I walked away from the table, mentally calculating how big a tip I would get from this order. I asked Adam to prepare the champagne while I carried out a few other orders. I brought the champagne to the eighth table.

The blonde was gushing about the plastic surgery she planned to have after the holidays.

I opened the bottle and filled the glasses as quickly as possible.

The blonde said, "Darling, you finally showed up."

After filling the last glass, I turned to leave and I bumped into Iden Black. He was wearing a white V-neck sweater and black jeans, his hair was neatly combed, and his face looked grumpy as usual. The familiar scent of a woodsy forest reached my nostrils. I froze for a moment, but I quickly caught myself and went to another table after a nice apology. Out of the corner of my eye, I could see that he was watching me. My hands began to shake. *What the hell is he doing here?*

I tried to focus on work and pleasant communication with guests. I had told him to disappear from my life and my thoughts. I was spinning like a bee.

Out of the corner of my eye, I noticed that the glasses on the eighth table were empty. I asked Rodriguez to refill the glasses because I needed to go to the bathroom.

Rodriguez, of course, gladly agreed to stand in for me.

In the kitchen, the head chef informed me that the dishes for the eighth table were ready. I had tuna steaks and Caesar salads for the girls.

When I approached the table, they were all chatting happily. The blonde's hand rested lightly on Iden's knee, and he placed his hand on the back of her chair. I served the dishes and went back to the kitchen. Returning to the table, I gave the dish to the nice guy and smiled. I gave the steak to Iden, said, "Have a good meal," and asked if there was anything missing.

As I was about to leave, a painfully familiar voice said, "I would like to try a traditional Lithuanian dish. What would you recommend?"

I turned around with a twisted face of pain, and our eyes met. Time stopped, and the memories came flooding back.

"Since you eat steak, I would recommend a traditional Lithuanian dish: Šaltibarščiai. It's cold soup with hot potatoes." My voice was barely audible.

"It fits well," Iden said.

I nodded and returned to the kitchen with my order.

"I can't do it anymore, Rodriguez," I said.

"What happened? Lu? Arm hurts?"

"Yes, my arm hurts a lot." *It's good that I can blame all the problems on my cast.* "I can't even hold the tray." I burst into tears, but the culprit was definitely not physical pain.

The manager was understanding and allowed me to go home. In the break room, I changed out of my work clothes and ran outside.

On my way past the bar, I stopped to say goodbye to Adam. He asked about my health and why I was leaving before the end of my shift. "Luka, I wanted to ask if you would like to go with me sometime—to the cinema or somewhere else?"

"You mean ... on a date?"

"Well, you can call it anything." Adam looked confused.

I was about to say that I wasn't going to start any relationships right now, but Iden came up to us and said, "I'd like a glass of whiskey."

Adam asked, "On ice?"

Iden shook his head and looked at me. He looked like he wanted to say something, but he held back.

The awkward silence was broken by Adam. "Luka, you don't need to answer right now. This offer has no expiration date." Adam smiled, and dimples appeared at the corners of his lips.

"Actually, I don't have any plans for tomorrow night." I smiled at Adam.

"Great. I'll pick you up at seven." Adam winked at me.

I smiled and said goodbye.

Iden was left standing at the bar with a glass of whiskey in his hands.

▪ ▪ ▪

On Friday, I could feel the anticipation of the weekend at work.

Serafina leaned against her desk and sighed, looking too tired to speak.

Mrs. Black was pacing around her office and scribbling furiously on her notepad.

Isabel secretly flipped through the magazine. "What are your weekend plans?" she asked.

I pursed my lips. "Well, tonight, my colleague and I will go to the cinema. I plan to spend the rest of the weekend in the dorm. I need to start writing the internship report. And what are your plans?"

"Are you going with Rodriguez?"

"No ... with Adam."

"Who is he? You haven't told me about him before." Isabel looked interested.

"Because there was and is nothing to tell. He's just nice to me," I said.

"Why do I think he thinks otherwise?" Isabel asked.

I looked up at Isabel and gave her the middle finger.

Isabel laughed and blew an air kiss.

That afternoon, an impromptu staff meeting was called. Anna looked tense, and Mrs. Black looked worried.

The manager stopped tapping her fingers on the table and looked at us. "Alvaro Rivera still hasn't decided whether he will cooperate with the Fashion Icon team or choose another company. We have to try hard to convince him." She looked at me. "Unfortunately for me, Rivera really liked our intern, Leia."

"Luka," I said.

She grabbed the bridge of her nose. "Yes, Luka. Luka, starting today, you are officially employed as my second assistant ... if you agree, of course."

Everyone looked at me.

"Of course!" I said.

"I thought so. And now let's go to a more important matter. Rivera is having a party at his villa tonight, and we'll be there too."

My plans for the evening changed in a matter of seconds. I texted Adam: "Hi Adam. I apologize, but I have to cancel our meeting tonight, I will be working late. See you next time."

Fifteen minutes later, I got a reply: "Hi, Lu. Too bad L. I'll wait for next time."

What will I wear?

CHAPTER FIVE

LUKA

"Elle, is this really the place?" I asked in disbelief, looking at the glass doors of the old building.

"It is. I have been here a couple of times. Let's go." Elle grabbed my hand and pulled me inside.

We went up to the third floor and reached apartment 12, Elle pressed the call button, and the door opened.

An elderly woman came out of the apartment. "You don't need to call like that. I can hear. I can hear."

"Hello, Joe. I'm sorry I came unannounced, but we have a problem. A beautiful evening dress is desperately needed for tonight. Can you help?" Elle looked hopefully at Joe. She opened the door wider and invited us in.

"Joe, this lovely lady is my best friend, Luka."

Joe held out her old, skinny hand.

"Luka, this is the most wonderful seamstress in Chicago, Joe."

I gently shook the old woman's hand and squeezed out a smile. "Nice to meet you, lady."

"Not a lady, just Joe." Joe motioned for us to sit on the flowery sofa. "Would you like some tea?"

"I'd be happy to drink a cup," Elle said. "Lu too."

I nudged Elle as the old lady hobbled off to the kitchen. "Elle, what are we doing here?"

"We save you money and try to get the most beautiful dress."

"I don't think she can make a dress in two hours." I shrugged.

"She has a lot of the most beautiful dresses, which customers didn't take or simply didn't like. Other customers just bring her their boring dresses. I think we will definitely find something."

Joe came back into the room with a tray of biscuits, fruit, and tea.

My stomach rumbled at the sight of the cookies.

"Eleonora, do you or your friend need a dress?" Joe fixed her ponytail and put on her glasses.

"Luka needs it. The work party is important to her today, and when she came to live here, she didn't bring any luxurious dresses—"

I said, "I really don't want to trouble you. I still have a couple of hours to look for a dress. We can go to a thrift store or look for something on sale."

"Girl, any other worries? I'm glad to help my grandson's crush." Joe smiled kindly at Elle, and she blushed.

"Wait, wait? Are you Martin's grandmother?"

"Yes." Joe smiled at Elle again. "OK, let's have some tea and cookies, and then we'll get down to business."

We spent an hour in a room with a huge wardrobe. A lot of hangers were attached to it. We drew and tried on various options. Finding a dress was complicated because I couldn't wear anything that didn't cover my injured arm.

Just when I had almost given up hope of finding something this amazing, Joe pulled out a black box. "I've been saving this dress for a special occasion." She opened the box and pulled out a silky, black, slightly shimmering, long dress. The left sleeve was long and slightly puffy, and there was no right sleeve. The dress flared from the hips and had a long slit on the right side.

"And this is beauty." Elle whistled. "Try it on right away."

I put on the dress, and I couldn't look away. The right leg could be hidden or exposed if I wanted to. The dress fit almost perfectly. It only needed a couple of extra stitches, and I looked perfect. "What if I tear it or cover it? The fabric is very expensive. I don't dare to take the dress."

"Everything will be fine. I trust you." Joe looked calm.

"Thank you so much, Joe." I gave her a big hug, and she hugged me back.

Elle and I returned to the dormitory and started on our manicures and pedicures. Moments like this, when I let Elle try out the latest makeup and hairstyle trends on me, happen very rarely. For two hours, she painted, combed, and beautified me in every way.

When I looked in the mirror, I didn't recognize myself. My hair fell in graceful curls into a ponytail. My green eyes were accentuated by soft evening makeup. My collarbones and cheeks glowed with a light mist. "Elle, you should have turned to the world of the beauty industry." I couldn't help but be surprised by what I saw in the mirror.

"It's not too late to change specializations." Elle seemed satisfied with her work. "Here, put on my long black stud earrings, and you're done."

"Good thing I asked you then and bought some black high heels. They match the dress perfectly." I stood in front of the mirror.

"Enough to admire yourself, miss. I called an Uber, and it is ten minutes away. Grab your mitten and conquer the world." She sent an air kiss.

"What are your plans for tonight?" I inquired. "Will you meet Martin?"

"Probably … although he's been a bit strange for the past few days." Elle looked confused. "Don't worry about me. Just have a good time."

I said goodbye to my friend and went out to meet my Uber. Twenty minutes later, I walked into the skyscraper where our office was located. Anna and Isabel were waiting for me in the lobby. Anna wore a long red dress and a short fur coat, and Isabel wore a short, sparkly cocktail dress.

"Hello, girls. You both look amazing," I said.

"Luka, you look enchanting. What elegance." Anna turned me around and looked at me from all sides.

The company's driver brought us to Rivera's house in the countryside. Guests and servants were bustling in the courtyard. I immediately recognized the models and designers adorning the covers of magazines. The photographers did not stop clicking their cameras. A couple of security guards were standing by the entrance, there was a real red carpet, and outdoor torches were burning. The scene was more like a scene from a TV movie than real life.

Stepping out of the Bentley, we were greeted by servants and the click of cameras. Anna looked charming and confident. She walked the red carpet with slow steps, turning every angle. I admired the elegance and lightness of this woman. Isabel and I walked a few steps behind.

Inside the house, there was no lack of pomp. Alvaro Rivera truly loved grandeur and beauty. The house stood out for its modern design, wide spaces, glass construction, and light colors. An elegant sculpture stood by the stairs, and a crystal chandelier extended down from the second floor. The house echoed with commotion and laughter. We gave our coats to the butler, and another butler immediately offered us champagne. Anna was saying hello to her friends and acquaintances, and Isabel and I followed quietly behind her.

In a large hall, there were tiny tables on the sides, a place for dancing in the middle, and a group of string instruments on the platform. The entire space was decorated with orchids in tall crystal vases. I pinched my hand twice to make sure I wasn't dreaming. Mrs. Black and Mr. Rivera sat at one of the tables. Mrs. Black, as always, wore black. A gorgeous, long, lace dress with faux peacock feather detailing accentuated her slender frame, and Alvaro Rivera wore a white tuxedo.

Mrs. Black, noticing us, beckoned us over. "Dear Anna, you have finally arrived." She kissed Anna and looked at us appreciatively.

"Rose, as always, you look stunning," Anna said.

"Alvaro, you're going to break more than one heart tonight." Anna slapped Mr. Rivera on both cheeks.

"Darlings, it's good to see you here," he said. "Who is this? Miss Luka, what elegance, what grace, what a dress!" He clapped his hands. "Turn around, show yourself. A real *preciosa*." Mr. Rivera grabbed my hand and began to carry me like a doll.

I felt my face turn red.

"Dear Alvaro, don't torture the girl. She'll get sick again." Mrs. Black pulled me out of my awkward position.

"It's OK." I squeezed out, embarrassed. "Mr. Rivera, your house is wonderful."

"Thank you, dear. Not too much pomp?" He spread his hands in all directions and quickly turned away. "Of course it's too much, but I'm already like that—all or nothing."

"Alvaro, can you show your modest abode?" Mrs. Black asked, and they headed for the door.

"Negotiations will begin," Anna said.

"Which companies have made an offer to Mr. Alvaro?" I inquired.

"Our biggest competitor is Fashion Industry. This is Mrs. Black's second husband's company. They parted not very amicably—and then Rose founded Fashion Icon."

"Mrs. Black's son's father's company is Fashion Industry?" Isabel asked.

"No," Anna said. "Iden's father died in an accident when he was two. He doesn't even remember his father. After his death, Rose married a second time, but the second marriage did not last long. Mr. Rich cheated on her with his secretary, and when Rose found out, she filed for divorce."

"Wow, her life is like the movies," Isabel said. "I have never met Mrs. Black's son."

"Iden was a very complicated child." Anna seemed embarrassed when she talked about him. "As a teenager, he had serious problems with law enforcement, and he could not control his rage. Rose sent him to a military academy in France. After graduating from the academy, he served in the legion. They were very angry, and Iden did not communicate with his mother for a long time. And now their relationship is not close." She sighed deeply. "However, Iden is a shareholder of Fashion Icon, and he has to communicate with Rose about business matters. Iden has his own architecture business, and he travels a lot."

I pretended that I didn't care about the topic they were discussing, but I tried to hear all the information. Isabel listened with fascination, and I could tell she liked Iden. *Oh, if only you knew what a dark man he is.*

"Mr. Black doesn't have a wife?" Isabel asked.

"Oh, Isabel. Why the curiosity? Have a crush on Iden?" Anna asked.

"No … no … anyway, I'm curious," Isabel said. "He's just so masculine and handsome. By the way, how old is he?"

"He turned thirty-three this year." Anna said.

I politely apologized to the girls and headed off to find a restroom. I took my time walking around and looking at the house and the artwork. All the luxury was fascinating, but it helped me understand that I did not belong to this world. I found a restroom and admired myself in the mirror. *Elle is a wonderful creator of beauty.* I returned to the banquet hall, but the girls were not at the table anymore. I pulled out my cell phone and started scrolling through Facebook.

"Bored?" asked a familiar voice. Iden Black was standing next to me.

"Please leave me alone." I wanted to go, but his hand grabbed my wrist.

"Don't run away from me. Please."

I froze at his touch.

Mrs. Black approached us and said, "Honey, it's good to see you here."

"Good evening, Mom." Iden's expression changed immediately. "I just asked Miss Luka to dance with me. With your permission." Iden dragged me to the dance floor.

Couples were spinning on the dance floor, and the band was playing Ed Sheeran's "Photograph."

Iden put his arms around me gently and turned me toward a group of dancers. I tried to look everywhere but not at him. At that moment, I felt a million different feelings: anger, fear, self-pity, tension. While dancing, time seemed to stand still.

"We never finished talking at the hospital." Iden whispered in my ear. His exhaled air tickled my neck, and I shivered.

"I think we have already said everything we wanted to say." I answered as calmly as I could, and my heart was beating like crazy.

"I want to compensate for the damage," he said as calmly as possible.

I stopped dancing and looked into his eyes. "To repay me for the *damage?*"

"I think I can help you. Tell me how much, and it will be transferred to your account immediately."

I could not believe my ears. "Bastard!" I ran to the bathroom and burst into tears. *Humiliated and hurt again. He took advantage of me, and now he offers me money like a whore?*

There was a knock on the door. I turned off the water, sank to the floor myself, pulled my knees in, and tried to calm myself.

After another knock on the door, there was a loud clatter. The door opened, and Iden burst into the bathroom.

I gasped, but I didn't move. I was as furious as a hundred devils. I clenched my fists.

He stood in front of me, and I moved closer to the wall.

"Shit," he said. "I … don't be afraid of me." He gripped his hair and stared at me.

"Leave me alone—or I'll start screaming." My voice was shaky.

"You misunderstood me. Shit." Iden slumped against the wall. "I can't find a place for myself. I'm not the monster you think I am. I'm very sorry for what happened. I'm still figuring out what happened there."

"Still trying to figure out what happened? You raped me!" I immediately covered my mouth, realizing that someone could have heard.

"I'm sorry for everything. Because of that night. I'm sorry a million times." He kept looking at me.

"Enough apologizing. It won't change anything." I got up from the floor, looked in the mirror, and wiped away my tears. "If your conscience will be calmer, I forgive you." I walked out, leaving him trembling on the floor.

I went to find the girls and tell them I was going home.

Anna said, "Who the hell was here?"

Isabel looked confused.

"Just a misunderstanding," I answered.

"You hit Iden right in front of Rose's eyes," Anna said.

"If I hit him, then it was for something. Don't ask. We cleared up this misunderstanding." I smiled. "I'll talk to Mrs. Black on Monday. If you don't mind, I'll call an Uber and head home."

"I'll take you back." Iden popped up behind us.

Anna and Isabel looked at me.

"Mr. Black, I thought we had said enough to each other. Thanks. I'm a big girl now, and I can go myself." I smiled as realistically as possible.

Before I realized what was happening, Iden grabbed me and threw me over his shoulder.

I started fighting and kicking. "Put me down right away. Immediately!" I ran my hands over his broad back and luxurious suit. "Anna, help me!"

"Have a good evening, ladies." Iden turned toward the door.

I slapped him helplessly. It was so embarrassing.

Everyone watched and applauded like in a circus.

A black SUV was parked by the front door. Iden forced me into the back seat and sat next to me. He told driver to go.

I continued to fight furiously. I reached for the door, but Iden grabbed my hands and asked me to calm down. I tried to kick, bite and otherwise get free.

"Buck all you want, but we'll still talk," Iden said calmly.

"Let me go, you bastard. It's a kidnapping. I'm going to call the police. Save me! Help! Sir, please stop the car. I need to get out." I kept kicking the front passenger seat.

Nobody paid attention to me. The driver drove in silence, and Iden looked out the window.

When I finally looked out the window, I realized that we were going in the opposite direction from my dorm. "You said you'd take me home! Where are we going?"

"I'll bring you home later. We are going to my place. Let's talk for a bit." Iden took out his phone and sent a message.

"I won't go to your house. This is a kidnapping!"

"Luka, I have something to show you. After this conversation, if you still want me to, I'll leave you alone." Iden looked at me, but I couldn't read his expression.

Looking on the terrain, I guessed that we were approaching Winnetka, an upscale town in Illinois. It was an oasis of peace in their lives of excess. We drove up to a huge metal gate that opened to reveal Lake Michigan beyond the lighted house.

At least it's a luxury, I thought.

The SUV stopped, and Iden got out and opened the door for me. "Will you go alone or be carried again?"

I got out of the car without saying anything. The evening was chilly, and my coat was still at Rivera's house. I wrapped my arms around myself and followed Iden to the front door. The house was modern and light and had tinted windows. The well-maintained yard was wide and lit up with outdoor lights.

Iden opened the front door and invited me in.

I slipped inside without saying a word. The interior was no worse than the exterior, and a minimalist style and earthy colors prevailed. The furniture was modern, and in the middle of the living room, there was a chic black sofa. A modern fireplace covered one wall, and the courtyard windows were covered with thin white curtains.

I could see the pool and Lake Michigan beyond the fence.

A bouquet of white roses was on the glass table next to the sofa, and surrealistic paintings hung on the walls. I recognized Salvador Dali's *Dissolved Time*—or at least a copy of it.

"Would you like something to drink?"

I jumped up and turned toward him, ready to attack.

Iden was not disturbed as he showed me a glass with a brown liquid. "I poured myself some whiskey. May I offer you some wine?"

"Whiskey," I replied.

While Iden went to pour the drink, I kicked off my high heels, which were tiring the hell out of my legs. I sat down on the couch and thought, *What am I doing here?*

Iden handed me a glass of whiskey, took off his jacket, and hung it neatly on the back of the armchair.

I could tell he was an orderly and commanding man. *He probably runs things according to a strict schedule, and every glitch makes the people who work for him tremble in fear.* "Why am I here?" I asked.

"Luka, you were high on drugs that night in Las Vegas, just like me." Silence fell again. "My people found out that I had been drugged by an enemy from the past. You were an accidental victim that night."

I listened even thought I was mad.

"They have photos from the room and are threatening to make them public. Of course they don't mean to hurt you—it's all about me—and you're an accidental victim. I am very sorry."

There was another long silence.

"What photos?" I asked barely audibly, but I understood what kind of pictures he was talking about. If Iden was telling the truth, I would most likely be a victim of a porn game. The kettle boiled in my head.

"Pictures of us ... having sex." He downed the rest of his whiskey.

I sipped mine too. The drink burned my throat, and I started coughing. When I looked up at Iden, he looked even more upset than I did.

"My God. If those pictures are released, if my parents see them, my father will kill me. I brought dishonor on my family!"

"Don't worry. I'm trying to fix it." Iden stood up, poured himself another glass of whiskey, and drank it in one gulp. "The worst part is that we can't track down the bastard. Before our first meeting at the Hilton, a package containing pictures was sent to my office. I really didn't expect to see you again. When I saw you, I recognized you as the girl from the hotel." Iden sat down. "When I woke up that morning at the hotel, you were gone. I remember almost nothing from that night, but when I saw the bloodied sheets, I knew something bad had happened. Then those pictures..."

"Can I see them?" I asked in a cold voice.

"I don't think that's a good idea—"

"I want to see them, and it's not a request!"

Iden stood up and walked down the hall. A few minutes later, he returned with an envelope and placed it on the table in front of me.

I took the envelope with trembling hands and looked at it for a long time.

Iden sat restlessly beside me.

Finally, I made up my mind and took the photos out of the envelope. Time stopped again. Images of that night flashed back: me on the floor, my face turned toward the camera, eyes like glass, Iden sucking on my breast. In the next picture, we were already in bed. He undressed my legs, and my face was like stone. There were maybe ten such shots. In the next picture, Iden's lips were tightly pursed, and I was trying to hold onto the edge of the bed. Tears were running down my cheeks. In the last photo, I am half naked—with bloody thighs and a bloody dress. A naked body was beside me, and one hand was draped over my stomach.

I shook, and I looked up at him. "But why do they need all this? Why me? Why?" I did not understand what was happening.

Iden looked at me with an icy face, sat down on the armchair, and sighed. "You just happened to be in the wrong place at the wrong time. Those photos prove that I'm a rapist." He clenched his teeth. "Why didn't you go to the police after that night, Luka? It was necessary to seek help. Any normal girl would have done that. I don't understand the reason for your silence." Iden was looking straight into my eyes.

I looked at him for a long time, but I could not speak. I turned my gaze to the glass wall and whispered, "I was afraid that no one would believe me. I blamed myself for drinking too much. I don't know. I'm trying to move on and forget that night." I turned to Iden. "If those photos are made public, I will not be able to stand it."

"Those who stunned us expected you to contact the law enforcement. It would have ruined me—and they still hope to. If those photos are released, there will be a scandal. You would be attacked by the media unless …"

"Unless what?"

"Unless we make a public announcement about the engagement … then this game would be meaningless."

"Have you lost your mind? What engagement?" I jumped up and started walking around the room.

"This is only temporary … until I find out where the person who organized all this is hiding. Once all the compromising material is removed, we will be able to announce that we have parted ways—and that's it."

"You're completely out of your mind. I won't get into these

games. I'll call an Uber and go home. What's the address?" I started looking for my bag.

"This is the only option, Luka. If the photos are made public, and we are a couple, we will simply be able to say that these are fake photos. We'll both stay out of trouble." Iden stood up and moved closer to me. "Think about it. Liam will pick you up."

I returned to the dormitory at two o'clock in the morning. Iden's chauffeur gave me his jacket and escorted me to my front door. He seemed like a nice guy, but he was 100 percent at Iden's pleasure.

After slamming my door, I took off my shoes and placed them in the shoe cabinet. After taking off my dress and changing into soft, heart-embellished pajamas, I curled up under the covers and fell into a fitful sleep.

CHAPTER SIX

LUKA

On Sunday morning, I woke up completely unrested. Elle did not come home that night. *She must have reconciled with Martin and stayed with him.* I tossed and turned in bed, thought about the conversation with Iden, and took a shower. I had fallen asleep without removing my makeup, and I woke up with black circles around my eyes like a panda. After the shower, I recovered a bit and decided to go for breakfast at the Corner Cafe. I thought pancakes with maple syrup would really lift my spirits.

The morning was chilly, and dark clouds floated across the sky. When I went outside, I wrapped myself tighter in my down coat. By the time I got to the cafe, my hands were shaking. Several elderly gentlemen were sitting in the cafe. I greeted the waitress and ordered American crepes with maple syrup. I was munching on my crepes and drinking my coffee when a gentleman at the next table caught my attention. There was a picture of Iden carrying me over his shoulder, and the headline was "Has Black's Heart Found Love Again?"

Cannot be!

I quickly finished my breakfast and ran to the nearest newsstand. I bought the newspaper and immediately started reading the article on the front page:

Sensation! A famous architect, 33-year-old Iden Black has been named Chicago's most desirable bachelor for several years. Yesterday, he was spotted at the home of designer Alvaro Rivera (30), a newcomer to the fashion world, with the beautiful Lithuanian Luka Ilgauskaitė (23), who works at one of the companies managed by Iden, Fashion Icon. According to the guests of the party, sparks really flew between them. We want to remind you that Iden Black dated and was engaged to famous model Mari Prescott (29) for five years, but Mari left him during their wedding and secretly married another famous architect Logan Toms (36 years old).

What a shit!

Below the article were some pictures of us dancing and him carrying me over his shoulder.

Oh my God, Mrs. Black is going to fire me!

Monday morning came to Chicago with fluffy snow and cold. I was going to work after a couple of lectures, and my morning started with a trip to the university. Before lunch, I took the elevator to the office. In the lobby, as always, the stony blonde looked bored. After seeing me, she said good morning and continued staring at her computer monitor.

Something new, I thought.

Isabel was drowning in file folders, but she immediately asked was happening with Mr. Black.

"Isabel, not now." I really didn't know what to say or how to make an excuse. "It's gossip. Journalists exaggerated the facts."

Mrs. Black opened the door and said, "Luka, come with me." She turned on her heel and returned to her office.

An ominous tone, I thought. I stood at my desk for a moment and tried to gather my thoughts. *She'll probably crack me like a nut. Well, Luka, enjoy your last moments at work.*

"Good morning, Mrs. Black," I said as boldly as I could as I stood in front of her desk.

"Sit down." Mrs. Black motioned to the chair in front of her.

An inauspicious start indeed. She seemed overly calm.

I slumped like a sack in my chair and waited to see what would happen next.

Mrs. Black looked at me for a long moment and then forced a fake smile. "Luka, honey, I've talked to Iden, but I want to hear the whole story from you." Mrs. Black folded her arms and looked into my eyes.

A shiver ran down my spine. *Did Iden tell her about that night in Vegas?*

"I don't quite understand what story you're talking about." I tried to pretend to be indifferent.

"Honey, you don't have to hide anything. I'm not really angry … not at all."

The office door opened, and Iden walked in. "Mom." He nodded to her, and when he came over to me, he pecked me on the lips. "Hello, sweetheart. How's your day going?"

I lost my voice. "He-llo. Good. How about you?" I barely squeezed out a logical sentence without raising my voice.

"It's good now." He smiled, took my hand, and sat down. "Luka, dear, I just talked to my mother yesterday and told her everything." Iden looked into my eyes as if he were waiting for understanding and approval.

"Everything?" I felt my face turning red.

"Yes, everything." Iden turned to Mrs. Black. "Everything about us and about the engagement party that we will hold on Christmas Eve."

Oh my God, don't do that. Don't do it! Iden is carrying out his plan without my approval?

Mrs. Black said, "I don't even know how to react. However, if the kind of love that Iden told me about yesterday really ignited between you, then I bless your relationship—and I will help organize the most luxurious engagement party." She clapped her hands and hugged us.

"I ... I—"

"Mom, if you don't mind, I'm taking Luka to lunch." Iden smiled.

"Of course. Of course." Mrs. Black looked very pleased. "Luka, don't come back to work today. You may not show up tomorrow either. Get settled comfortably in your new home."

I looked questioningly at Iden.

He intertwined his fingers with mine and led me out of the office.

I managed to grab my purse and coat as I passed my desk.

Isabel looked at us in disbelief, and I shrugged apologetically.

The stony blonde was sitting in a daze when she saw us holding hands. *At least Serafina will no longer feel superior to me.*

Once we got into the black Audi SUV, I said, "Iden, what the hell? Have you completely lost your mind? We? What else are we? Engagement? Did you hit your head? Sir, take us to the hospital. This gentleman needs a health check as soon as possible."

"Calm down," Iden said. "After yesterday's article in one of the most famous American newspapers, there was no other way out."

I shouted "But I did not agree to participate in this circus. I said I'd think about it, and my 'think about it' always means no!"

"I think we both don't want this circus, but there is no other way out. We'll announce the engagement over the weekend. Luka, I don't know how long it will take, but I will fix everything. It's only temporary. Later, you can live as you want and spit on me."

"What about my family? How will they react? After all, they are alive, and they have feelings. My mother thinks I will be an old maid and that I need a husband. Can you imagine how happy she will be that I found a husband? And then it will go through because I will get a divorce." I was always confusing English words.

"We can visit them. I'll get to know them, and they'll calm down."

"And then, after a month, two—or who knows how much time—I will say that we broke up? My parents won't take me home." I burst into tears. "They don't have the same views as your mother."

"Don't worry about it. I will take all the blame. Let's go eat. We have a lot to do later."

We returned to Iden's house in Winnetka at ten o'clock that evening. Five inches of snow had fallen that day, and it was very cold. I was glad to enter a warm, dry space. My phone rang, and I ran into the library to answer it.

"Where the hell are you?" Elle shouted.

"Hello, Elle. I forgot to write you that I won't be back at the dormitory tonight."

"You're not coming back? Where are you?" Her tone changed to curious.

"I'm at a friend's house. Long story … don't ask anything." I tried to stay calm.

"Lu, what friend? You have a boyfriend, and you don't tell me anything?"

"Elle, I will tell you everything when we meet." I was getting really very upset.

"OK, I'm burning with impatience! Rodriguez was looking for you today. He wanted to hand over next week's work schedule. I found it. You will be working on Christmas, and I was so hoping that we would celebrate Christmas together."

"There's still a week until Christmas. We'll figure something out." I tried to be as cheerful as possible. "OK, I can't talk anymore. I have to go. Bye, Elle."

"Bye, honey. Have fun with Mr. Mysterious." Elle laughed.

Iden was staring out the window with a glass of whiskey in his hand.

I went to the living room, sat on the sofa, and looked at his back. "Or maybe I could live in a dormitory?"

Iden turned and said, "If we live separately, no one will believe we are in our love. This is the best way." His phone rang. He looked at it and slipped it back into his pocket. "Come on. I'll show you where your room will be."

I followed Iden to the second floor, which was just as beautiful as the first. The size of the room assigned to me was like two rooms in my native house.

The room was bright, and there was a large bed by the wall. The triangular floor-to-ceiling window was decorated with white curtains that fell elegantly along its sides, and it perfectly matched the design of the furniture. If I looked carefully through the window, I could see the lake. All the furniture was white, and it looked very chic. There were two more doors in the room. The first one led to a spacious bathroom with an elegant bathtub in the middle of the room. It had four legs that resembled the paws of a lion. One wall was mirrored with mosaic pieces, and there were two elegant wash-basins. In the corner, a flower reached the ceiling. Chandeliers hung from the ceiling. Behind the second door, I found a wardrobe with clothes in it. Confused, I turned to Iden. "Is this someone's room?"

"No. This is your room now. You can use everything in your wardrobe. I asked a designer I know to buy everything you might need while you live here."

"I didn't ask you to buy me anything. I have my own clothes, and they are enough for me."

"If we're going to pretend that we're a couple, you must look good. But do as you desire. Good night." He left the room.

I wandered around the room for a long time and explored everything. The room looked more like a princess's room than a common man's room. Everything was so luxurious and posh. In the dressing room, I touched the fabrics of all the clothes. They were all so soft: silk, cashmere, and the devil knows what kind of fabrics. The clothes still had tags. I glanced at some of the prices and gasped when I read that a sparkly dress that would barely cover my butt cost fifteen thousand dollars. After receiving such a price shock, I fell onto the bed and wondered what would happen next.

In the morning, I was woken by bright sunlight coming through the window. Opening my eyes, I tried to understand where I was. Frightened, I sat down and looked around. Lake Michigan was looming outside the window. *In my new room at Iden's in Winnetka.* Since I hadn't brought any clothes from my dorm, I had to wear the new ones. I pulled on a light cashmere sweater, deep blue jeans, and ankle boots. I put my hair in a loose ponytail and smelled the perfume I found in my bag. *How did he know the size of my shoes and clothes?*

When I went downstairs, I found a note on the kitchen table: "You will find what you need for breakfast in the fridge. I will be back soon. A." I found sandwiches and coffee and went to the living room. In the corner, there was a fir tree that was two meters tall. The whole room smelled like a forest. Maybe a dozen boxes with various Christmas decorations were placed next to it.

"Wow. At least it's a tree." I whistled. "I'll take care of you in a moment, beautiful, but first, I need breakfast." Satisfied with the day off, I fell on the soft sofa and turned on the TV.

After breakfast, I listened to music that creates a Christmas mood: *Egidijus Sipavičius's* "Snow Is Falling." I started decorating the Christmas tree, singing, and dancing loudly. For a moment, I felt like I was at home—a house that smelled like a forest, beautiful Christmas toys, sparkles, and Christmas songs—and the upbeat mood enchanted me. As I danced, I turned toward the hallway.

Iden was leaning against the wall and looking at me.

"I didn't hear you come back." I was embarrassed. "How long have you been standing here?"

"For a while. Do you like it?" He pointed to the tree.

"I like it. In Lithuania, we only decorate the Christmas tree on Christmas Eve." *Why the hell am I being so nice to him? Luka, he is a bad person.*

"OK."

"Take it." I handed him a beautiful glass bubble. "Hang it. This is your Christmas tree."

"I do not know how. I'm not a specialist in decorating Christmas trees." He laughed.

What a beautiful smile you have.

"Just see where there aren't enough bubbles and hang it." I shrugged.

Iden hung the toy and turned to me. "As well?"

I bowed my head.

Iden moved closer and reached for my head.

I froze and held my breath.

Iden looked at me and backed away hastily. "There are thorns in your hair." He held out his palm, which contained several thorns.

"Apparently, it happened when I was decorating the Christmas tree."

Iden scowled and said, "Pack your suitcase. We have to be at the airport in an hour."

"Why?"

"We will fly to Lithuania … to see your parents. I need to get to know your people so that everything is done 100 percent correctly. It's better to think about everything in advance to avoid any unforeseen gaps later." He left the room so quickly that I doubted whether he had been there or was just playing with me.

"Of course." I sighed. *After all, everything is just a game. No one cares about my family or my feelings.*

After that, everything was like a movie. I finished decorating the house, out of breath, threw some clothes in a suitcase I found in the closet, and stood outside. Since we flew on Iden's private plane—otherwise, the rich, it turns out, don't know how to live—we were in Vilnius exactly ten hours later. As is usual, at that time of year, Lithuania was gripped by the cold. There was a lot of snow outside, and we couldn't take a step without long boots.

Iden was huddled up getting off the plane, and I was so happy I didn't feel the cold.

We arrived at my parents' house after a three-hour drive since the traffic was terrible. When I entered my parents' yard, I was filled with excitement. It was seven at night, and my parents had finished working. The light was on in the house. I turned to Iden and whispered, "I don't think this is a good idea. They're good people, Iden. Let's not drag them into all this shit."

"Let's finish what we started." Iden took my hand. "Everything will be resolved later, and your parents will forget about me."

But will I forget you?

CHAPTER SEVEN

LUKA

"Hello, Mom. Surprise!" I said to my mother as happily as possible as soon as she opened the door.

"Luka." My mother caught up and grabbed me in her arms, and she started kissing me, hugging me, and calling my name.

"Mom, you're going to suffocate me." I tried to joke.

"How are you here?" Mother could not believe it. "Why didn't you say anything about coming back? For long? Maybe forever?"

"We just decided to come." I excused myself without going into a deeper discussion.

"And who is this gentleman?" Mom looked at Iden.

"Mom, this … this is my … my fiancé, Iden." I managed to get the last words out.

"Who? Fiancé? I hear well, don't I?" Mother looked surprised.

"You hear well, Mom." I spoke even more quietly. "Iden, I told my mom you're my fiancé." I spoke to him in English, and he handed Mom a bouquet of flowers he'd bought on the way. In English, he said, "Nice to meet you ma'am," and he kissed her hand.

The whole day resembled a traditional happy family reunion. Iden only spoke English, but he got along with my parents as best he could—with the help of my translation. My sister came with her family. I had missed her little twins very much, and I spent the whole evening playing with them. Iden brought perfume, jewelry, fishing gear, a bunch of the latest toys, and all sorts of other goodies. Everyone was so impressed with the abundance of gifts. My mom smiled so much, and it made me sad to think that this whole circus would end sooner or later, and my parents would be very sad. I also managed to meet Arn. He agreed to come after being asked a lot— even though he had a fight with our father.

"Arn, how are you?" I asked when the two of us were left in the kitchen.

"Somehow. Is it that obvious?" My brother smiled. He was gaunt and had black eyes.

"You look sad and tired. I would never say that, but maybe I can help?" I asked in a soft voice.

"I'll manage everything myself." Arn hugged me for the first time in a long time and kissed my forehead.

I took one step closer to my brother.

"I'm glad you're back," he added sadly.

"If you still need help, always reach out." I nudged my brother and returned to Iden.

In the evening, my mother made a bed for us in my room. She wished us both a good night and closed the door.

Iden looked around the room, studying framed photos and other things from my childhood.

"How will it be now?" I asked to distract him from focusing on his surroundings.

"We're going to bed," Iden answered calmly as he took off his clothes. "I'm too tired to think." He fell on my cramped and hard bed, covered himself with a blanket, and instantly disconnected, gesturing with his hand that there would be enough space for me too. I undressed, slipped into my warm pajamas, and curled up in the corner of the bed. I stayed as far away from Iden as possible—even though one part of my body was reacting very strangely to sleeping with him.

The flight had exhausted both of us, and I logged off without agonizing for too long. The whole night, I dreamed that he was caressing me, touching me, hugging me, and stroking my hair. I liked it, I won't lie, although I was well aware that it wasn't appropriate to act like that. I felt excited.

When I woke up in the morning, I didn't understand why I couldn't move. I opened my eyes and saw that Iden was hugging me. His heavy arm rested on me, and one leg was draped over mine. I was afraid to even move. *And what to do now?*

"Good morning, Luka. How did you sleep?" Iden kissed my hair.

"Good morning. Thanks. Good. How about you?" I closed my eyes.

"Good. I rested." He didn't lift his hand. He just squeezed my stomach even harder and gently traced a straight line from the navel up with his fingers.

A shiver ran down my spine, and the place just caught fire. I didn't know my body. I understood that it was a rising lust, although I realized that it should not be. *He is a bad man.* I was dizzy, and I had to do something. "Would you please let me go?" I finally said.

"If that's what you want." He rolled over on his back.

I quickly ran to the bathroom, locked myself inside, and started smiling. I raised my eyes to the mirror; I was not the same girl who had left to find happiness in America. My big green eyes were shining, my cheeks were red, my heart was pounding, and my breathing was fast. I involuntarily ran my hand along the same line on my stomach where Iden had touched. I shuddered at the memory of his touch and smiled again.

When I returned to the room, Iden was sitting at my desk, examining a photograph. "Who's this?"

It was a photograph of me as a child. I was wearing braces and thick glasses. I was ashamed again. "It's me. Quit staring." I prayed these days would pass quickly.

DECEMBER 23, 2018

We returned to Chicago on Christmas Eve. Iden didn't touch me for the rest of our stay in Lithuania, and he was pretty quiet. I enjoyed the silence. The journey home was silent, but we exchanged strange glances sometimes. Iden was focused on his tablet. I kept wondering if he realized that I liked his touch.

It snowed even more in Chicago. I walked into the house and brushed the snow off my down coat.

Iden turned to me and spoke for the first time in ten hours. "Tomorrow is our engagement party. If you want, you can invite your friends. My mother is organizing the party at the Hilton restaurant." He went to the study and slammed the door. He seemed angry with me. *It seems to be more of a pain for you than for me.*

In the morning, Iden walked around like he had sold the land.

I just flirted with him and asked him to be ready in a few hours. I invited Elle, Martin, and Rodriguez to the party. I would tell them the reason for the party when they arrived. At half past three, I started getting ready. I soaked in the bath, put on some light makeup, curled my hair into neat curls that fell lightly over my shoulders, and put on a short, red, silk dress with an open back and black pointed shoes. I went down to the living room, stood by the glass wall, stared into the distance, and thought about my murky future.

"You look beautiful." Iden approached. "Only these are missing." He put a box in my hand.

I opened it and saw beautiful teardrop-shaped gold earrings with sparkling diamonds.

"Thank you, Iden. You really didn't have to."

"It doesn't matter ... just wear them. I think they'll do just fine." He turned away from me to pour himself a glass of whiskey.

At that moment, I felt very bad again. I put on the earrings and pretended not to care. "I'm ready, we can go."

Iden looked up at me. "One more thing." He took out another box and held out a white gold ring with an impressively large gem. "You are my beloved fiancée—and how are you a fiancée without a ring?" He took my left hand and put the ring on my finger.

The ring was heavy but graceful. I was thrilled. If I didn't know it was all fake, I'd be the happiest woman in the world. I started to smile, and I looked up at Iden. His expression was eerie. His lips were pursed, his eyes were angry, and he looked like he was in a lot of pain.

Without saying anything, he turned and walked toward the front door.

Blushing with embarrassment, I followed.

A flock of media had gathered outside the Hilton.

When our Audi SUV pulled up, Iden got out first, straightened his suit, and opened the door for me. He took my hand and helped me out. He put his arm around my waist and let them take a few photos. Everyone was told that it was a private celebration, and only a few journalists would be allowed inside.

We went inside. My heart was beating faster and faster. He looked like he was about to have a panic attack. The banquet hall was full of people—none of whom I knew—and I looked around with wide-open eyes. The chic hall was decorated with flowers and crystal candlesticks, and round tables and chairs. I saw cards with names on the tables and luxurious dishes. A live band was playing on the stage. My head began to spin.

"My sweet cookies. I knew there was something going on between you when I saw you in this restaurant." Alvaro Rivera grabbed me in his arms, kissed my cheeks, and squeezed Iden's hand tightly.

"Thank you, Mr. Alvaro. Everything happened very quickly and unexpectedly," I said.

"There's no need to be ashamed. I'll want to hear all the details," Rivera said.

Iden kindly apologized and took me to meet other people he knew. For an hour, we said hello and listened to greetings. Finally,

Iden picked up a glass of champagne and handed me another, and we went to the stage. He told the musicians not to play anymore and asked for everyone's attention.

"Good evening. Today, we are gathered here for a special occasion … to celebrate the most beautiful holiday of the year and to celebrate love." Iden turned to me and took my hand. "I met this charming lady last summer. She impressed me with her modesty, elegance, sincerity, and light. When I started thinking about her furrowed brow every time she's angry, her damn big green eyes when she's scared, and her warm smile when she's happy, I knew I wanted to see that every day for the rest of my life. So, after a lot of effort, we are standing here together." Iden smiled at me so sincerely. "And Luka agreed to be my wife." He cupped my face with his hands and kissed me. His lips were warm and smooth. I froze, but my heart did not listen. I opened my lips and accepted the kiss. Iden pulled his face away and put his fingers to his lips. He seemed as confused as I was.

When everyone in the hall clapped and shouted, his face turned red. Iden took my hand, and we walked off the stage.

The congratulators came in droves, and I finally familiar faces. Elle and the boys were approaching us.

Elle hugged me and looked back at me and Iden. "Luka, what was that all about?"

"Surprise!" I grinned as if I had won the lottery. "Elle, Martin, and Rodriguez, this is the great love of my life, Iden Black." I hated lying to my best friends.

"Hello." Elle shook Iden's hand. "We want to congratulate you on your engagement." Elle hugged me again and whispered, "Our conversation is not over yet."

Rodriguez greeted us very formally. Deep in my heart, I cried like a child.

The party went on late, and I drank a few glasses of champagne to relax and act more realistically. I was chatting with Anna and Isabel, and Iden was discussing plans with Mrs. Black. I felt the tension.

A strikingly beautiful woman with dark hair, green eyes, and slim, long legs approached us.

Iden's expression changed from his usual scowl to icy, and Mrs. Black looked petrified.

"Iden, honey, why aren't you answering my calls?" the woman asked.

"Mari, what are you doing here?" Iden said through gritted teeth.

I remembered Iden calling me Mari that night and the article about how his ex-fiancée was named Mari. *He loves Mari. Is this the same Mari?*

Iden's nostrils flared like a bull's, and his chest heaved more violently than usual. *Yes, it's really the same Mari. She is really beautiful—even more beautiful than in the photos.* I felt like a little mouse who didn't fit in at all in the company of these beautiful people.

"Iden, I don't think you want to marry that gray mouse when I'm here. I came back for you. It's over between Logan and me. Don't make that mistake. After all, I know you still love *me*." She said the last word while looking at me.

Iden turned to me and told me that Liam would take me home. He then grabbed Mari's hand and led her out of the hall. I shrugged and apologized to the girls, and I told them I was very tired and was going home. I told Liam to get the car. I went out into the cool evening by myself and held back my tears. I couldn't understand why I felt that way.

A cab stopped, and Rodriguez opened the window and asked if something had happened.

Without thinking, I opened the door and got in. I needed to cry on a friendly shoulder. I asked the driver to get us out of there as quickly as possible, snuggled into Rodriguez's coat, and started pouring out my heartache.

Rodriguez rented a small room above a garage in Lemont. Rodriguez's house was about an hour away. As we drove, I calmed down and looked at the road. Although there was one more tear that shouldn't have been shed, it was much better than at the beginning of the trip. Once we were at his house, he suggested wine or a beer. I chose beer. I settled comfortably on the sofa, covered myself with a blanket, and sipped my beer.

"Where is your fiancé?" he asked.

"Somewhere," I answered.

"What's up, Lu? You are somehow different. Is it real?" Rodriguez looked puzzled.

"Everything is more real than you think." I realized that, despite everything, I was starting to like Iden, but his heart was occupied. The ground began to slip from under my feet. I felt jealous, and that horrible feeling was gnawing at me.

"Are you angry?" Rodriguez asked.

"You can say that." I pursed my lips. "His ex-fiancée came to the engagement party. Iden he told me to go home with the driver, and he left with her."

"Heartache?" Rodriguez looked at me. "I can see that it hurts. Come closer. Crying will help." He hugged me.

I put my head on his chest, and we sat like that until I had no more strength to cry.

I cried about everything—and not just about that night. I cried the most about being so stupid. A small part of me began to believe in a relationship that didn't exist. *How could I have been so deceived? Did I really think a man like Iden would pay attention to me? Why am I so naïve?*

IDEN

"You're such an idiot, Iden." Liam looked angry. He walked around me and fired angry lightning bolts. Liam sometimes looked twenty years older than he really was, and his sermons wore out even the most patient man.

"I don't understand." I was really angry.

"Can you at least guess where she could be?" Liam asked.

"I called her friends, and she is not with anyone." I sighed.

"I told you that you have to finish this whole performance with Mari immediately. Decide which one you want. He turned on his heel and went outside.

I paced the room restlessly. *Mari crawls under my skin like a snake. I don't know if I want her, but it's fun to see her so humbled. This is a great opportunity to get revenge on her husband. Maybe a small part of me still wants the feeling of freedom that I experienced only with her, but another part of me wants to pursue Luka. Luka is a very dangerous woman, but she does not know it. She could destroy a happy man's life with one finger, but she could also make that man the happiest man in the world. I am completely lost.* "Damn it." I punched a hole in the wall. *Shit.*

I shamelessly fucked Mari tonight, but I was thinking about Luka. It made me sick to remember Mari's blissful face.

Bitch.

I don't understand what is happening to me. I can't find a place for myself. I'm angry with myself, and I'm angry with Luka. *Where the hell are you? I really want her to suffer like I am now. I want to hurt her and completely control her and make her obey me. I can't help myself.* I run my fingers through my hair and walk along the terrace. *Luka will pay for this joke. No one treats Iden Black like that—no one. Luka, you will understand who is leading this parade. I will not forget this, and I will not let it slip through my fingers. Luka, where are you? You haven't been home for almost a day.*

LUKA

I opened my eyes, and it was already light outside the window. I slept on Rodriguez's sofa. I smelled freshly brewed coffee. My head was heavy from the beer and the crying, and I was in no rush to move. However, a full bladder forced me to get up.

"Good morning. You're up early." I smiled at my friend. "By the way, merry Christmas." I kissed him on the cheek.

"Good morning, chica. Merry Christmas to you too. Here's fresh coffee for the most charming girl in the whole world." Rodriguez handed me a cup of coffee with a smile on his face.

"Thank you. I really needed that. My head is heavy from yesterday's alcohol." I smiled.

"When you fell asleep, your fiancé called. I have no idea where he got my phone number."

I rolled my eyes.

"Don't be afraid. I didn't tell him that you were with me. Let him suffer." Rodriguez smiled. "I told Elle that you were here. She will be here soon."

"Thank you. You are a true friend." I smiled and hugged my friend. I sipped my coffee, stared at my hands, and contemplated my alleged engagement. *Maybe I should stop playing this stupid game now?*

An hour later, Elle came to us with Chinese food and a terribly funny Santa Claus hat. She brought normal clothes because I was still wearing the red dress. We had lunch, and the three of us sat down like before. Rodriguez had to go to work, and I was forced to stay there, although I would have really liked to go to work too. Elle and I drank two bottles of wine, and I relaxed a little again. *It's time to go back to your pretend home.* Just the thought of having to crouch in that manicured cage gave me chills.

I took a cab back to my supposed home. The gate was open, and a couple of Audi SUVs were parked in the yard. It was already well after four o'clock in the evening. The lights were on in the house. I stood at the front door since I didn't have a key. I put the bag of yesterday's clothes by the front door, went around to the back gate, and walked out onto the snowy shore of Lake Michigan. The wind was blowing fiercely, and I walked slowly, leaving my footprints in the snow. I wanted to distract myself and realize what a mess was brewing in my head. I walked about half a kilometer, got tired, sat down on a bench, and looked at the setting sun. All kinds of thoughts and contradictions were running through my head. I couldn't figure out what I was feeling and what I wasn't feeling anymore—and whether it was right or not. I heard crunching in the snow and turned to see Iden walking toward me.

"Where the hell have you been?" He pulled me to my feet. "Why didn't you come home all night?"

"You were busy, and I decided to celebrate the holidays with the people I want to be with."

"What other people? What the hell are you thinking? We are a very happy couple who just announced our engagement!"

"A fucking happy couple? I'm about to show you what a fucking happy couple we are!" I growled, pushed Iden, and ran toward home.

Iden was a step behind me. "What did you think of throwing out again?" He grabbed my hand.

"Let me go, animal. I'm not your fucking property!" I tore my hand from his embrace, turned around, and continued toward the house. "What a man. What nonsense. What a character!" I said loudly in Lithuanian, gesticulating with my hands.

Iden laughed.

That laugh of his completely pissed me off. I turned around and pointed at him. "Don't laugh at me!"

Iden pulled me closer and kissed my lips.

I tried to control myself. I hit his chest and shoulders, but finally I gave in to my feelings and responded to the kiss.

Iden tightened his grip on me and used his tongue to massage my tongue and my bottom lip. One hand touched my hair and my ear, and the other held my waist.

I could no longer think soberly. I gave in to emotion. I wrapped my arms around Iden's neck and sighed.

Iden pulled his lips away and looked at me with his dark eyes. "Peace?" he whispered.

"Over my dead body," I answered.

Iden smiled and started me kissing again. We stood like that until we were completely frozen.

When we got home, I rushed to the fireplace to warm my hands. I kept replaying the kiss in my head and smiling.

Iden wrapped me in a blanket and then brought me a cup of hot chocolate and marshmallows.

"Thank you," I said. "Why do you behave like this?"

"How's that?" Iden asked.

I shrugged. "You're so good to me."

"Maybe because I want to be like that," he answered gently.

We drank hot chocolate in silence and stared at the fireplace.

Iden started teasing me about my childhood, friends, school, and anything else that interested him. I had to tell the embarrassing story of my first kiss and the time I fell into a rosebush while riding my bike—and my braids got tangled in it. There was no way to get them out. Dad had to cut them with hedge shears.

Iden burst out laughing, clutched his stomach, and fell on the floor. It was great to see him so relaxed and happy. It was completely different from what I had seen before.

He got up and walked over to the Christmas tree. He took a package from under it and brought it to me. "This is for you. Merry Christmas, Luka." He kissed me on the cheek.

"Thank you. You didn't have to." I smiled. "I don't have a present for you."

"Never mind. There will be more than one Christmas." Iden smiled.

I opened the package, which was quite heavy. Inside was a beautiful music box. I opened it and heard a familiar tune playing, and the ballerina inside began to spin. I smiled. "Thank you. She's perfect. I used to take dance lessons, and I really liked dancing, but I had to give it all up."

"Why?" Iden asked.

"My sister had a fight with my parents about money, and then my dad said that I couldn't go to dance school anymore because it caused arguments at home. I don't want to think about it anymore." I sighed. "I'm tired. I'm going to sleep."

Iden helped me stand up, and he put an arm around my shoulders and led me upstairs. We walked into my room, and I turned to him. His face was no longer as radiant and relaxed as it had been before.

"Iden, why are you so grumpy?" I asked gently.

"You can go to bed now," Iden replied coldly.

"Did something happen? You were happy downstairs—"

"Enough!"

I flinched and could not believe the change in him.

"We were being watched by the paparazzi because of what you did yesterday when you went out for a night out with who-knows-who. Now they have enough information and photos that we are a perfectly matched pair of lovers. The words were simply spat out by lovers and the perfect couple. If you want to communicate like this, we will communicate like this—when we are alone. Do you understand?" Iden walked off sternly and closed the door.

I collapsed and sobbed, silently biting my lower lip to stop myself from crying out loud. After fifteen minutes, I forced myself to stand up. I locked the door and then locked myself in the bathroom. I fell asleep, curled up in a ball, and felt sorry for myself.

After staying in bed on Sunday, I got up early on Monday, quickly got ready, and went home. In the lobby, I greeted the building supervisor and conveyed my wishes to his family. When I took the elevator to my office, I was greeted by the annoying stares of my coworkers. Everyone looked at me like some kind of prostitute who got my job through Iden's bed.

Anna and Isabel treated me kindly. Mrs. Black had gone to Florida for a winter vacation.

In the days leading up to New Year's, I walked around corners to avoid Iden. I quietly went to work and went home again.

On New Year's Eve morning, I found Iden in the kitchen. I couldn't avoid meeting him. He told me to get ready for the evening because we had to go to party with his friends. I was in the office for half the day, and then I decided to treat myself by going to my old workplace. The restaurant was full. My colleagues were happy to see me and served me *cepelinai* (potato dumplings). I was happy to spend a few hours with them.

When I got home, I showered and put on a black jumpsuit. I couldn't wear a bra because it only had thin crisscross chains instead of straps and a bare back. I put my hair in a ponytail and made my eyes brighter. I put gloss on my lips and put on the tassels that Elle gave me. I put on red high-heeled shoes, red mittens, and a black fur over my shoulders. I went down to the living room and poured myself a glass of whiskey. I decided to have fun like I'd never had before. I got a text from Iden on my phone: "Liam will take you." Of course, how could it be otherwise? I took one gulp of whiskey, shook myself off, and went to find Liam.

He was standing by the door, waiting for me. "Miss, with your permission." He opened the back door of the SUV.

"You don't need all those missus and other blah blah blah, Liam. How much older are you? Ten years? We are from the same stratum—you may even be from a better one—so we are equal. I'm fucking Iden's puppet."

Liam blushed like a beet and closed the door.

We reached the luxury hotel near the Millennium Park after an hour. The streets of Chicago were clogged with traffic. Everyone rushed to meet the New Year.

After stopping the car, Liam jumped up like a bunny and opened the door.

I forced a smile and walked boldly into the hotel. The party was taking place on the top floor. I left the elevator still full of determination. I tossed my coat theatrically to the supervisor and walked toward the crowd with my head held high. The person I was interested in could be seen from afar: a dark, sleek suit, carefully gelled and slightly tousled hair, and his posture oozing with arrogance.

Mari was standing next to Iden, holding his hand, in a dress that barely covered her ass. I stopped the waiter and grabbed a glass of whiskey from the tray. I finished it without taking a breath. I took another glass of whiskey and a glass of champagne from another waiter. I poured the whiskey for myself, without even shaking it, and thought it was pretty good. Bees started whistling in my head, and I felt even braver. I clutched my glass of champagne and strode toward my target.

Iden's eyes narrowed when he saw me, but I wasn't scared.

I raised my chin even more and moved my butt to join their company. "Good evening," I said a little more kindly. "Honey." I smiled at Iden and took a graceful sip of champagne.

"Honey, can we talk?" Iden said through gritted teeth.

I surveyed the men standing beside the beautiful couple and saw a handsome young man. "Are you dancing?" I asked, looking into his eyes.

"Yes, I am." he said with a smile.

"Maybe I should have the honor of asking you to dance with me?" I arched my already arched eyebrows even more.

The stranger smiled kindly and held out his hand, accepting the invitation.

I took another sip of champagne and forced the glass into Iden's hands. The contents of the glass spilled onto his fancy suit.

When we entered the dance floor, "Don't Stop the Party" was playing. *Pitbull is my favorite.* We both felt the rhythm of the Latin music and started dancing happily. All my problems floated away, and only the music and the fun feeling of returning to something long forgotten remained. My companion had a great sense of rhythm and knew a lot of dance steps. If I turned a little to the side, he immediately caught the angle and performed the desired movement. We danced for the whole song, and then "Lambada" came on. We danced as if we were the most experienced dancing couple. It was so fun that the smile didn't disappear from my face.

Before the song ended, Iden stopped us, grabbed my wrist, and led me to a quieter space. "What the hell are you doing?"

"I was having fun, honey. Isn't that what we're here for?" I asked sarcastically.

"Get ready now. Go wash off that whore makeup and act like a normal fiancée." Iden's hands were balled into fists.

"Don't be afraid. I won't fuck anyone today," I said coldly. "Except for that hot guy I danced with. I think he's just as good in bed as he is on the dance floor."

"Don't you dare!" He punched the wall, right next to my face. His breathing was ragged.

I could see him holding back his anger, but I couldn't stop. My heart hurt so much, and I wanted him to hurt too.

"What's wrong, honey? Don't like to share?" Even though I was scared as hell of his fury, I raised my chin. "Or maybe let's try the four of us? Call Mari—who so faithfully clings to your hand—and I'll call that hot, brown-eyed beauty." I licked my lips. I hated myself for doing this, but part of me burned with anger and wanted more pain—more of everything.

"Shut up!" Iden hissed. "Don't make me say something I'll regret later."

It was time for a blow below the waist. I moved so close to his lips that I was practically touching them. "What, shall I be raped by you again like some kind of animal?"

Iden jumped away from me like he was being scalded. He ran his fingers through his hair and kicked a chairs. "Shit, shit, Luka." He was screaming like an animal being slaughtered.

I cringed a bit, but I couldn't show how I really felt.

"Why are you doing this? Why?" He jumped toward me and practically pinned me against the wall.

I held my breath and closed my eyes. I really thought I was going to die.

"I curse the night I met you. Get out of my sight." Iden ran toward the door.

I don't know how long I leaned against the wall, but when I finally moved, half the guests had already left. Liam drove me home, and I didn't even get to wish him a happy New Year.

I went upstairs and sat on the bed. *You've achieved what you want, Luka, but what's next?* Was I happy to make such a mess? No, I really wasn't. I went downstairs and got a bottle of whiskey. I put on "Diamonds" by Rihanna and started a ritual of self-pity. I drank straight from the bottle—sip after sip—and I danced. I drank more than half the bottle, and I became weak. I could no longer think logically. I wanted to end the damn guilt, the pain, and my miserable life. After a couple more sips, the room began to spin. I lost track of where I was. I took one last sip, and I dropped the bottle.

I slowly staggered to my feet and headed for the stairs. The image floated, and the floor rippled. I grabbed the railing and started to climb up. Someone grabbed me from behind and pressed a smelly rag to my nose. I was so drunk that I couldn't resist. I knocked everything off the chest of drawers in the corridor. Then there was complete darkness.

JANUARY 3, 2019
IDEN

I spent two days drinking, wandering around Chicago, and looking for company. In a way, I didn't have a sober moment. After arguing with Luka on New Year's Eve, I just went crazy. I was shaking with anger and wanted to forget, and the best way to forget is alcohol.

Mari crawled after me like a tick. She knocked on the apartment door, but Liam kicked her out.

Liam and I spent the night together, and when I woke up in the morning, I started drowning my heartache in whiskey again. Finally, Liam dragged me out of the apartment and told me to go home. Home was like a curse to me. *Luka hates me, but I hate myself more. And where is my life going? And why am I going through so much for some village girl? Liam is trying to make a human out of me. What a kind bastard.*

Liam said, "Get a grip, man. You look terrible."

I held my throbbing head in my hands. *Saint Peter explains how to live.* "If I was interested in your opinion, I would ask." I frowned at him.

"Don't act offended." He looked at me.

Hercules. "My head hurts. Shit, I need painkillers." The car ride was starting to make me sick.

"You look like a little girl now." He laughed sarcastically. "Like a little puppy that has just been weaned from its mother."

Go to hell, Liam. "Where's Luka?" I finally dared to think about her.

Liam shrugged. "I don't know. I drove her home after the party, and then I didn't see her."

"We need to talk to her," I said. *Shit, it really gives me a headache. I won't drink anymore.*

"Do *you* need to?"

"Go to hell," I roared.

"You will lose Luka, for sure, and you will die lonely."

"I'm terribly angry at her," I said. "She twisted my brain like a snake. One moment, I want to try to love her, and the next I want to kill her." I sighed.

"I think you *already* love her."

Love? What does love look like?

At home, things had been thrown from a chest of drawers, and photo frames were strewn in the corridor. A half-filled bottle of whiskey and Luka's shoes were in the living room. I took the shoes upstairs. The light was on in the room.

"Something's wrong," I said. "Liam, Liam!"

He said, "What happened?"

"Check the camera records. Something is wrong. Her phone is here—and her passport too." My heart began to beat faster. My hangover evaporated when I shook out her purse and saw her passport and all the personal belongings she never left the house without.

Liam rushed into the study and shouted, "Iden, we have a problem. She was kidnapped on New Year's Eve."

I stood there with Luka's shoes in my hands.

CHAPTER EIGHT

LUKA

I woke up with a terrible headache, nausea, and an unpleasant taste in my mouth. I tried to open my eyes, but there was no way I could. I started to wrestle and realized that my hands and feet were tied. I was blindfolded. "Save me. Help me. Save me!" I screamed in all the languages I knew.

The door opened, and someone grabbed my hand.

I started screaming and kicking. I realized how painful my whole body was.

"Good morning, beauty."

I pressed myself against a wall. "Where am I?" I groaned. "Please let me go now!"

"Calm down, kitty. Show your claws?" They touched my leg, and I kicked again. "You'll stay here for a while, but rest for now."

I started screaming and kicking, but I was unable to defend myself.

They pressed my knee, stuck a needle in my shoulder, and injected something.

"Where am I? Why am I here?" I started to cry. "Please let me go…"

The voice began to fade and become weak. It was dark again.

It's quiet, dark and cold. Am I awake? Most likely. Very uncomfortable. I don't know how long I've been here or how long I've been asleep. Did someone miss me? Is anyone looking for me?

"I'm sorry, but I need to go to the bathroom." I groaned loudly.

The door opened, and heavy steps approached me, took my hands, and lifted me up. I was carried to a cool room and was placed on the floor. Without shoes, my feet were cold.

"I'm sorry, but I'm wearing very uncomfortable clothes. Could you free up my hands and eyes?"

Silence. The shoes squeaked, and after a few seconds, I was able to massage my hands. They removed the bandage from my eyes. I squinted from the artificial light, and my eyes hurt a lot. Finally, I saw a tall man standing next to me. His face was covered by a mask, and he was dressed in black and wore black boots. We were in a very small room with a toilet and a sink. The peeling paint on the walls testified that no one had lived there for a long time.

"I'm sorry, but could you leave or at least turn away?" I asked in a very soft voice.

He went out the door, and I quickly got out of my overalls and did my natural chores. I was very relieved. I looked at myself in the mirror; my makeup was gone, my eyes were black, and my hair was loose and tangled.

The door opened, and the man walked in. He took me by the hand and led me to another room. There was a mattress on the floor, and the windows were boarded up. The man sat me down on the mattress and handed me a tray with a cup of tea and a sandwich. I was very hungry, and I cut a sandwich without any hesitation and drank some tea. "Why am I here?" I tried my luck again.

"Don't ask." He knelt down, tied my hands behind my back again, and put a bandage over my eyes. He left sitting me like that, and he left.

I started moving my arms, trying to free myself, but I had no luck. It hurt my wrists, and the knot didn't budge at all. *Shit*, I thought. I felt someone entering the room again. They turned me on the mattress, and I started screaming and kicking. Another jab in the shoulder, and I logged off again.

▪ ▪ ▪

My mouth is very dry. I try to raise my head, but there is no strength. I blink. There seems to be no blindfold, but the room is blindingly dark. Tears roll down my cheeks. Why am I here? I don't understand why. I try to move the knot again. The knot finally loosens. I manage to get one hand out. I sit down and untie my legs. I stand up, but I can't see anything. It's completely dark. Touching the wall with my hands, I move forward and try to find the door. Damn, it's dark. I feel a doorknob, turn it very quietly, and the lock clicks. I slowly open the door, and it is dark in the corridor. I quietly press against the wall and see light coming from the other room through the crack in the door. This damn abandoned house is very confusing. I walk quietly down the corridor, and I start to panic because I can't find the front door. Finally, I find a room with an open window. I try every possible way to open it, but it won't budge. Finally, I strain so hard that I lose my balance and fall.

▪ ▪ ▪

The door opened, and a man rushed over to me, "You tried to run away?" He punched my lip, and I fell to the floor again.

I got into a defensive stance, jumped on top of the bastard, and pummeled him with my fists. "Let me go, you big pig!" I growled and punched him.

He hit my fists away with one hand and punched my right cheekbone.

I shook like a sack of potatoes again, my eyes flashed, and I tasted the blood in my mouth. Before I passed out, I thought, *Are all my teeth in place?*

I tried to open my eyes, but one eye was swollen shut. My hands were firmly tied again. I did not understand whether it was day or night because of the blindfold. My lip hurt, and I could still taste the blood. I tried to roll over on my side, but I felt nauseous. I curled up into a ball, and for the first time in years, I prayed to God to make it all end.

I don't know what day it is today, how long I've been here, or when I last ate or drank. Damn weak. I tried to sit up, but my head began to spin. I collapsed onto the mattress. I started to scream. *I still don't understand why I'm here.*

I heard a crack, and the door opened. He removed the bandage from my eyes. I opened my right eye with difficulty, and my left tried to get used to the light. I was seated, barely holding my head and body upright.

The masked man put a bottle of water to my lips.

I sipped a little.

He put a sandwich to my lips, but my appetite was gone.

I fell back onto the mattress and stared at the ceiling. Even though the windows were boarded up, the room was quite bright.

The supervisor didn't say anything this time. He just injected something into my hand and left.

I watched the sun shining through the crack, and I started humming a traditional song. I hummed and stared, and big tears rolled down my cheeks. I felt frozen. Although my family was not believers, I wanted to believe in God. I wanted him to have mercy on me.

When I opened my eyes for the hundredth time, it was dark. *Has no one missed me? Is anyone looking for me? Does anybody care where I am? What do my parents think? Am I going to end my life here, alone, hungry, and cold?*

The door opened, and a tall man with a dark mask illuminated the room with a flashlight. "Get up!"

"I'd love to get up, but I can't," I answered almost sarcastically.

He picked me up, but my legs wouldn't support my weight. I was dragged into another room with a chair stood under a lamp. He dropped me on the chair like a sack of potatoes. He tied my legs to the legs of the chair and my hands behind my back to the back of the chair.

I sighed.

Another masked man came in. "Hello, kitty." He laughed. "Oh, how beautiful are you?" He whistled.

"Thank you." I spat at him.

"You still haven't lost your sense of humor, have you?" He slapped me and cut my lip again.

I licked off the blood with the last of my strength. "Either let me go—or it's over!"

"No, dear, you are still needed alive." He stood in front of me. "Your brother owes my boss a hell of a lot of money. It's been five fucking days, and he doesn't even know his sister is here. He escaped from Lithuania with his companion. Can you imagine?"

I freaked out. *Arn? Am I here for Arn?*

"We sent him several messages with warnings that we have you, but he disappeared." He began to laugh.

"All because of that damn wrecked vehicle?" I asked.

"There were several million euros' worth of cocaine in that damned vehicle, and it exploded with the car. Since your brother spit on his little sister, maybe your fiancé won't?" He took out his phone, turned on the camera, and handed it to the other guy. "Now be a good girl and ask for help."

"Don't you dare bring this up, Iden." I tried to free myself, but I was very weak, and my head kept spinning.

"Kitty, do you want to scratch again?"

I already knew what would happen next. The tall man punched me in the stomach, and I curled up as much as my bound arms and legs would allow. I gasped for air, but I was still silent.

The bastard hit me again, this time in the face.

I screamed inside, but I didn't make a sound.

He then punched me in the nose.

I kept silent.

One more to the stomach, and I fell with the chair. I stared at my abuser with wide eyes, but I didn't make a sound. I felt liquid running down my face, probably blood, but I no longer felt any pain or cold. I just watched and waited for the end.

Finally, the masked man decided enough was enough and pulled me up in the chair. My head with a bunch of bloody hair was bobbing around like a rag doll. The little guy put the bag over my head, injected me with a new syringe, and carried me back to the room where I had spent the past five days.

My whole body hurt. I was lying on my side, and one side of my body was completely frozen. I heard a noise in the house. Someone was struggling and shouting. I heard glass breaking. *A shot? Was that a shot? Maybe. What's the difference. Maybe they finally shot each other, and now I can die in peace.* I wanted to turn over onto the other side—my right side was numb—but my body wasn't listening anymore.

Finally, I heard the door open.

"Iden, I found her!"

Is that Liam?

I heard footsteps and a question: "Is she alive?"

They removed the bag from my head, and I could finally breathe normally. I could feel the dried blood in my nostrils. I opened my better eye, but the image was blurry. My body didn't listen to me at all.

"What did those animals do to her? I will kill them! I will kill all of them!" Iden shouted.

I was lifted up and carried somewhere. I could smell Iden's scent, and for the first time in my life, I felt safe.

▪ ▪ ▪

I recognized the smell of bandages and medicine, and I heard the beeping of a machine. I opened my eyes. *I'm in a hospital. I wasn't dreaming. Iden really came for me.* I wanted to turn my head, but every part of my body hurt. "Ugh." I tried to roll onto my side. It felt like there was an open wound in the place of my stomach.

"You woke up. How are you feeling?" Iden asked.

I managed to turn my head a little in his direction.

Iden had a patch on his left eyebrow, a corner of his lip was black and blue, and his beard hadn't been shaved in days.

"I really want a drink," I said.

Iden put a straw in a bottle of water and put it to my lips.

I sipped it greedily. "Thank you."

"You're welcome," Iden said. "How are you feeling?"

"I'm fine now," I answered dryly. "Thank you for saving me. I'm very sorry that you had to get involved in the problems caused by my brother."

"Did they hurt you in any other way?" Iden looked at me with pity.

I understood what he was asking. "No, they didn't rape me … if that's what you mean."

Iden was sitting on the chair next to my bed, propped up on his elbows, and he took my hand and pressed it to his forehead. "I didn't know you were kidnapped. I really didn't understand. When we had a fight … when I told you to get out of my life that night … I stayed in an apartment in the city for several nights. I didn't think someone would kidnap you. When I got home, I saw a mess in the hallway, your shoes strewn across the living room, a bottle dropped on the floor." Iden pulled my hand away from his forehead. "I went up to your room and saw that your documents and phone were still in the room. At first, I thought you were at a friend's house, but when we looked at the video cameras, I realized something was wrong." He sighed. "I didn't even realize you had been kidnapped for two days."

"It doesn't matter … I'm alive. I'll get better."

"On the fourth day, I received an email with a video of you being sliced like an apple. What did they ask you to do that you refused to do?" Iden looked flustered.

"To beg for help directly to the camera." I looked at Iden and didn't understand why he was there. "OK, thank you for saving me, but why are you here? I think we told each other everything on New Year's."

"I think we said some things to each other that we shouldn't have said." Iden traced lines on my arm with his finger. "You got it all wrong … I mean, for Mari's sake." Iden looked up at me.

"That doesn't make sense," I said.

"Can you not argue with me for once? You've been talking nonsense. I've been silent, you've been silent, I've been silent, you're gone. I've been silent, and now I'd like to say whatever it takes to make you finally understand me." Iden looked confused.

"OK, I'm listening." I put my head down.

"I lied to you," he said very quietly. "I remember everything from that night, and I understood what I did."

There was silence.

Iden looked down at his shoes and took a deep breath. "When Mari left me, I was very angry. I hurt other people, especially other girls. That night, part of me realized what I was doing, but another part of me was in a daze. The next morning, I swore to myself that I wouldn't do it again. I felt so bad. I tried to look for you, but I couldn't find out anything about you. I expected law enforcement to knock on my door and arrest me for rape, and I certainly wouldn't have defended myself because I deserved it. But those photos. When I saw you on the street, you looked so different, so real. You were doing your hair in my car window." Iden looked at me. "I don't know if I still love Mari, but I know that I want to try to love you—if you'll let me try."

"I don't know what to say." I was so confused. One part of me was happy as a child, but the other part remembered all his ugly words and behavior.

"Don't say anything." Iden stroked my hair. "I'll wait as long as it takes—just give me a second chance."

We looked at each other without saying anything until I fell asleep.

▪ ▪ ▪

I woke up the next morning feeling refreshed. Iden was sleeping on a chair, and his head was resting on the edge of my bed. I smiled.

A nurse came through the door, and when I motioned for her not to wake him, she tilted her head in understanding and smiled. "Your fiancé was very worried about you." She checked my blood pressure. "He hasn't taken a step away from you since the moment you got here."

"I don't even ask how long I've been in the hospital?"

"Today is the third day. For the first two days, we cleaned your body and tried to recover your strength. Those kidnappers put you on a lot of strong sedatives, and we had to remove them."

"I understand."

The nurse left the ward, and Iden looked up. "Good morning." He yawned. "How are you feeling?"

"Good. I just really want to go home." I looked into Iden's eyes.

For the rest of the time I was in the hospital, Iden never left my side. I had visitors every day, and Elle, Rodriguez, Isabel, and Anna were the most faithful. There were a lot of flowers and teddy bears in the ward. Mrs. Black made the whole hospital staff jump. I laughed heartily again at her facial expressions if something was not done according to her wishes. Mr. Alvaro Rivera kept shedding tears because of my bruises. I was surrounded by beloved people, and Iden sat quietly in a chair in the corner as my friends tried to cheer me up.

I was finally discharged. My side still hurt, it turns out one rib was broken, and I had to hide my face under large sunglasses, but I felt good overall. When I left the hospital, I put on sweatpants, Ugg boots, and a down jacket with a hood. Reporters gathered outside the hospital, but Iden did not speak to them. He quickly put me in an Audi SUV, and after a forty-five-minute drive, we were home. The house still had the Christmas decorations, including the Christmas tree.

"Why didn't you undecorate the house?" I asked.

"That's the least of the problems that need to be solved." Iden turned away.

I stood in front of the mirror and took a good look at myself. My eyes were black, the bruise around my right eye was still blue, a patch was stuck on my nose, and there was a huge scab on my lip. I pursed my lips and was not satisfied with what I saw.

Iden walked over to me and gently touched the scab on my lip with his thumb. "Does it still hurt?"

"No." I bit my lip. "I just look like I've been hit by a truck."

"You look charming, as always." He gently puckered his lips. "Let's go rest."

We slowly walked upstairs. My room was filled with white roses, and we snuggled on the bed.

"You know, the press is full of articles about your kidnapping," Iden said in a serious voice. "I managed to hide why you were kidnapped, but when I find Arn, it won't end well for him."

"Tell me if he's OK. In general, where is he? My family has no idea where he and Paul went, and I still can't believe that Arn didn't do anything about my abduction."

Iden gently twirled a strand of my hair on his finger and told me about his childhood, how he grew up without a real father, and how his mother wanted a normal family so badly that she married a man she barely knew. He was not a good husband, but he was a good father. After his mother's divorce, Iden joined bad company, started using drugs, and got into all kinds of trouble.

"Once, when I was seventeen, my mates and I went to a party. I dressed well, and I drank a lot. We all behaved the same way." It seemed like an unpleasant memory. "We sat in a car, and I drove because I felt the most sober. We drove to the club, still drinking bourbon in the car, and a moose ran onto the road. I was drunk and distracted, and I did not react in time. The car rolled several times. We all got a good shake, but the seat belts saved us—except for Scott. He was sitting in the middle of the pickup and was not wearing a seat belt. When we rolled, he went out the window and died." Iden paused and stopped twirling my hair.

"If it's hard for you to talk, don't say it," I said.

"No, everything is OK. I want you to know." Iden smiled. "After the accident, I was almost put behind bars for involuntary manslaughter. Because my mother was famous, she sent me away. That's how I ended up in France ... at the military academy. I was very angry at my mother for pushing me out of her life like that. I closed in on myself, and I became angry. The military academy turned out to be good for me. I learned to control my anger and achieve my goals. Later, I served in the legion, saved money to start a business, and enrolled in an architecture program. That was how my business was born." He looked at me and smiled.

"What about Mari?" I asked.

"Well, she's my past." He pressed his lips together and rolled his eyes. "We met in Milan. We started dating. I liked her because she did not take the world seriously. Everything was a joke to her. At the time, I also lived like that. I cared about parties and having fun, but being together brought us good things. We both got serious, and my business started to succeed. I think she was comfortable with my company and my last name. We planned a wedding. I loved her very much, but she didn't show up on our wedding day." He shrugged. "I put an end to my personal life and started working. And now Mari is asking to be together again. I'm just taking advantage of the situation to get closer to Logan and get the photos back."

"Is Mari's husband the organizer of all this?" I raised my eyebrows.

"Yes, I think he is. We've been at odds ever since I left his company to start my own. He wants to destroy me because of my relationship with Mari. Mari left him for reasons only known to them. Logan has done a lot of wrong, especially to you. I'm not really going to leave it at that. Logan has to answer for everything he's done. I can thank him for one thing … because of his revenge, you appeared in my life. Of course, our introduction was not how you would have liked."

Iden looked so young and handsome. His eyes reflected pity, but he did not pity me. He pitied all the evil. He rarely showed his feelings, but this moment was living proof that he could be different.

"And how are the two of you feeling now? Meeting after so long?" I felt very uncomfortable asking such personal questions about Mari, but I couldn't help but ask.

"I care about her," he replied.

My heart was cut again.

"But I care you more," he said.

I didn't say anything. I just hugged him and snuggled against his chest. Iden was open. I couldn't help but rejoice at this progress in our fragile and new relationship. A small, barely visible fire of hope burned in my heart. Could our feelings become real? Could we solve everything and be happy? I didn't want that moment to end, but all good things come to an end someday.

CHAPTER NINE

LUKA

The next two months passed like one day: home, work, internet conversations with my family, meetings with Elle and Rodriguez, and work parties. Iden's people had been intensely searching for traces of my brother and his friend, but so far, the search had been fruitless. The last traces were cut off in Sweden. My parents were desperate, and my father even said that he had forgiven Arn's sins so that he would return home safe and alive.

I still lived with Iden, and we spent all our free time together. We tried to get to know each other, get closer, and fix the mistakes we had made before.

Iden tried to be gentle and understanding, staying in my room until I fell asleep because I was still afraid of outside noises, and then he would go to his room. We only got close enough to stealthily kiss or touch each other. Although everyone around us thought we were the perfect couple and were looking forward to the wedding, the reality was not so sweet. Sometimes I wanted more, but Iden avoided my touches. He was afraid to get close. It drove me to despair. I felt inferior. I didn't understand why he was like that: one moment, he was kissing, and the next, he was running away.

After the successful presentation of Alvaro Rivera's winter

collection, the spring season was planned. The whole office worked intensively; we were looking for the perfect place for the presentation, coordinating the advertising campaign, and looking for the most professional models. After work, Iden and I would usually go to a new restaurant for dinner, and on the weekends, we would travel around Chicago, take a yacht out on Lake Michigan, or just walk along the lake. That time together was more like a movie plot, but it was not real life. We were as happy as we let ourselves be. I would look at Iden's profile and daydream, just waiting for the moment when he would say he loved me and Mari was in the past, but he was closed and secretive. There were no more open conversations like after my abduction, but I did not pressure him. I wanted him to open up on his own.

April brought warmer weather to Chicago than usual. I could confidently wear a dress and enjoy the kisses of the sun. Iden worked a lot on a hotel construction project, and he often stayed late at work. Our presentation was only a couple of weeks away, and we rushed to plan everything. I worked from home over the weekend while Iden was at a business meeting in Michigan. I sat down to refine the pitch list and got a text from Iden:

> Iden: *I won't be able to get back to you today. I have an urgent meeting with an investor.*
> Luka: *That's too bad. I already roasted the duck.*
> Iden: *Leave it for me to taste.*
> Luka: *Duck?*
> Iden: *And a duck.*
> Luka: *Pervert.*
> Iden: *Sleep well and dream of me.*

It was well after eleven o'clock when I closed the computer, rubbed my tired eyes, and went to bed. *It's strange that Iden isn't home.* I couldn't fall asleep. I was tossing and turning, and I decided to go to his room. I turned on the night light and looked at his cuff links, perfume, and photos of him with his friends. His bed was covered with dark blue linen, and there were two bedside tables. His room had a large triangular window, and it was painted a darker tone than mine. I sat down on the bed, and the corner of a photograph caught my eye. It was a picture of Iden and Mari. *He still loves her*, I thought. I wanted to crumple up the damn photo, but I put it back in the book and put it away. *It's no wonder that our relationship hasn't developed into something more, and we're still pretending to be a relationship. Is it my fault? Maybe he is too disgusted to touch me? Am I still here because he feels like he owes me?* I smelled Iden's scent on the bed, took a deep breath, and fell asleep hugging his pillow.

▪ ▪ ▪

I felt the bed sag. Iden was getting dressed on the edge of the bed.

"Hello," I said in a sleepy voice.

"Hello. Did I wake you?" Iden crawled under the covers and hugged my waist.

"No," I said. "I thought you wouldn't come back."

"I told you I missed you." He played with my hair. "And why are you in my bed?"

"I don't know." I was embarrassed, and I wanted him to touch me and kiss me. I pressed myself against him. "Maybe I missed you."

Iden smiled and gently touched my lips.

I pulled him close and kissed him back. A part of my soul wanted more—more than Iden could give—and it made me sad as hell.

Iden gently touched my shoulders and back, and he caressed my thighs. My hands were sliding up and down his shoulders. Iden rolled me onto my back, and I wrapped my legs around his hips, panting loudly.

"Luka, what are you doing?" He pulled his face away from mine.

"I want you," I whispered. I was blushing with embarrassment at having my fake fiancé on my neck.

Finally, Iden said, "Really?"

I nodded.

Iden started kissing my lips, my neck, my collarbone, and my breasts. My heart was pounding so loudly that I thought it would jump out of my chest. Iden gently removed my nightgown, leaving me in just my underpants.

Intuitively, I covered my breast with my hand.

"Don't hide. Please." Iden gently pulled my hand away and traced a map of kisses down to my belly. My breathing sped up to the max, and that spot began to throb. That feeling drove me crazy. Iden gently pulled down my panties, and I started to hide again. Iden returned to my lips and sucked on them. We kissed slowly and dreamily. He gently touched my sensitive spot with one hand, heating it even more. I felt his sex on my thigh. I began to squirm from the pleasant sensation, wanting more. Iden stopped kissing for a moment and looked into my eyes again, as if waiting for approval. I pulled his face closer and kissed him twice. Iden settled more comfortably between my legs and slid inside very gently. He moved gently and slowly, taking his time. I put my hands on his back and his shoulders. This time, it wasn't scary. It wasn't unpleasant, and it wasn't painful. This time, I felt passion and great pleasure, which slowly turned into a pressure in my stomach. Everything was different; it was bright and beautiful.

For a long time after everything, Iden drew maps on my body with his fingers. He kissed me, spoke nice words, and said he wanted to make up for the time when we became victims of evil games. This time, I felt different. I felt happy and full. I felt love. For now, that love was unrequited.

▪ ▪ ▪

The alarm clock went off, and I opened my eyes. I turned my head and two dark eyes were staring at me.

Iden smiled. "Good morning."

"Good morning," I answered. "How long have you been staring like this?"

"When you started snoring, I couldn't sleep anymore." He smiled.

"Was I snoring?" I blushed.

Iden started cooing and straddled me.

I tried to free myself, but he was stronger than me. "Stop! Stop! I'm afraid of being tickled."

I was writhing like crazy.

Iden grabbed my leg and kept tickling.

I finally got out of his arms and sprinted to the bathroom.

Iden was not far behind. He pressed me against the shower wall, looked into my eyes, and gently ran his fingers over my cheek.

"Iden, I'm going to be late for work."

"And who cares?" He slowly kissed my neck.

"Your mother will fire me." I pursed my lips.

"I will employ you at my company. Just where a diligent secretary is required."

Iden continued to touch down my collarbone toward my stomach and then up to my lips. I let out a deep sigh, and Iden returned to my eyes and sat me on his hips. I ran my fingers through his dark hair and looked into those dark, innocent eyes. Iden kissed my lips softly again, whispered, "I want you," and pushed himself inside.

He moved gently, taking his time, repeating in my ear how beautiful and perfect I was, caressing my buttocks and waist with his hands. He bit the corner of my ear and tugged gently.

I gasped with pleasure. There was a storm in my belly. I gripped Iden's shoulders tighter and encouraged him to move faster. It wasn't enough. I wanted more. When I finally felt that blissful relief, Iden grunted, opened his eyes, and looked at me with misty eyes. I was shaking from the orgasm I had just experienced and the sight of it and the knowledge that I could make someone feel so strongly.

After a shower, I showed up at work at almost ten o'clock in the morning.

Isabel saw me, and she immediately knew that something was up. "You're glowing today."

"Me? I didn't notice." I smiled widely, and my cheeks turned red as I remembered what Iden and I had been up to last night and this morning.

"You smile every time you look at your phone," Isabel said.

"Don't think about it," I said. "How was your weekend?"

Isabel began to tell me about her weekend adventures, and she had many.

The rest of the day went by as usual. Mrs. Black was driving everyone from office to office. I brought her the latest issue of a magazine, called a photographer, and did a million other things.

A couple of hours later, Mrs. Black opened the door to her office and cried out, "What is this nonsense, Luka?"

"Mrs. Black, what happened?" I jumped up from my chair, and it fell thunderously to the floor.

Isabel jumped up from her desk and looked at me. "On the internet, all the media outlets are sharing spicy photos of you and Iden!"

I googled Iden's last name, and when I pressed the search button, the entire search field flashed with headlines: "Forced love or deliberate business plan?" I stared at the titles for a minute and clicked on the articles and pictures from that night. The article said that I was an exchange student—an innocent sheep—and Iden had taken advantage of me. Fearing responsibility and gossip, he came up with a twisted plan to marry me in exchange for silence, but he still spends his free time with Mari.

After reading the article, I sat down and looked at Mrs. Black. She looked furious.

"I ... I ... I don't know how to explain it, but—"

"I don't care if you don't know how to explain it," Mrs. Black said in a shrill voice. "Come to my office right now."

Isabel sat at her desk with her head down and looked at me sympathetically. She had probably read the article too.

I followed Mrs. Black into the office, and I had no idea how to get out of the situation. "Mrs. Black, this is definitely not what it says."

"Did he actually rape you?" she asked.

Don't cry. Just don't cry. "Mrs. Black, I love your son, and those pictures are just a misunderstanding."

Mrs. Black approached the glass wall, massaging her temples with her fingers, and said, "Luka, I have to know. What's going on between you? Why is Mari's name still mentioned? He's still with her?"

"I don't know," I answered. "And if that's the case, then he loves her more than he loves me."

"What are you talking about? Love? What is going on between you?" Mrs. Black looked confused. "From the first moment in that restaurant, I understood that something was happening between you. Iden is different besides you."

"Mrs. Black, I think you should talk to Iden yourself," I said dryly. "I would like to return to my work ... if you don't mind."

"Of course, of course." She waved her hand and turned to the glass wall, letting it be known that I could go.

I returned to my desk and slumped in my chair. My face was burning, my heart was pounding, and my hands and feet would not stop shaking. I read the article again and again. *Spending time at Mari's ... Mari's ... Mari ... I started looking at the photo gallery of Iden and Mari. An evening at a restaurant, a club, a party ... A photo from an evening in Michigan caught my eye ... It was yesterday. Mari is standing very contentedly, her arms wrapped around Iden, and he whispers something to her ear. In another shot, they are kissing. I can't look at it anymore, but I can't turn the damn article off.* Something broke in my heart again. *I gave myself to him tonight of my own free will. He keeps me by his side and actually spends time with Mari whenever he gets a chance.* I got up from my desk and ran to the bathroom. I threw up and hugged the toilet, horrified at my bad choices. I decided to put an end to it. *My studies are over, and no one is keeping me here anymore. Iden left for New York today, and I have time to make the right decision.*

I went back to my desk, finished all my work, and wrote my resignation letter. When Mrs. Black went home, I put it on her desk. When I got home, I threw my most comfortable clothes and my personal belongings into my backpack and my duffel bag, took off my engagement ring, and placed it on the nightstand. On a white piece of paper, I wrote a few words to Iden:

> I don't want to continue this game anymore. I don't think you're happy living a double life either. Last night doesn't mean anything—it's just that we both got what we deserved. Tell everyone about your engagement break, and you won't have to secretly date Mari anymore. Don't look for me.

I folded the sheet in half and placed it next to the ring. When Liam went to the car wash, I walked to the nearest cab stand and left. I couldn't go to Elle or Rodriguez; they would look for me there first. I texted them that I was fine and would be in touch shortly and turned off my phone. I didn't want to return to Lithuania because I couldn't stand the pressure from my parents. I decided to go to the bus station. I left my SIM card in the cab so they couldn't track my phone signal. Maybe I was being too dramatic, but a small part of me hoped they would look for me. I bought a ticket for Los Angeles. When I was on the bus, which was going far away, I realized that I was going to miss Chicago like crazy. My heart had been broken again.

APRIL 12, 2019
IDEN

While I was still in New York, I saw a newspaper article and twenty missed calls from my mother.

Shit, no time.

I called Luka, but her phone was off. *She must be very angry with me after seeing those pictures of me kissing Mari. I was a fool not to explain the situation to her. I could have told her everything, and there would have been no unnecessary arguments, especially now that our relationship is as real as it can be.*

I got up again, canceled all my appointments, and flew to Chicago. There were no lights on at home, and I was very worried.

"Luka, Luka?" I rushed up the stairs. She was nowhere to be seen. I found a note and the engagement ring next to it.

"Shit!" I started throwing things around the room.

Liam tried to hold me back, but I broke the mirrors with my fists. He hit me, and I fell to the ground with my hands over my head.

"Calm down, Iden. What are you doing? You won't get her back that way."

Go to hell! "Where is she?" I jumped to my feet and grabbed Liam's collar. Blood flowed from my fingers.

"You won't get her back like this." He pushed me into a chair.

"What should I do?" I couldn't understand why I was so stupid. *Donkey, I'm a donkey.*

"Get a grip, Iden. Get rid of Mari—and let's start looking for Luka."

"It's easy for you to talk. I'm short of breath." I clutched my chest. I started looking around the room. *Maybe I'll find some clue about where Luka is. Or will she come back? She's gone.*

"I'm going to call a private detective. Maybe he can help." Liam left the room.

I was left with bleeding hands and a broken heart. *Luka is more important to me than I thought. I really love her, but why didn't I admit this to myself earlier? Everyone saw it—everyone told me—but I was too stupid and stubborn to admit that I loved her. Luka is a smart girl, and she will not put up with my nonsense. Have I lost her forever? My worst nightmare has come true. I lost her. I lost my love. Luka, where are you?*

APRIL 20, 2019
LUKA

It's been a crazy week. When I arrived in Los Angeles, I rented a small, cozy apartment. Good thing I had enough savings to start a new life. Then I went out to get to know the city. I allowed myself to rest and think about the future without hurrying to see the city. I spent the evenings quietly on the coast of the Pacific Ocean.

A few days later, I contacted Elle and Rodriguez. *I haven't told them where I am yet, but the most important thing is that they know I'm fine. I still haven't told my parents about my broken relationship, but I can't continue this silence any longer. I'm going to have to let them know.*

At night, when I returned to my little place, I could not sleep for a long time. I felt sorry for myself. I kept thinking about Iden, what he was doing, and who he was hanging out with. For some reason, I always imagined that he was with Mari, and they were both making fun of me. That feeling suffocated me so much that I couldn't sleep. At the beginning of the new week, I started looking for a job. I scanned the entire classified section of the newspaper and circled the attractive offers. It took me half a day to create a detailed CV and send it out.

On Monday morning, I decided to go for a walk and have a lei-surely breakfast at a cafe that was close to my apartment. I was sitting with my elbows on the table, reading a magazine, when I caught sight of a photo of Iden and Mari and the headline "Chicago's Most

Wanted Groom Spends More Time with His Ex-Fiancée." *A really great start to the week.* Tears welled up in my eyes, and as I looked at the headline and the happy faces staring out of the magazine, my heart felt like it was going to jump out of my chest. I closed the magazine and took a deep breath. I closed my eyes and tried to calm down. I flinched when the phone rang.

"Luka is listening," I said as calmly as possible.

"Hello. We are calling from the Markus Company. We received your CV and your request for the secretary job." The soft voice sounded very pleasant.

"Yes, nice," I said.

"If you are still looking for a job, we invite you for an interview tomorrow." I heard the rustling of paper. "If it suits you, we will be waiting for you in the office at exactly nine o'clock in the morning."

"It fits perfectly."

"That's cool, Miss Luka. See you tomorrow."

"Goodbye." I ended the conversation with a smile on my face.

For a moment, I went back to last year when Anna called and invited me for an interview.

I was slowly making my way home when a hairdresser's sign caught my attention. *Time for a change,* I thought, and I went inside.

■ ■ ■

On Tuesday, I got up a couple of hours earlier than planned. I carefully combed my shoulder-length hair, cut short in a light war style and lightened gray. I put on light makeup—I managed to hide my black eyes—and put on a blue dress and platform sandals. I looked pretty good, even though I was pretty wet. I took the subway to the Markus Company, which was located in an industrial part of Los Angeles. The nine-story building was not luxurious, but the lobby was neat and modernly furnished.

A middle-aged woman at the receptionist's desk smiled kindly and asked what she could do to help. I introduced myself and was escorted to Mrs. Maffin, the woman who had called me yesterday.

Mrs. Maffin was a good-looking woman of about forty-five, with close-cropped, raven-black hair that stuck out in all directions and calm, sunken eyes. She wore a classic-cut black dress and low-heeled shoes.

"Good morning, Miss Luka Ilgauskaitė. It's very nice to see you." She shook hands firmly.

"Good morning." I smiled. "And I'm glad to see you."

"Sit down, please." She motioned to the massive wooden chair in front of her desk. "So, Miss Luka, I read the CV you sent. Coming from Chicago?"

"Yes," I replied.

Mrs. Maffin settled more comfortably in her chair. "Do you have a husband, a friend, children?" She looked at my CV.

For a moment, I hesitated. *Should I tell the truth that I'm a loser who just broke up with my fiancé? Can I call him my fiancé? Was it even real? Maybe I've been living in my own fantasy world until now?* "No, I haven't," I replied dryly.

"Of course, you're still very young." She smiled. "What are your future goals?"

"My immediate plans are to find a job that I like," I answered completely without joy.

"Who brought you here, Luka?"

I shifted in my chair and looked at Mrs. Maffin with sad eyes.

"Got it. Are you running away from something and want a fresh start?"

Check. "Yes, I want a new beginning." I felt tears welling up in my eyes.

Mrs. Maffin moved the box of tissues closer to me and sighed sympathetically.

I tried not to cry.

"The Markus Company has been creating advertising for many

years. We mainly work with the fashion industry, but there are also other orders." Mrs. Maffin looked at her work calendar. "If you are satisfied with creating advertising and managing documentation and communicating with customers, this job is yours." She smiled.

"Really? Do you want to employ me?" I was so happy.

"Yes." Mrs. Maffin smiled broadly again. "Welcome to the Markus family. Come on. I'll show you where your office is and introduce you to the boss." Mrs. Maffin stood up and walked over to the door.

After leaving her office, we walked down the corridor to another door. Behind them was a larger hall. On the left side of the door was written "Advertising Manager, Miss Liza Smith," and the other door was decorated with the inscription "CEO Mr. Nick Markus." Next to that, as far as I understood, was the door of my future office.

Mrs. Maffin knocked on the CEO's office and invited me in. The office was quite spacious, and there was a stack of documents on the table. The room was bright and clean. Sitting behind the table was a handsome man, maybe forty years old, with light brown, curly hair, greenish-gray eyes, and a freckled face. He was about six feet tall.

"Nick, please meet your new secretary, Luka Ilgauskaitė." Mrs. Maffin pointed at me.

I approached Mr. Markus with a smile and shook his outstretched hand.

"Good morning. It is very nice that you are joining our team." He smiled. "You are not local? A very interesting surname."

"I am from Lithuania. I graduated from Chicago, and now I'm here." I smiled.

"Very good." He clapped his hands. "I really need extra working hands. Starting today?"

"I can start today." I was happy.

Mrs. Maffin led me to my new office. The cabinet was small, the walls were light gray, and there was a white table, a leather chair on wheels, and two red armchairs. On the wall hung a painting of a field and a couple of shelves with files. Outside the window, I could see the street and the tops of the palm trees. I stood by the window and looked into the distance. I realized it was a new day, a clean slate, but I didn't feel happy. My heart ached just like it had a week ago.

The first week was easy and fun. The small staff was very friendly. In the mornings, Liza and Karl from the Advertising Department went to drink coffee. They openly sympathized with each other, and I liked seeing happy people around me.

In the middle of the week, I logged into my social networks for the first time in more than two weeks and found tons of messages from my sister, Elle, Rodriguez, Mom, Anna, and Isabel. My sister and mother asked me where I was and whether I was sick. I told them that I was working a lot and didn't have time to call or write. "I'm very sorry, but it's a very busy time right now. Is there any news about Arn and Paul?" I told Elle and Rodriguez that everything was fine and that I was already working. They kept asking where I was, but I didn't want to reveal that I was staying in Los Angeles. I told Isabel and Anna that it was too difficult to stay in Chicago, and I apologized for not saying goodbye. I got friend requests from Liza and Karl. I stared at Iden's Facebook profile for a few moments, turned off the app, and got back to work.

The week was coming to an end, and Liza and Karl invited me to go to Malibu for the weekend and have fun and relax on the beach. *Why not?*

On Friday evening, we packed our bags into Karl's Toyota Prius and set off. Karl's friend had a beach house in Malibu. After a couple of hours, we reached our destination and found ourselves on the fabulously beautiful Pacific coast. Karl's friend Steve was shorter than me, a little stocky guy, but he was a very friendly and warm person. In the evening, we had fun swimming in the ocean, playing volleyball, and sitting by the fire. For the first time in almost a month, I was truly happy with the company and the roasted marshmallows. Karl kept taking pictures of me and Liza, and we had fun posing.

The games with the camera reminded me of Rodriguez, and it really broke my heart that my best friends were not with me. I wished I could introduce them to my new coworkers.

I woke up in the morning to the sunlight coming through the window. I woke up refreshed. During the long dinner by the fire, we had shared our life stories and memories of our friends. I put on a short white linen dress and ran my fingers through my shoulder-length hair. I opened the patio door and walked out to the beach. I was greeted by the sound of seagulls and crashing waves. I put on headphones and played some romantic music. As I was walking on the beach, I got a message:

> Elle: Are you in Malibu and cut your hair?
> Luka: How do you know?
> Elle: Karl uploaded a photo to his Facebook account and tagged you.

I sat down on a dune and downloaded the Facebook app since I had deleted it in frustration. Pictures of yesterday's fun flashed on my wall: me in a white bikini, catching water bubbles and having fun splashing them with my hands, sitting on the shore, and watching the sunset n. The next photo was of Liza and me jumping in the waves, my short hair flowing around my face. One of the most beautiful photos was me sitting by the fire, curled up in a blanket, smiling and blowing an air kiss right into the camera. In that photo, my eyes were laughing, my cheeks had a healthy flush, my hair was naturally wavy, and the wind was blowing lightly on my face. The campfire danced happily behind me, and I looked so happy and relaxed. Above the photos, Karl wrote, "A fun start to the weekend with charming girls." I thought, *Sooner or later, I have to get back into my social life. Why not today?* I uploaded the picture of me by the fire as my profile picture. *If we continue to live, then we must live properly.*

The rest of the weekend was very fast and fun. We spent a lot of time at the beach and traveling around Malibu. Liza and Karl walked around holding hands and kept denying that they were a couple, and Steve and I kept teasing them. On Saturday night, we went to a seafood restaurant, and then we went to a bar for drinks and dancing. I put on a knee-length yellow dress with straps, tucked a flower behind my ear, made my eyes brighter, and put on platform sandals. Liza wore a short white dress and high-heeled sandals, and her red hair was in a messy bun. We both danced like crazy and drank cocktails with umbrellas. Karl kept taking pictures of us—even though I didn't want him to, and he definitely got some good shots. We returned to the table and the waiter brought a bottle of Cristal champagne.

"We didn't order it," Karl said.

"That gentleman at the bar is serving you." The waiter pointed to a man standing at the bar.

I turned, and to my surprise, Iden was leaning against the bar. He had one hand in the pocket of his dark jeans, a drink in the other, and a white short-sleeved T-shirt that exposed the tattoos on his neck and forearm. The second one looked recent. His hair was slicked back, and it looked really hot.

"Oh shit!" I turned to the companions.

"What happened, Lu?" Liza glanced at the bar and then looked at me.

"Nothing … everything is fine." I was very confused, but I pretended not to care.

"I wonder who that man is and why he's giving us champagne," Steve said.

"I know him a little." I giggled. "Maybe he's just saying hello." I finished my cocktail in one gulp and showed the bartender that I wanted another one.

I drank half of the new cocktail, and Liza got us back on the dance floor. We started moving to Jennifer Lopez's "On the Floor."

I relaxed and had fun on the dance floor. After a few more selfies with Karl's phone, I excused myself and walked toward the toilet. While I was waiting in line, I checked Facebook and the pictures of this evening. I was smiling everywhere and had rosy cheeks. *Karl is a victim of social networks*, I thought.

"Good evening, Luka."

I heard his painfully familiar voice, but I didn't move or turn to him.

Iden moved closer and stood behind me.

I could smell his perfume and hear his breathing. My body reacted immediately. My skin became wrinkled, my heart began to beat faster, my cheeks changed, and my breathing increased. I braced myself with all my might and continued to stand like a statue. Iden was standing right next to me, and I could feel the warmth of his body on my back.

He snuggled completely against my back and lightly ran his fingertips down my arm from wrist to shoulder.

I shook.

He leaned closer to my ear.

I could feel my breathing, and I barely kept myself from fainting.

"No matter where you are—no matter where you hide—I will always be a step away from you, Luka." The air he exhaled gently tickled my ear. "And that night meant a lot more to me than you can imagine." He pressed his lips to my ear, put one hand on my left shoulder, and ran the other hand up and down my arm.

A tear fell from my left eye, and with all my strength, I pulled myself out of his trap. I ran into the bathroom. I kept feeling his touch and his smell. I didn't like the feeling I got from being around him. I felt completely weak. I stood at the edge of the sink and looked at my reflection in the mirror. *You won't fail me a third time, Mr. Iden Black.*

When I left the bathroom, Iden was nowhere to be seen. I went back to my friends. They were having a good time at the table. We ended our evening drunk from too much alcohol and sore legs. It was the wee hours of the morning, and we stayed on the beach until five o'clock that evening. We finally said our goodbyes to Steve and headed back to Los Angeles. While we were on our way home, I had time to go over the meeting with Iden a million times. He, as always, managed to shake my world to its foundations. My healing wound opened again, and the feelings tore through me. I couldn't lie to myself and say that I didn't feel anything for him. That would have been a lie. It was hard to admit that I missed him and longed for him. The calm music in the car stirred my imagination.

Sunday night hit me again with my loneliness and thinking about that person who only hurt me. I didn't want to think about him anymore. That night, I tossed and turned, wondering why he was here. A bad feeling permeated my body from head to toe, but I promised myself that I wouldn't give in to his charms. *I won't be his toy anymore.*

CHAPTER TEN

LUKA

Monday morning was hazy and hot. I put on classic khaki shorts, a white blouse, and fringed sandals. A new client wanted to create an advertisement for a new hotel. I straightened my hair a little more and lightly highlighted my lips with a pink pencil.

At work, my colleagues and I had coffee and discussed our great weekend in Malibu. Mrs. Maffin was very glad that we had become friends. The CEO arrived at half past ten. He invited Liza and me into his office to discuss some advertisements we had presented.

I said, "Mr. Markus, maybe we should film the perfume commercial on Thursday, and we still haven't found a suitable model for the shoe commercial."

Liza agreed with me.

"What is wrong with the designer?" Nick asked.

"According to him, a model's legs should have charisma." I held out my leg.

Nick laughed and tilted his head. "OK, I understand. Girls, we're going to the conference room in ten minutes. The CEO of the hotel is coming." Nick looked focused.

This order is probably very important to him.

I returned to the office and put the observations about the perfume advertisement in the work calendar. At times, my mind wandered back to Saturday night. My body felt longing, but I realized that I couldn't give in to my feelings. I had to move forward.

Nick poked his head into the office and invited us to go to the conference room. Liza joined us. As we walked, we discussed a basketball game because the CEO was a big fan.

A couple of stocky middle-aged men were in the conference room. We greeted them and sat down at the table.

Nick started talking to the taller man about opening a hotel.

Liza and I sat at the table and waited for the meeting to start. I was sitting with my back to the door and was smiling kindly at one of the men, and he asked what I thought about the design of the hotel. I looked at the photos for a few moments and said, "I think the hotel is unique in its modern design. I really like that there is no lack of light in the rooms, the space is perfectly used for mirrors and lighting, and there are no heavy details."

The door to the conference room opened, and Nick jumped out of his chair. "Good afternoon, Mr. Black." He held out his hand.

I froze, afraid to turn around and see if it was the same Mr. Black I was thinking of.

"Good morning, Nick." Iden's voice cut through my heart like a knife. "Forgive me for being late."

"Everything is fine. Please sit down."

There was an empty seat to my left. I shifted in my chair and looked straight ahead.

"Miss Luka, my assistant, was just telling us her observations about the interior of the hotel."

"Really? It is very interesting to hear the opinion of a charming lady," Iden said very slowly, emphasizing each word.

Liam—Iden's bodyguard, driver, and friend—looked at me. He was and barely smiling.

"Darling, extend your thought," said the man in front of me.

I took a deep breath and forced myself to smile. I spread out the pictures of the hotel on the table and looked at them again. "As I said, the design is very elegant, not overloaded. I would say that an elegant lightness would also be suitable for hotel advertising, but our colleague Liza can tell you more about that." I smiled at her. "My idea would be that during advertising, you should emphasize the uniqueness and grace of the hotel so that the guests will feel at home, but at the same time, they will receive the highest-quality services at a reasonable price." I smiled. "And now I pass the floor to Liza."

Iden's closeness and smell drove me crazy. I sat still with my hands on the table. Iden was asking Liza something, but I didn't hear anything. I just thought about his smell and how I would like to be in his arms again to feel his closeness and warmth. I felt a gentle touch on my arm and looked up at Iden for the first time in half an hour.

He looked at me calmly and said, "Excuse me, your hand is on the picture." He smiled.

I quickly took my hands off the table and put them on my knees. For the rest of the meeting, I just sat there and answered specific questions. I listened to Iden's every word, every breath. It was the greatest martyrdom, and with every word, my heart was bleeding more and more. My mind understood that I could not dream about him because he was a bad person, but my heart and body were drawn like a magnet to be closer to him.

Eventually, everyone rose from their seats, shook hands, and wished each other a good day. I humbly followed the etiquette of politeness. I turned to Nick, and he smiled at me. I turned to say goodbye to the culprit of my heartache. His eyebrows were furrowed, and his lips were pursed. His eyes were like two black coals. I held out my hand and said, "Have a good day, Mr. Black."

Iden shook my hand, took a step closer, leaned closer, and whispered, "So you're warming that bastard's bed right now?" He was looking at something behind me with wide eyes. I followed his gaze and realized he was looking at Nick. I was startled by such accusations.

"I'll kill him—and you—if I have to." He turned and stormed out of the office.

Liza approached me, and I even flinched at her touch. "Isn't that the man who sent us champagne on Saturday?" She looked suspiciously at the door.

"It is," I replied dryly.

"A naughty guy," Liza said. "Did you see the way he looked at you? It looked like he would eat or kill you. Either he really likes you—or he's a sociopath."

I shook my head, walked to my office, sat on the windowsill, and wondered what Iden was up to. I looked up when Nick entered my office.

"Luka, forgive me for interrupting. I wanted to ask, if you don't have any plans this evening, would you agree to go to a restaurant with me?"

I turned around with wide eyes.

Nick laughed. "It's not a date, Lu. Don't be afraid. I have to meet several shareholders of this firm, and I need company because they will be coming with their girlfriends. Maybe join us? As a colleague, of course."

"Of course I can join." I smiled. "What time—and what is the dress code?"

"I'll pick you up at seven. Put on an evening dress. We'll have dinner at one of the most luxurious restaurants on the boulevard." He smiled and left the office.

After returning home, I took a shower, curled my hair, and applied light makeup. I chose a short, black, slightly shiny, backless dress that fastened at the neck. I put on pointy red heels and painted my lips with red lipstick.

Nick gave me two thumbs-up as he opened the door of his BMW. The restaurant was full of famous people who could be seen in gossip magazines and television screens. We had a nice dinner with the shareholders, and since they were visiting from New York, Nick suggested they extend the evening at the Warwick nightclub in Hollywood.

We went to the club at eleven thirty, and a crowd had already gathered there. I was impressed by the club's authentic design solution: high ceilings, crystal chandeliers, dark blue suede sofas, matching white stone tables, and Persian rugs. There were flowers everywhere and a lot of wood and candlelight, which reflected in the mirrors. My first impression was that we had returned to the past or found ourselves in a fairy tale. We sat down at a reserved table, and when Maroon 5's "Sugar" came on, we all hit the dance floor.

After a few dances, we went back to the table to freshen up. It wasn't long before one of our guests took me back to the dance floor. As we were moving along to the pounding music with the whole mass of people, having a good time, some guy wrapped his arms around me and grabbed me. I tried to free myself from his grip and kicked his leg, but he pushed me toward the wall and roared incoherently while flailing his arms. He was completely drunk. I thought I was going to get punched, and I ducked.

Iden knocked the man down, and when he got up, he hit him again. The guy's friends got involved in the fight. Iden fell on his knees after receiving one blow after another, but he quickly regained his balance and knocked out both opponents. More drunken men got involved in the fight. It didn't matter who was hitting whom; what mattered was that they were hitting someone. There was a commotion in the hall, and I heard threats, curses, and breaking glass.

While everyone was chanting and grinding each other's faces off, I went back to the table, drank the rest of my drink, and apologized to everyone. I told Nick I'd take a cab home and walked outside, leaving everyone behind. I didn't want to be there to see what happened next. I walked out to the street and tried to find a cab, but my efforts were fruitless.

IDEN

I couldn't find peace again all day. Isn't she sleeping with that asshole Nick? Fucking cunt.

I was stomping on the terrace of a recently purchased house and drinking whiskey. I don't know how long I was walking like that, kicking chairs, when Liam appeared in the yard. As always, he was self-righteous and annoying.

"Where did you leave the mood?"

Are you kidding me, dude? "Did you see how Luka was smiling at that bastard Nick? He even drooled while looking at her. Now I really regret not wiping that stupid smile off his face."

"She was smiling for her boss." He straightened the chairs and rolled his eyes.

Is his brain overcooked or what? "That sponger is drooling when he looks at her." Isn't *Liam really so blind that he doesn't notice anything?*

"I think you're the only one drooling when you look at her." He snorted at his wit.

I stopped and turned to Liam. "What are you talking about?" I got nervous and thought Liam might be right.

"I say how it looks. Today, I thought you would eat her with your eyes." He snorted again.

Do I look that stupid around her? "Liam, I'm really sick." I drained the entire glass and poured myself another. *I've been drinking like a horse lately.*

"Are you trying to forget her or yourself while drinking?"

"Both her and myself." I sighed. "How should I behave? I want to apologize, but she doesn't even talk. Then I get angry and say all sorts of horrible things. There's that Nick. Luka is like candy—everyone wants to tuck her into bed."

I hate myself. How can I expect her to love me? And I want her in my bed.

"I know they're having fun at the club right now with the share-holders of that ad agency and Nick." Liam coughed.

"With Nick?" The glass in my hand shattered into a million pieces. I gritted my teeth and looked at Liam with wide eyes. *This evening is not going to end well.* I started galloping down the terrace toward the parade ground.

Liam remained standing there.

"Are you going together or something?" I roared.

Liam just shook his head and followed.

We reached the club after half an hour. On the way, I was screaming and blowing like a bull. I couldn't stand still. I was determined to grind Nick into flour if I caught him getting too close to Luka. When I entered, the first thing that caught my eye was the image of some mullet pushing Luka toward the wall and getting ready to hit her. I ran up and punched that guy in the chin. Luka squealed, and I jumped on top of that sack of potatoes and started punching him. He stood up and fired back. We fought each other like two wild bulls. One for him, one for me, one for him, one for me. I tasted blood in my mouth.

Liam stood back and watched how things would end.

I felt a kick in the back. *His friends joined our fight?* "You piece of shit."

Liam came to help, and there were two of us against eight slugs. Maybe six minutes later, everyone was on the ground. I was hit in the back of the head with a glass, and something exploded in my ears. I had to shake my head to avoid losing my balance.

Liam brushed the worm away with one hand and helped me to the car.

"Where is Luka?" I groaned.

"She left ten minutes ago," Liam replied, spitting.

"Shit, how is she? I don't know where she lives. We need to find her right away." I spat blood into my sleeve.

Down the street, I saw her stopping a cab.

LUKA

After ten minutes, a white Lexus SUV pulled up next to me. Liam was driving. The back door opened, but I ignored it and continued to look for a cab.

Iden jumped out of the car, grabbed my arm, and pushed me into the car. My wrist was so crushed that I thought the bone would break. "You bastard! Let go. It hurts!" I hit him in the chest with my free hand.

"Calm down and shut up!" Iden let go of my hand for a few seconds, and then he grabbed my hands while the other massaged the back of his head.

His lip and eyebrow were cut, and blood was pouring out. His shirt was torn and dirty. Although it was dark in the car, I could see his frown. He was really in pain.

Liam was sitting there too. It was uncomfortable, and I could swear I smelled blood.

For the first time in my life, I did what I was asked to do. I kept quiet.

After five minutes, Liam asked for my home address. I said it very quietly and turned to the window. I sat in silence all the way home. Iden kept one hand on my arm and the other in his hair. His head was turned toward me, and he was staring blankly.

Liam stopped right outside my house and turned off the engine.

I silently thanked him, took my hands out of Iden's palm, and left the car. It was dark on the street, and only the outdoor lamps gave off a dim, yellow light. I ran up the steps and started looking for the key. I heard the car door slam.

"Luka," Iden said in a tired voice.

I turned away.

He was standing right next to me. "I'm sorry for everything."

I nodded and was about to take a step out the door when my legs went numb. I turned to Iden and said, "If you want, you can get ready at my place." I left the door open and headed for the stairs.

Iden followed in silence.

I unlocked the door to my modest apartment, kicked off my shoes, and turned on the desk lamp.

Iden didn't fit in this space at all, and neither did our relationship. I offered to sit on the couch. Iden shook like a sack and put his hands behind his head.

I went into the bathroom and grabbed a first aid kit and clean towels. I put them on the table next to the couch, filled a bowl with warm water in the kitchen, and returned to Iden. I put on a towel and sat down on the table across from Iden. "Can I?"

Iden removed his hands from his head and looked at me with such a sad look that I felt guilty for the way he looked. His left eyebrow was split, and so was his lip. Blood was still oozing from the cuts. A bruise was forming under his left eye. The cheek on the right side of the face was red and swollen. Blood ran down his face. His white shirt was bloody and torn. One sleeve of his jacket was torn.

I moved closer to Iden's face and gently began to clean the blood away. He flinched but tried not to move. I kept pulling the cloth and cleaning his eyebrow and lip. I applied an antiseptic and put a bandage on it. Iden didn't say anything; he just kept quiet and stared at my face, swallowing from time to time. As I parted Iden's hair, a pained grimace twisted his face.

"Oh my God, that's a pretty deep wound." I gasped. "You need to go to the hospital."

I was about to stand, but Iden grabbed my arm and pulled me back to the table. "No need. Everything's all right. Just clean it up. It will heal."

"What happened? This is definitely not a fist job."

"A guy broke a glass on my head." His face was contorted in pain.

After fifteen minutes of gasping and pleading for him to go to the hospital, I had cleaned and covered the wound as best I could. The water in the bowl was bright red. I poured it all down the sink and pulled a bag of ice from the freezer. I placed it on the back of Iden's head.

He was sitting with his head against the back of the couch and his eyes closed. As I bent down to add the bag of ice, Iden opened his eyes—and our eyes met. My heart began to beat faster, and I couldn't escape his gaze. Iden didn't say anything; he just stared and kept quiet. That silence and repentant look made me feel very uncomfortable. I closed my eyes and was about to pull away when Iden kissed me. It was too much, and I jumped back. He stood up so fast that he staggered.

"Iden, I think it would be best if you left," I said, almost crying.

"Lu, please forgive me," he said very quietly.

"You hurt me once, and then we got into a relationship based on lies, and I believed you." I was sniffling. "I believed we could actually be together, and you were secretly seeing your ex-fiancée. I've been fooled again—for the second time."

"Everything was wrong. Please just listen to me."

"Iden, please, I'm begging you. No need. I had to leave Chicago to get away from you and all the scum that's after you."

"I did not want that. You think this is easy?" Iden spread his hands and looked into my eyes.

I shouted, "Is it difficult for you? You're a damn fool who chases after a married woman's skirt and fucks his naive and gullible fake fiancée at the same time!"

"When will you finally realize that I don't need any others, Luka." Iden ran his hand through his hair. "I was wrong. I just thought Mari was still important to me, that I still had feelings for her, but I was wrong." Iden looked like he was losing hope.

"I don't want to hear you or see you anymore. Please leave." I turned to the wall and tried to control myself.

"Luka, I was a complete idiot." Iden stood with his head down.

"Until you left, I didn't understand what you meant to me." He sighed. "Luka, if necessary, I will beg on my knees. I will do everything you want—just forgive me, please." Iden fell to his knees in the middle of my living room and cupped his face in his hands.

I didn't know what to do or how to behave. My heart wanted to run to him and tell him how much I still loved him, but my mind told me not to give up on him. I was numb, and I struggled to control my feelings. Tears rolled down my cheeks. I fought myself. I couldn't bear to look at Iden on his knees, and I reached over and touched the top of his head.

Iden pulled his hands from his face and looked at me questioningly.

"Stop. Let's go to sleep. I have to go to work tomorrow, and it's already past three in the morning." I held out my hand to him.

Iden grabbed my hand, and I helped him stand up. Although he was a tall, sturdy man, he looked like an abused child.

"Can I stay here?" he asked.

"If you want, you can stay." I went to the bedroom. I was too tired to argue with him. Iden followed like a cat. I grabbed my pajamas and went to the bathroom, leaving him on the bed. When I returned, he was still sitting in the same place. I went around the bed from the other side, and I opened one eye.

Iden looked very confused.

"Are you going to lie down—or are you going to sit up all night?" I asked.

Iden gave a half smile and went to the bathroom. He returned with his shirt fully buttoned He took it off and placed it neatly on the back of the chair, and he did the same with his pants. He carefully climbed in next to me and grunted in pain.

"You should have gone to the hospital and stitched up that wound; it's going to get infected."

"Shh." Iden made himself comfortable in the bed and wrapped his arms around me. "Good night, Luka."

I fell asleep within seconds. It felt so good to feel Iden next to me again and to hear him breathe. It seemed that the last difficult period did not exist.

It was very hot in the morning. Iden was sleeping with his arms and legs wrapped around me. I couldn't move, and if I tried to, he would immediately hug me tighter. The alarm went off for the second time, and I was still in bed.

"Iden, wake up. Let me go."

He continued to hold me.

"Iden, I have to get ready for work," I said.

"Don't go to work. Stay with me." He closed his blue eyes and frowned.

"Hurts so much?" I touched his bruised eyebrow.

"Your presence heals better than medicine."

I felt his cock on my leg.

Iden's hand gently touched my bare stomach, sending shivers down my body.

I started laughing and squirming.

Iden started to kiss my ear, and he hugged me even tighter. "It's so good to wake up next to you in the morning." Iden purred in my ear, and I smiled the biggest smile.

He continued kissing me, swaying me, and caressing me.

I turned and kissed him on the lips.

Iden ran his hand over my cheek and kissed my nose. "I love you," he whispered, looking into my eyes.

I wrapped my arms around Iden and kissed him on the lips, and he winced but returned the kiss. I ran my hands over Iden's body, trying to remember every muscle and mole. He caressed me with his hands and lips for a long time. I couldn't take it anymore. I wanted to feel that fullness with him inside me. I slid my hands down gently, using my hips and thumbs to pull down my shorts.

He sighed heavily, and without waiting for anything, he took my nightie off.

"I miss you so much," he whispered.

I pulled him closer. "I want you."

Iden kept kissing my lips, forehead, nose, and eyes. Shivers ran through my body, raising my passion even more.

Iden slid in with a sudden movement that made me gasp, and he began to move back and forth at a fast pace. I clawed at his back and felt his pace. My entire body shook, my legs tensed, and a wave of relief rippled through my stomach as Iden snarled and gritted his teeth in relief. I gasped for air, and Iden kissed my shoulder softly.

"You're amazing, you know that?" He rolled away from me.

"I'm going to be late for work."

"Liam will take you. Can you get ready in twenty minutes?" He took out his cell phone, and I hurried to the bathroom.

I got ready in eighteen minutes. I put on a pink bell-shaped dress and high-heeled sandals, my hair was still wavy from yesterday, and I applied mascara.

"You look wonderful."

"Thank you." I blushed. "And you're not going to get up?" I arched an eyebrow questioningly.

"No." He replied got out of bed naked.

I gulped as I looked at his penis and his muscular body. "I will be in bed all day today. My head hurts a lot."

"It's all because of me," I said.

"It's my fault." He held my face in his hands. "Don't be sad, and don't get involved in adventures." He poked my nose.

"What does your new tattoo mean?" I touched the black birds.

"That my lucky bird ran away." Iden smiled and told me to go downstairs so I could make it to work on time. He fell back into bed and pulled the covers over his head.

A white Lexus was parked outside. Liam opened the door and said, "How is he, Miss Luka?"

"All scratched and blue." I sighed. "He has a big wound on his head, but he wouldn't agree to go to the hospital."

"Iden Black is like that. He'll always get what he wants—no matter the cost."

"Stubborn."

Liam laughed and looked in the rearview mirror. "I'm glad you reconciled. He was a real splinter when you left."

We both burst out laughing.

Liza met me at work and began to interrogate me about last night because Nick had spilled everything to everyone in the morning. I kept evading the answer. I simply said that I had known Mr. Black for a long time, and he wanted to protect me from the abuser. Liza looked at me suspiciously and shook her head. She said that she would figure it all out—sooner or later.

Karl agreed with her.

"Conspirators." I went to my office with a smile on my face.

Later, we reviewed the final documents for the implementation of perfume advertising and went to lunch at a cafe across the street. Karl kept saying that I was a real man beater, and Liza teased me about where and how long I'd known Iden. I just laughed at my friends' efforts. When we got back to the office, I found a bouquet of red roses in my office. I opened the handwritten card: "Much more ... I." I smiled and put the card in my purse.

Liza almost tripped when she entered the office and saw the roses. "Is it from him?" She touched and smelled my flowers.

"From what, Liza?" I crossed my arms.

Liza, like a little girl, could not stay still. "From Mr. Black?"

"Maybe from him, maybe from someone else." I raised my eyebrows.

"Luka, tell me now, or—I swear to God—I will force the answer out." Liza crossed her arms, blew her lips, and gave me a stern look.

I started laughing. "These flowers are from my boyfriend." I smiled and stuck out my tongue.

"You have a boyfriend? Since when?" Liza sat down on the chair and opened her eyes.

"Since then," I answered. "I just have to. We were separated, and now we are trying to be together again." I sighed.

"Why do I have to beat everything out of you with a stick?" Liza kept getting angry. "Satisfy my curiosity—and tell me who he is?"

I got more comfortable in my chair and started thinking about how to describe Iden. "Well, he's a real handsome man, such a magazine boy. Sporty." I pictured his naked body in my mind and smiled. "He is very intelligent, lustful when he wants to be, and very romantic and gentle. Small talker. He understands women perfectly." I smiled. "But he's jealous and possessive as hell. He's sometimes a real tyrant, and he can be inflexible, stubborn, and hard-nosed."

Liza listened in amazement.

"This probably isn't about me?" Iden stood in the doorway. He wore dark ripped jeans, a white T-shirt, and black boots. His face was covered by black sunglasses, but the wound on his lip and bruised cheek were clearly visible. He was leaning on the door frame, arms and legs crossed, looking relaxed, with a crooked smile on his face and his hair in a bun.

Liza jumped up and said, "Mr. Black, how nice to see you."

Iden gently shook Liza's hand and walked over to me. He leaned against the table, took my hand, and kissed it.

Liza was speechless, and I was no less surprised.

"What did you come up with?" I asked.

"I just brought something." He pulled out a ring from his pocket—the same one he had given me when we were engaged. Iden put it on my finger, kissed my hand again, and got up from the table. "Don't take it off again. We'll meet this evening." He smiled at Liza and left.

Liza turned to me and said, "What the hell is going on here?"

I covered my mouth with my hands and started to cry. I felt my cheeks heating up.

"Luka Ilgauskaitė, you are a liar. You ran away from him in Chicago? He was the apple of your heart? Did you decide to change your life fundamentally because of him?" Liza came over and hugged me. "I'm so glad you came here. I haven't seen such drama in a long time."

We started laughing.

The next few hours at work passed like minutes. I kept looking at my hand—again decorated with a ring. At the end of the day, I had another chat with Mrs. Maffin. She was going to visit her sister in Atlanta, and she asked me to do some of her chores. I left the building, and Iden's big smile was waiting for me on the sidewalk. He was leaning on a beautiful Harley-Davidson.

"Wow!" I said as I came closer.

"Do you like it?"

"Ignoring the fact that it's a potential killing machine? Yes, I like it very much." I whistled.

Iden grabbed me my waist, pulled me between his legs, kissed me on the lips, and smiled. He put a helmet on my head and another one on his head. "The most important thing is safety." He tapped my helmet.

I laughed.

Iden sat on the motorcycle, and I slung my purse over my shoulder and followed suit. After he started the engine, I flinched. The sound and vibration were overwhelming. I held Iden tighter and was glad to have the chance to snuggle up to him.

We joined the general bustle of the street, and I looked around and enjoyed the warm wind on my skin. Iden took one hand off the motorcycle's handlebars and placed it on my palm. It was a very intimate moment that I put in my memory chest. We finally hit the highway and headed away from the city. I realized we were heading toward the famous Hollywood sign. We arrived at the observation deck just after the sun reached the horizon. I jumped off the motorcycle and realized that my legs were like jelly.

"What are we doing here?" I asked as Iden removed my helmet.

"I wanted to bring my fiancée here and show her the famous sign." He smiled.

"If I remember correctly, our engagement was fake, so I am a free girl." I shrugged.

Iden glared and pulled me closer. "You mean, you don't have a fiancé?" He raised an eyebrow.

I shook my head. My handsome fiancé smiled, gracefully got down on one knee, and took my hand. "Miss Luka, beautiful and incorrigibly stubborn, will you do me the honor of becoming a part of my life, to endure my pranks, jealousy and endless love for you? Do you agree to be my wife?" He uttered the last words with great concentration.

I smiled widely and nodded.

Iden stood up, cupped my face in his hands, kissed me passionately, hugged me, and buried his nose in my hair.

I had a hard time realizing it was real.

The sunset was perfect for our mood. We took pictures and fooled around with some selfies. *I will definitely make a photo collage.*

On the way home, we stopped by a pizzeria for dinner. I felt like I was in a fairy tale, but in real life, fairy tales end quickly. As the character in my favorite series, "Lawrence," said in the final episode: "There are no happy endings. If you are happy, it's not the end." My heart felt that all this happiness, coming unexpectedly, would soon crush me like an avalanche because Iden came like a whirlwind, sweeping everything around him and crushing his enemies. I looked at his wide smile and thought, *How long will we be happy this time? How long before a black cat runs across the path of our life together? How long will he want this fairy tale? When will I become his enemy again? After all, from love to hate is only one step.*

CHAPTER ELEVEN

LUKA

I opened my eyes and made up my mind. I turned my head, and my handsome fiancé was sleeping next to me. His muscular, tanned body was barely covered by a blanket. Iden slept peacefully on his stomach, and I admired the view. His split eyebrow and lip were almost healed, and the bruise under the eye was no longer visible. He'd been spending a lot of time in Los Angeles lately, only returning to Chicago for a few days. It seemed like we were living in a fairy tale. He behaved nicely, he was humble, and he listened. Sometimes I even thought that he was not the Iden I knew before. He was trying to be the kind of man I wanted.

I quietly got out of bed and went to the shower. *As sad as it is, today is Monday, and I have to go to work.* After showering, I wrapped myself in a towel and returned to the room. I was thinking about what to wear.

"Morning, sweetie." Iden hugged his pillow and smiled. "Were you going to run away from me quietly?"

"Some people have to work to survive." I rolled my eyes.

"You know you can't work." Iden rolled onto his back. "I'm going to Chicago today. I'll be back in a few days."

"Of course, your life is there." I sighed. "I'll get dressed and make breakfast soon." I smiled.

We discussed his hotel promotion over breakfast. As much as I didn't want to, Iden still insisted that I make it. Everyone in the office was already discussing my personal life, but Iden didn't budge. Before leaving for work, Iden pulled his keys out of his pocket and tossed them to me.

"What's this?" I asked after catching them.

"Here you go," he said while putting on his jacket. "I don't like that you take cabs and subways. It's not safe."

"You bought me a car?"

"Yes, I bought it. After all, you are my fiancée." He shrugged. "And, by the way, there's something else." He pulled a key with a pendant from his other pocket. "Here is the key to our house. It's quite a squeeze in this small space. I will send the address later."

"Wait, wait. We didn't agree to this." I was angry. "This is my home, and there is enough room here for both of us."

"I understand that this is enough, but why suffocate in an apartment when you can live a little more comfortably?" Iden came closer and took my hands. "I love you, and I won't spare you anything." He raised my hands and kissed them.

We went outside. At the curb, next to Iden's Lexus, was an exact same model SUV. It was bright white, and as far as I could tell, it was for me. "Wow. What if I damage it?" I was scared. "I haven't driven a car for almost a year. Besides, the traffic in America is terrible."

"It's going to be OK." Iden squeezed my hand encouragingly and led me to the car. "Sit down and drive." He kissed my lips.

With shaking hands and feet, I got into the car and smiled at Iden. I screamed inside with terror and fear.

Iden encouraged me to drive, and I slowly moved. The car smelled clean and leathery. I was happy with the interior and the freedom of movement. I was driving slowly, and I was repeatedly honked at by other drivers. I parked the car in the parking lot next to the office building. At the same time, Karl's Prius entered the lot.

Liza jumped out of the car and whistled when she saw my new wheels. "Girl—and the car? Did you rob a bank?"

"No, it's not mine. It's Iden's."

"If Mr. Jealous becomes bored with you, I can gladly take him over."

Karl grimaced.

We all started the morning with a cup of steaming coffee. I got a text from Iden in the afternoon:

> Iden: Liam will help you move stuff out of your apartment. Go there after work, and he will be waiting for you.
>
> Luka: I still don't understand why we can't live in an apartment.
>
> Iden: I thought this problem was already solved.
>
> Luka: OK.

He was back to his old self again. *Where has my sweet and romantic Iden gone? Dominant as ever. And they say life is difficult with women? Men are bigger drama kings than women. I think Iden can claim the title of Drama King 2019, and he deserves to take first place.*

In the afternoon, Liza and Nick went to shoot a shoe commercial. Once we found the right model, we could start. Nick was happy that the shoot was going smoothly, and Liza and I were laughing as we watched the shoe designer running around with the shoes in his hands, prodding the young model back and forth. He reminded me of Alvaro Rivera; both of them had such bright personalities, but this one was also spoiled to infinity.

As the workday was coming to an end, I had to pack up for the trip home. With shaking legs and hands, I sat at the steering wheel and came back in a huff.

Liam was already waiting at the house. "Good evening, Miss Luka." He smiled.

"Hi, Liam," I replied. "Why did Iden leave you here?"

"He said you have a ton of unnecessary stuff to move." He chuckled, mimicking Iden's mannerisms.

"Iden's jokes are very funny," I said sarcastically, and we went to the apartment to pack my stuff.

After five hours, all my personal belongings were packed into boxes. I took one last look at the walls of my cozy apartment and slammed the door. We took the highway toward the coast. It was already dark when we entered Santa Monica, a coastal city west of Los Angeles. The streets were full of palm trees, happy faces, and lots of sand. We arrived at a residential area right next to the beach. Liam stopped at a metal gate that opened itself, and a little farther along the palm-lined road, I saw a large, beautiful, white house. In the middle of the courtyard, there was an illuminated fountain and a lot of vegetation. The house was not modern; it was reminiscent of an ancient mansion. Four large columns held up the balcony, and the front door had floor-to-ceiling windows.

I stopped the car at the side of the house and got out. I had the key in my hand and was smiling widely. *Is this our new home?* Liam moved the boxes from the cars, and I went up the stairs. There was a swing, a table, and a flower on the front terrace. I unlocked the door and took a step inside. After turning on the light, I saw a wide hall and an oval staircase. The stairs went up on both sides. In the middle of the hall, there was a small table with a bouquet of wildflowers on it. The living room was an equally large space. By a large window, there was a massive dining table with eight chairs, a glass sideboard, a solid wood chest of drawers, and luxurious lamps. The high ceiling was decorated with crystal chandeliers. Dazzling white curtains covered the huge window. A widescreen TV was attached to the other wall, and there were several shelves with souvenirs. A soft, leather couch was flanked by two modern armchairs and a small coffee table. The house was so impressive.

It was already after midnight when Liam finished carrying the boxes. We said good night, and I was left alone in that huge house. I went up to the bedroom on the second floor. The room was painted in a soft gray color, and the king-sized bed was decorated with a canopy. The windows covered the entire height of the room. From the balcony, I could see the ocean. I took a shower and got in bed. I still hadn't heard from Iden.

In the morning, I woke up well rested and much earlier than the alarm clock. I put on my sports clothes and went for a run. I went out through the patio doors and saw a huge terrace with soft armchairs, hanging chairs, and sunbeds by the pool, palm trees, and a cozy terrace that was decorated with garlands. After enjoying the perfect garden, I went for a run on the beach. After running, I swam in the pool and got ready for work.

At work, we had to start the creative process for Iden's hotel ad. I was really excited. I put on a white, short, loose dress and my most comfortable platforms. On the way to work, I listened to Lithuanian hits. I felt so free and independent when I could drive the car by myself. I had forgotten how much fun it was.

We started the day with coffee and a chat. I told Liza and Karl that we had moved to a house in Santa Monica, and they were eager to come visit. I called Elle that afternoon. I missed her a lot. She was visiting Martin's relatives in Latvia. She still hadn't decided whether to stay in the US or return to Lithuania. She had a great job offer in Lithuania, but Martin was here. My best friend had been very sad lately. "How was your vacation?" I asked cheerfully.

"Good. We just returned from Riga. I walked so much that my legs ache."

"But I think you've seen a lot. Have you decided on the job offer in Lithuania?"

"Not yet." She sighed. "If we were to go back to Lithuania together, I would choose Lithuania."

"Yes, that's right." I paused. "I don't think I will return to live in Lithuania." I fell silent. *Of course, this will not be enough for Elle.*

She will torture me until she finally finds out the truth, and then she will really grind me into flour.

"Why? What has changed in a few weeks?" Elle didn't understand.

"I made up with Iden," I said.

There was a long pause.

"You what? With Iden? With *that* Iden?"

"Don't yell at me." I snapped. "Yeah, with *that* Iden. It's my life and my decisions, Elle. I love him." I still couldn't say those words to Iden's face.

"All right, all right, just don't do it." Elle said. "You and your well-being are important to me. He already hurt you once, but what if he does it again?"

"Elle, I'm still confused. Don't be my conscience," I said quietly. "We figured it all out. We are living together again, but I don't know what will happen later." I sighed and made myself more comfortable in the chair.

"He moved to Los Angeles with you?"

I think I made it clear that we live together. "It was like that in the beginning. And now we've moved to Santa Monica ... to Iden's house."

"He bought a house in Los Angeles? Because of you?"

"For himself. He said there was not enough room for him in the apartment." I laughed.

"And how did Iden's mother and your family react to your reconciliation?"

"We haven't told anyone yet." I covered my face with my hand. "But it will have to be said when I make up my mind." I sighed again. "Did you visit your housemates and my parents? Did you give up waiting?" *I don't want to talk about Iden anymore.*

"Yes, they were very happy. Your mother is very unhappy. She worries about Arn. So many months have passed, and there is no news from him. Are you still mad at him?"

"Of course I'm angry. His stupidity could have killed me! On the other hand, he's my brother. I hope he is alive and well."

Nick knocked on the door and showed us that he was waiting for us in the conference hall. "OK, Elle. It's time for me to go to the meeting with the customers. Best wishes to Martin."

After saying goodbye to Elle, I was very upset about my brother. *What kind of sister am I to not care where he's gone? Iden's people are still looking for him, but it is only because of Arn that they kidnapped me, beat me, tortured me, and demanded money from Iden. My brother is still hiding. He didn't even apologize to me. It took months before I was no longer afraid of sleeping alone at night, and it was even longer before I dared to walk the streets in the dark. As always, Arn is the main cog in my family, and my mother is more worried about him than about me or my sister.*

At the end of the workday, I stopped by Target and did a little grocery shopping. Iden had hired a housekeeper, but I felt uncomfortable having other people being concerned about my well-being. *After all, I am a simple girl from the province who has worked hard all my life.* At home, I made a late dinner, sat on the terrace, and read a book.

The phone rang, and it was Iden.

"Hello," I said. "I missed you. Where have you been?"

"Hello." He sighed and said something to another person. "I was very busy. My phone ran out of power, and I just charged it. Don't be angry. Have you settled in yet? Is everything all right?"

"Yes, I'm just sitting on the terrace and admiring the sunset." I could hear the roar of the ocean and see the sun setting over the ocean. "I just miss having you around."

"I'll come back to you soon. I have to go to a meeting." After a moment, he whispered, "I love you, Lu."

"Goodnight, Iden," I said. *I still can't tell him I love him. I'm afraid. I seem to trust and understand that our relationship is real, but a part of me remembers all the bad things that happened.*

I sat on the terrace for another hour and went to bed with a restless heart, but I could not understand why I was worried.

Iden returned on Thursday night. I was already asleep when he woke me up and wrapped his strong arms around my waist. A hot wave of feelings flooded my body.

"Hello, beauty." He cuddled me and purred in my ear. "I miss you."

"Hello." I smiled. "I thought you wouldn't come back today." I patted his hands.

"I'm back—now sleep." He kissed my hair and made himself more comfortable.

I woke up in a good mood because I had felt Iden's body heat and smell next to me all night, which was very soothing. I got up, put on a robe, and went to the kitchen to prepare breakfast. I turned on the radio and scrambled eggs while listening to music. My school dance song, "Beautiful Girls," was playing as two arms wrapped around me.

"Good morning." Iden gently swayed to the beat.

"Good morning. Breakfast will be ready soon." I smiled. "As I can see, you slept well."

"I really did." He tucked my hair behind my ear and kissed my neck. "The reason for my good sleep is standing next to me."

Shivers ran through the body, and my heart began to beat faster. Iden's hands were driving me crazy. Every touch caused a real storm inside me. Next to him, I stopped thinking, and everything around me lost its meaning. *It wasn't until I fell in love with Iden that I understood what love is and how it hurts when you lose it.* I turned off the stove and turned to Iden.

He stole a kiss from me and smiled.

"I love you," I said quietly, looking into his eyes.

Iden tilted his head and said, "I know." He wrapped an arm around my waist, grabbed my neck, pulled me close, and sucked on my lips.

I wrapped my arms around Iden and held him close.

Without waiting for anything, he grabbed me and carried me to the couch in the living room. He tore off my robe and nightgown, and he began to travel with kisses down my neck—all the way down to the thighs and up again. Each kiss heated me from the inside, made me shiver, and raised my passion. The thin fabric of my panties was completely wet. I shuddered at every touch and gently caressed Iden's cock, which was already ready. I deftly pulled down Iden's shorts and spread my legs flirtatiously, beckoning him to come to me. "How long will I have to wait?" I asked out of breath.

Iden settled me between my legs, grabbed my hair with one hand, and pulled my face close to his body. Burning with shame, I tasted a man's body for the first time. I licked his cock like candy in slow motion, and Iden's breathing picked up with every movement I made. I really had no experience with oral sex. I'd only seen it in movies or read novels that detailed the process, and I didn't know if I was doing it right or not. Judging from Iden's reaction, it went smoothly.

After that, everything happened like in a movie. Iden pulled away from me in a sudden movement and put me in a puppy position on the couch. He penetrated me from behind and rhythmically moved back and forth while I gripped the back of the couch to keep from losing my balance. Iden kept slapping my butt, and then he grabbed my hair and pulled me close. His free hand cupped my chest and kept moving until I couldn't take the heat rising inside me anymore. I was shaking with pleasure. Iden finished and collapsed on top of me. He kissed my shoulder and tried to catch his breath.

"Our breakfast got cold," I said.

"I've already had breakfast," Iden replied.

We both started to laugh.

"You're so beautiful after sex." Iden stroked my cheek with his thumb. "So radiant and with sparkling eyes." He kissed my lips.

"And tangled and sweating." I started to blush. "I'm going to be late for work. I'm going to prepare myself—and you can make the coffee." I pointed at the kitchen and walked to the shower naked.

There was only an hour left before work. I quickly got ready and drank hot coffee while standing up.

Iden was laughing at me in his sweatpants and a T-shirt. "I'll take you to work. I'm going to the gym." Iden calmly tied his shoes.

"Since when have you been going the gym here?"

"Since I spend more time here than in Chicago." He straightened up. "Are you ready?"

I pursed my lips and grabbed my purse.

We went out to the yard, holding hands, and I almost jumped on Iden from the sight I saw in the yard. Arn was sitting on the stairs, leaning against a column, and his eyes were closed. He was unshaven, dirty, and ragged. "Oh my God, Arn." I rushed over to my brother.

He opened his eyes. "Luka?" He stretched out his hands.

I jumped into my brother's arms and started crying.

Arn patted me gently on the back.

Iden came closer and waited for me to calm down and pull away from my brother.

"Hey, man." Arn held out his right hand to Iden, but Iden punched him in the face.

I rushed over to Arn and screamed, "What the hell are you doing here?"

Iden stood there, his face contorted with anger, and stared at Arn. "Here's to you for the kidnapping of Luka, asshole." He turned around, went inside the house, and slammed the door behind him.

"Lu, don't be mad at him." Arn struggled for his words. "I'm really crazy. I'm up to my neck and included you. I really didn't think they would find you and kidnap you." Arn began to cry, and he covered his face with his hands.

Sitting next to my brother, I hugged him and said, "You told those mobsters that your sister has a rich fiancé?"

Arn tilted his head, letting me know I was right.

"How could you do this? Why?"

"I'm really sorry, Lu." Arn's voice was gravelly, and he looked miserable.

"Where is Paul?" I asked.

"We broke up in the Netherlands." Arn's gaze was filled with horror. "We were supposed to meet at the airport in New York and travel together to Los Angeles to look for you, but he didn't show up or contact me." Arn grabbed my shoulders and cried. "Lu, I think he was tracked down and killed by that mobster. And they will kill me."

I listened to my brother's story about how he and Paul had been hiding in Russia and Europe for months and that they didn't know about the drugs in the car. The mobsters found Arn and demanded money; otherwise, they promised to deal with all his relatives. Arn and Paul had some savings. Paul was going to sell his apartment, but it would not have been enough to repay the debt.

Finally, the mobster's henchmen came to Paul's apartment, cut off his finger, and threatened to kill him. Arn got scared and said that his sister lived in the USA and had a rich fiancé. He thought he would waste some time like that, but Paul panicked. They ran away, and the mobster's henchmen found me.

I finally got up from the stairs and held out my hand to Arn. "Let's go inside, have a snack, rest, and then I don't know ..." I couldn't think of how to help my brother. "Didn't you try to contact the police?"

"Of course not. After all, they are mafia. The police will not help us." Arn seemed angry.

We went inside.

Arn fidgeted awkwardly with the bag in his hands.

Iden was sitting on the couch where we had made so love that morning, watching football with his legs stretched out on the table.

"Iden, are you still taking me to work?" I asked calmly.

Iden lifted his legs and turned to me. "I'll take you." He stood up, came over to me, and looked into my eyes. "Is everything all right?"

"It's OK," I answered, even though a pot of panic was boiling inside me. "If you don't mind, Arn will stay here."

"OK," Iden said. "I'm going to go to the study to call someone, and you show your brother where the kitchen and the guest room are." He tapped my forehead.

I took Arn to the second floor and showed him the guest room and the kitchen.

Iden appeared in the living room fifteen minutes later, having already changed into a pair of tight dark jeans and a light T-shirt. "We can go. You're already late."

"Liza called. I told her I punctured a tire and am waiting for you to come pick me up." I shrugged.

We left Arn at home and got into Iden's Lexus.

Iden looked at me. "How did Arn find out where you live?"

"As far as I understood, Facebook showed that I was in Los Angeles." I shrugged again. "I don't know, Iden. I'll ask him later."

"It's OK. Don't worry. I'm just curious how he tracked down where you live in the second largest city in the US." Iden looked puzzled.

I was almost an hour late for work. Nick and Liza had gone to the Advertising Department to watch the filmed and edited shoe commercials. Out of breath, I hurried to them and apologized for being late. Everyone was lamenting my flat tire, and I was blushing about such an innocent lie. Finally, after 101 revisions, we decided what we still needed to fix and change before we could show the finished version to the client.

I made lunch half an hour shorter than usual because I had to prepare some contracts for Nick. At half past five, I got a text from Iden: "I'll be at your office in forty-five minutes." I had just finished the last contract when a new message arrived: "I am waiting for you." I turned off the computer and went downstairs.

Iden was waiting in the car. He was in a bad mood.

"Hello, dear." I pecked him on the cheek.

"Hello," he replied dryly and without even looking at me.

"Iden, is something wrong?"

"No, it's nothing." He was gripping the steering wheel so hard. I could feel the tension emanating from his body. I didn't like his state. "Any problems with work?" I tried to understand what kind of hornet had stung him this time.

"It's OK, Luka. Don't worry." He smiled and continued to look at the road all the way home with a serious expression.

I was rambling on about advertising for the hotel and what we were going to make for dinner, and Iden wasn't even listening. At the mention of Arn, he frowned like he had bitten a lemon. For a moment, I thought the two of them had a fight.

When the car stopped, I got out and ran home.

Iden followed me, twirling the car keys around his finger.

My heart felt that something bad had happened, but I did not understand what trouble had befallen our home.

"Arn, we're back." I shouted happily, taking off my shoes. "Arn?"

"He's not there," Iden said from behind me.

"How come he isn't there?" I didn't understand, and I stared into his eyes. They were red. *Was he crying? Did he take something?*

"He's gone, Luka. He's gone." His expression was incomprehensible. I didn't understand if he was angry with me or with my brother. I was really starting to suspect that he was drunk, but I couldn't smell the whiskey.

Iden entered the living room and poured himself a glass of whiskey. I definitely knew something was wrong because Iden wouldn't drink for no reason. I followed him, put my hand on his shoulder, and hugged him from behind.

His body did not respond to my tenderness.

"Iden, I'm not mad at you for hitting Arn this morning, and I certainly don't blame him for disappearing again." I sighed. "Don't be so sour. I don't feel comfortable being with you like this."

Iden turned to me with a wry smile and laughed with his hand over his mouth. "You think I blame myself for hitting your brother—and that's why he left without saying goodbye?" Iden laughed.

I smiled and said, "Then what else could you be angry about?"

Iden took a few deep breaths, placed the empty glass on the table, and grabbed my hand.

I winced. "Iden, are you crazy?"

"Let's go, bitch! You'll see for yourself what I'm angry about." He pulled me so hard that I tripped and scraped my knee on the carpet.

"Stop doing that. I'm in pain."

He dragged me to the study.

I sat on the ground with my head down and cried, not understanding what was happening.

Finally, Iden came over and pulled me to my feet. Every time he touched me, I flinched like a wild animal. He forced himself around his desk, gripped my face tightly, and turned on the computer screen. A camera recording showed Arn in the office with a few other guys. He took Iden's checkbook out of the drawer, wrote something, said something else, and went outside.

I didn't understand anything. I just stared at the screen, and then I raised my tearful gaze to Iden.

He was as mad as a bull.

"Iden, I don't understand."

"You do not understand? Your appearance in my life is not without reason, Luka? Right? Mari was right. You're just another whore who wants to get laid. Did you put those drugs in Las Vegas yourself? Yes? Did I blame Mari's ex-husband—or was it unnecessary?"

I could not believe my ears.

"Answer me!" he shouted.

Swallowing my tears, I tried to control myself. I wrapped my arms around myself and tried to find a logical explanation for his accusations but no thoughts came to mind. I wanted Iden to believe me, but how could I prove my truth without any solid evidence? "I really don't understand what you're accusing me of."

"You damn liar." Iden started pacing the room and running his fingers through his hair. "I was a complete fool. I trusted you. I thought it was all my fault, but you twisted bitch and your cursed family!"

I flinched at his raised voice.

"I ran after you like a puppy. And for what? To hatch the twisted plan with your brother and ransack me?"

"I really don't understand what you're talking about." My hoarse voice sounded really unconvincing. "Iden, I didn't do anything you're accusing me of. It's a misunderstanding. I didn't invite Arn. I didn't know." I shook my head.

"Enough! That damned asshole, your brother—if he's even like that to you—stole ten million dollars from me today."

I gasped. "That can't be true. He may be stupid, but he's not a thief!"

Iden turned on me in a fit of rage and spat the words in my face. "You planned everything carefully with him. How could he know where we live? From where?"

I shivered, curled up, and pressed one hand to my heart.

"From Facebook? I couldn't think of a more stupid explanation."

"Iden, I really didn't know anything. I didn't know anything." I fell to my knees in front of him and wrapped my arms around his leg. I cried and told him I didn't know anything. I grunted with every word he said and tightened my grip on his pants. The ground began to slip from under his feet, and the accusations drove him to despair.

"Get up. I hate looking at you!"

Shivers ran down my spine. I stood up and moved closer. "Iden, sweetie, I love you, and it really isn't and wasn't as you say." I touched his hand with my trembling hand.

Iden turned around with a contorted face and slapped me so

hard that I had to lean against the table to keep from falling over. At that moment, my heart broke into a million pieces. I put my left hand to my sore lip and pulled back to see blood on my fingers. I stared at my bloody fingers and was speechless. The absolute limit had been crossed.

Iden stood white-faced, looking down at me with glassy, dark eyes. His chest heaved like a bull's.

I stared at my bloody hand and slowly made my way past Iden, trying to regain my composure. He stayed in the study while I climbed the stairs on shaky legs.

I pulled out a couple of suitcases from the closet and slowly folded my clothes into them. I put my personal belongings inside as hot tears rolled down my cheeks. My body was shaking. When I packed everything, I saw that my white blouse was stained with blood. I didn't have the strength to change. I ordered an Uber, grabbed my bags, and headed downstairs. I put on low-heeled shoes at the front door and stuffed my other shoes into my suitcase.

Iden came into the hall.

I didn't even look at him. I licked my lip, which was still bleeding, and slipped the ring off my finger. I walked over to the table and placed the ring and the house and car keys on it.

Iden didn't even move.

I stared at my shoes, grabbed my bags, and walked out the door. I walked down the street and found my Uber.

The driver got out and put my bags in the trunk.

I sat down and took one last look at Iden in the doorway.

That's over now. Everything is over. No one will save us this time. I dictated the address of my old apartment to the driver. *Good thing I had paid several months in advance, and I have a place to stay.*

Iden took a few steps toward the car as we pulled away, and I realized how badly I had hurt him. Tears rolled down my cheeks, and my imaginary world shattered. I was an empty vessel. Once again, he had trampled me like a worm.

IDEN

I was alone again. The first day passed terribly slowly, but the anger had taken hold of me so strongly that I was pacing the house. Liam didn't interfere, and he kept his distance. The sight of Luka putting the ring down and walking out the door stood out in my eyes. I wanted to cry, and I did. The anger was taking a toll, and I craved bloodshed and revenge. I got drunk that evening, and I drank all week.

A few days later, Mari appeared again like a snake. This time, I sent her far away. It should have been done a long time ago. Drugs didn't ease the pain or fill the emptiness inside. I had fun with the whores, but when it came down to business, it pissed me off. *What the hell am I doing?*

Liam didn't agree with my laziness or my demand that the lawyers give Luka an ultimatum about the stolen money.

"Do you understand that she has no way to repay such an amount?" Liam snapped angrily, looking at the broken mirror on the floor.

"I don't care. I want her to suffer the way I suffer." I stomped my foot like a child.

"You're a complete asshole." Liam's eyes widened.

He was telling the truth. I was an asshole. I behaved like an asshole because no reasonable man would be deceived like this. "I want her to disappear from the face of the earth."

"Are you punishing her—or yourself again?" Liam asked.

Shut up. Stop being so righteous. "Who cares? She could find a new victim." I couldn't give up on Liam. I leaned my hand on the table and thought about Luka's face. God, how I hated my damned mind and my heart that longed for Luka. She was like the strongest drug for me, and she was my driving force.

"What if everything is not as you think?" Liam asked.

Sometimes I don't understand why Liam works for me if he is so smart. He is intelligent, savvy, good-natured, and completely self-controlled. And I, as far as I can remember, have always been un-yielding and unbreakable. I looked up at Liam, and for the first time in a week, I thought he might be right. *Shit! What if he is right?*

CHAPTER
TWELVE

LUKA

It has been exactly eight weeks since my brother's visit. It's been a nightmarish eight weeks since the painful breakup with Iden. I never counted time before, but counting time has become a kind of therapy.

After moving into the old apartment, it took a few days to heal the wounds before I could go back to work and behave like nothing happened.

Liza couldn't be fooled, and for the first week, she diligently lent me her shoulder to cry on.

A week later, Elle returned from Latvia and immediately came to see me. There were days when we were lying in my bed, I was screaming, curled up in a ball, and Elle just sat and comforted me as best she could. In the middle of the third week, I decided to call my mother and tell her what Arn had done. My mother, of course, didn't believe me; she said it couldn't be because her son was, well, "not a thief."

My brother sent me to hell, my ex-fiancé broke my heart three times, even physically, this time for good, and my parents disowned me because they can't accept the truth that their son stole money. I have received several messages from Iden's lawyer saying that I have to return the money my brother took or I will be sued.

I'm in total shit, and I don't know how to go on with my life. When I wake up in the morning, I can hardly open my eyes. I feel so tired. I masterfully play a happy woman during the day, but when I come home, I cry and feel sorry for myself until I fall asleep. For my birthday, Elle and Rodriguez decided to spend the weekend with me in Los Angeles. Liza and Karl also came. As Friday was approaching, my mood was completely ruined. At work, my colleagues greeted me with a cake. I almost cried, but it was not from happiness; it was from the realization that exactly a year had passed since my normal life turned into a complicated mess.

In the afternoon, Rodriguez appeared at work with Elle and Martin and their suitcases. I was happy about the arrival of my friends, and my mood improved a little. Liza and Karl had a great time interacting with them. Nick heard about our plans for the weekend, and I invited him to join if he didn't have plans. He gladly agreed.

A few hours later, we all gathered at Boardner's Bar. I had reserved a table, and we didn't have to wait in line. Elle dressed me up like a doll, curled my hair in small waves, and applied bright evening makeup. I was wearing a bloodred dress with a plunging neckline, a massive necklace, dangling earrings given to me by Elle and Martin, and black pointed shoes. Nick complimented my appearance as he helped me out of Karl's Prius.

The bar's dark environment made me feel like I was in old America. The music created an illusion of the past. Without waiting for anything, we fell into bright red leather chairs and ordered cocktails. After three sex in the beaches, it got bad, but I wanted to have fun. We went out with the girls to the dance floor and danced until we had enough energy. Refreshed with cocktails, we continued our musical journey, including the boys. Rodriguez and I danced and went crazy.

Throughout the evening, Nick smiled at me and made me dance when he saw the opportunity. After the sixth cocktail, I practically stopped thinking about Iden, all the troubles that had befallen me, and my hard part. Even Nick seemed prettier and cuter when I was drunk.

At exactly midnight, the DJ congratulated me on my birthday. My cool friends couldn't think of any other way to congratulate me. Rodriguez popped the champagne and poured it into glasses. Everyone took turns toasting me and giving me kisses. Nick gave the last toast. He hoped I would not look back and only go forward and believe in love again and let it into my life. I stood and listened to Nick's words. I got their point, but I felt damn lonely at the moment.

I was drinking my champagne and having a good time chatting with Nick when Iden came to our table. A drunken blonde was clutching his arm.

"Good evening," he said proudly. "I see you're having a great time." He raised his glass of whiskey.

I looked at him in horror.

"Luka, my dear Luka. Happy birthday. You gave me your virginity last year. What will you give one of them this year?"

I understood that he was drunk, but I wasn't going to listen to such humiliating words. I jumped up, grabbed Elle's glass of champagne, and threw it in his face.

Iden wiped his face, looking furious, and his entourage squealed in terror.

"Get away from me," I growled.

"Pay off the debt—and then go to hell!"

"That debt is not mine; it is my brother's. Get out of my way!" I pushed him away.

Iden grabbed my arm and whispered, "Spend one night with me and let me do whatever I want with you—and there will be no debt." He smiled.

I couldn't believe my ears. I hit him in the face so hard that I thought I broke my hand. "Shut up, Iden. I am ashamed of my brother and of you. You're disgusting."

He said, "You just gave up your one chance to solve this problem with beauty—and now you all will suffer!"

Nick walked over to me, put his hand on my shoulder, and pushed me behind him. He stood up for my honor like a true gentleman. "Mr. Black, I don't think this is the place and time for such a conversation."

"And who are you? A *lawyer*?" Iden pressed his fists to his sides.

Nick said, "If I understand correctly, you no longer have the right to be interested in Miss Luka's life, and I am asking you to leave our table."

Liza and Elle were sitting with their eyes wide open, Rodriguez was clenching his fists under the table, and Karl was drinking his fifth drink and waiting to see what would happen next.

Iden grinned like a mental patient and poked Nick in the chest. "I ask again, who are you to dare to explain how I should behave?"

I shuddered, but I could not let this circus continue. I stepped into the space between them, tilted my head, and looked into Iden's face. "He's my boyfriend. And you can go on your way or hit me again. After all, you are good at that."

Iden took a step back and rolled his eyes at us. His companion tried to drag him onto the dance floor, but Iden yanked his arm out of the poor girl's grasp and punched Nick in the face. "I will kill you. I will kill both of you!"

Infinity Ink's "Infinity" started playing, and the dance floor plunged into darkness. Colored lights flashed, and smoke was released.

Nick staggered into me, and I fell onto the bench, and then Nick punched Iden in the face.

Karl and Rodriguez tried to separate them, but they punched each other ten times before Iden grabbed Nick's neck and smashed his forehead right into his face. Nick fell back onto the table, and the girls started screaming. Iden jumped on Nick like a beast and tried to deliver a decisive blow, but I caught his fist with my hand.

Iden turned to me with red eyes, messy hair, and a bloody face and gave me that look he used to give me. It only lasted a moment. He was so disgusted by being touched by me that he withdrew his hand as if he had been stung.

"Stop, please," I said.

The security guards tied Iden's hands behind his back. Iden did not resist and was led outside.

Nick was panting heavily. After half an hour, he finally sat down.

"Nick, I'm so sorry. Why did I tell him you were my boyfriend? I wanted to hurt you, and he beat you." I started crying.

"Don't worry. It's been a long time since I've felt this good." Nick laughed. "Really, so much adrenaline has built up that I feel like a tough guy—even though I've been beaten." He tried to smile.

"Tomorrow, you will curse me," I said sadly.

"It's good that tomorrow is the weekend." He laughed again.

Nick and the boys went to the bathroom to clean up and came back with a bag of ice for his eye. No matter how I tried to talk everyone into going home, my friends were stubborn and would not leave. I went home alone. I apologized to everyone, and I told them to have fun until morning and not to be sad for me.

I couldn't find a cab for a while. Maybe it was the alcohol—or maybe it was my Lithuanian temperament—but at the last moment, I changed the direction to Iden's house in Santa Monica. I really hoped I would find him there. When I approached the house, the gate opened. I asked the driver to stop, and I paid him. I walked to the front door and rang the doorbell.

A few minutes later, Iden opened the door. His hair was matted, a trail of coagulated blood ran down from his eyebrow, his lip was cut, and blood was running from his nose. Nick had beaten him up quite a bit. Iden's white shirt was torn, bloodied, and unbuttoned.

I licked my lips and took a step inside. "I came," I said. "You said one night, and the debt will be gone. I'm here. Do what you want with me." I raised my chin, even though I was crying inside.

"You're here?" He seemed surprised, but he didn't move.

"I came to pay." I touched his chest with my hand, dropped my handbag, and kicked the door. I started kissing his lips softly.

Iden didn't move or respond to my kiss; he just stood there and watched.

"Why are you silent? Do you no longer want to do everything you can think of with me?" I released my dress from my shoulders, which slid down my hips, and I was left standing only in my underwear.

Iden took a step closer, put one hand on my neck and the other on my face, and looked me in the eyes for the first time since we broke up. "You were my great love." He pressed me against the door.

I was trapped between his arms, and I stared into his eyes.

"And now you have come to pay for the money stolen by your brother?"

"Isn't this what you asked for, Iden? After all, I'm the last bitch who colluded with her brother and the others to profit from you." I swallowed and unbuttoned my bra with one hand. It fell to the floor. In a trembling voice, I added, "Now fuck me all you want, and we will be settled."

Iden pressed me tighter against the wall, and his hand gripped my chest painfully. His other hand grabbed my hair, and he bent his head and sucked on my lips. I could taste his blood and hatred. He bit my lower lip several times, but I remained silent and suffered the humiliation.

Turning me around to face the door, he tore off my panties and pulled out his penis in a sudden movement and went inside. Nibbling on my neck and shoulder, he moved faster and faster, seemingly intent on leaving a mark on me. I didn't make a sound, but a tear rolled down my cheek. That's all.

Iden finished inside me and shuddered. He backed away, dropped a bunch of cash at my feet, said "You can go," and disappeared into the house. Swallowing my tears, I put on my dress and ran away.

After returning to my apartment, I lay down on the couch in the living room.

An hour later, the friends who came home. Rodriguez fell on the couch next to me, and Elle and Martin lay down in my bed. My ears were ringing from the amount of alcohol I'd consumed, but I couldn't stop thinking about tonight, about Iden, and about what he'd done. He hated me more than I imagined and accused me of things that didn't exist, but I couldn't prove that he was wrong.

After tonight, I no longer want to prove anything to him. He erased the last ray of hope in my dying heart, trampled my femininity, and wounded my soul and body with his indifference. I was just a whore for him tonight, and my purpose was to work for money. What have I come down to?

IDEN

I couldn't sleep all night. I felt like a bastard. I sat on the terrace and thought about what I would say again. After all, she came. I could have fallen on my knees and begged for forgiveness, but I got up again. Once again, I couldn't get over my ego.

What a moron you are, Iden.

I fucked her like some kind of bitch. I watched her brood and suffer, and my damned ego was overflowing. The main thing was revenge for her being with that bastard Nick. I didn't care about anything else but wanting to teach her. But what did I learn? I learned a lesson myself.

What is happening to me?

I no longer understand reality. Lately, I've been in conflict with everyone. Everyone is talking about the old Iden being back. Mom is going crazy.

I've lost her. I've lost her now.

And why the damned poets don't describe how terrible the suffering of love can be. It is better to tear off the fingernails than to suffer like this. I hate myself for everything I did to her. I hate it. I don't understand how I could do this. I know I can be very cruel, but I would never dare raise a hand against a girl, much less Luka. What I did tonight is unforgivable. I dishonored her. I dishonored her faith in me, in herself, and in our love.

"Hey, man. How are you?" Liam asked.

"Hello. It's bad. I finally did it." I almost started crying.

Liam sat down next to me. "What happened?"

"I kicked Luka out—"

"I don't want to know this." Liam shook his head.

He had had enough of my adventures, misfortunes, quarrels, and anger. More than once, I had to be shaken so that I would come to my senses. He always had to listen to my sins.

If I could only turn back time!

As we watched the sunrise, I realized I had ruined our relationship. It was beyond repair. *Enough stalking her and watching her apartment windows—she will never come back to me. I have lost her forever. She was my light, and I am the spawn of the devil who knows how to destroy all that is beautiful. I ruined everything with my own hands. I am my own worst punishment. I am in purgatory on earth. I lost Luka. I lost my love.*

LUKA

I couldn't lift my head in the morning. As soon as I put my feet on the ground, I rushed to the toilet and emptied the contents of my stomach.

When Elle woke up, she started laughing and joked that champagne and cocktails don't seem to appeal to me as much today as yesterday, and that's why I decided to get rid of them. I stayed in bed for half the day and swore to God and all the saints that I would not drink another drop.

In the evening, we went to the city. I called Nick, but he didn't want to join us. He said that his eyes were too red to show them in public, but his mood was definitely not unusual. We went to a Chinese restaurant and then a movie, and then we stumbled into a bar where we inevitably had to make friends with beer.

On Sunday morning, I didn't feel as bad, but I promised my friends that, after this weekend, I wouldn't drink another drop. Everyone, of course, laughed and said I would be talking like that until next time. That evening, I accompanied them out to their cab.

Elle hugged me and shook me tightly. "It's your turn to visit us in Chicago."

"OK, OK. Don't break me." I laughed.

Rodriguez hugged us both. "It was good to meet you, chica. Really, come visit us." He kissed my cheek.

Martin was more reserved. He stood at a distance, but I motioned for him to hug me.

I returned to the empty apartment. I felt bad, I was tired, and my stomach hurt. I decided to lie down. Surprisingly, I didn't wake up until Monday morning. I couldn't remember the last time I slept so well. I felt rested and full of energy.

I showered, ate breakfast, and threw up again before heading out the door. The last time my stomach was so upset was when I caught a virus. On the way to work, I ran to the store and bought mineral water.

Liza was waiting for me in the office with coffee. The smell of coffee made me feel nauseous, and I rushed to the toilet. When I got up, Liza was standing with her arms crossed and looking at me questioningly.

"What?" I asked nervously. My stomach continued to tighten, and the cold shook my body.

• "Are you pregnant?" Liza rolled her eyes.

"What are you talking about?" I laughed, but at the same

time, I realized that the last time I had my period was more than a month ago.

Liza must have caught my thought, and she took a deep breath.

I went to my desk, opened the calendar, and started counting the days.

I gasped. "Oh my God."

"Did you take a test?" Liza was looking at me with wide eyes.

"No, I didn't. Shit, Liza. What should I do?" I felt hysterical and looked around for help—as if someone could solve the problem for me.

"Don't be nervous, dear. Don't be nervous." Liza went into her office and returned with her purse. She gave me pregnancy test. When I looked at her questioningly, she shrugged. "I just have to because of everything."

With trembling hands, I took the test, hid it behind my jacket, and went to the toilet. Liza followed me. We disappeared behind the toilet door like secret agents. I locked myself in the stall and read the instructions for five minutes.

"Lu, pee on the damn test," Liza said.

"I will right now … don't rush me." I took the test out of the box with trembling hands.

I finally relented and soaked it in urine. I left the stall, put the test on the sink, and counted the minutes. Each second passed so slowly that it seemed as if the second hand had stopped.

"Lu, oh my God, it's positive," Liza said.

The test had two bright red lines.

"What do I do now?" I panicked and gripped the edge of the sink. Time stopped, and the horrible word *pregnancy* and the realization that I was expecting a baby hung in the air. I couldn't believe I had been so irresponsible and stupid and not protected myself properly.

Liza hugged me, and we stayed like that for ten minutes. I was in shock and didn't realize what was happening. I went to my office and sat on the windowsill for half a day, involuntarily putting my hand on my stomach.

At the end of the day, Liza came to my office and said, "What did you decide?"

"I don't know, Liza. I can't raise a baby alone. I won't be able to handle it on my own. And how will I survive alone?" I panicked even more. My panic was probably reflected in my eyes.

"I understand you, but won't you regret it later?"

"No. After all, Iden hates me. This child may have been conceived in love, but I don't want it to grow up in hatred." I sighed. "I will have to go to Chicago because my doctor is there. I have not yet processed the documents for treatment services at the hospital here.

"You don't have time to deal with anything here." Liza looked so worried. "You have to go to Chicago as soon as possible."

"I think so too," I answered. "I'll call my doctor tomorrow and make an appointment." Liza and I were silent for the rest of the day.

The next day, I vomited and felt sick. I called my doctor, and she agreed to see me on Friday. When I got to work, I asked Nick for a few days off because of health issues. I told him I had to go to Chicago to see my doctor. Nick didn't mind.

That evening, I called Rodriguez, told him I was coming to Chicago, and asked if I could stay with him for a few days. He said he would be happy to wait for me at the restaurant since he worked late on Thursdays. The flight to Chicago wasn't long, but I felt bad the whole trip. I was happy that I managed not to get sick in the plane cabin.

I missed Chicago and its streets. As much as I liked Los Angeles, Chicago was a part of my soul. I was happy to be back. I took the subway to the restaurant and listened to my favorite songs. By the time I reached the restaurant, it was dinnertime, and my stomach was demanding food. I went inside. Nothing had changed.

Adam greeted me with a big smile and gave me a tight hug. My other former coworkers were all so kind. I asked if there were any free tables and sat at the corner one. It was a couple of hours before Rodriguez's shift ended. I ordered a roasted steak because I really wanted meat. When the food was brought, I greedily took a bite, and my stomach started flipping. After the third bite, I ran to the bathroom and got sick . I returned to my table with an empty and upset stomach and didn't even notice Liam sitting at my table.

"Good evening, Miss Luka." I was surprised to see him.

"What are you doing here?" I asked. "And forgive me for being rude. Hello." I smiled.

"Everything's all right. I often come here to eat. Your traditional cuisine is very tasty. Are you moving back to Chicago?"

"No ... I'm just here for a few days." I put my hand over my mouth and pushed the plate away from me. "I'm sorry. I have health problems that I want to solve as soon as possible."

"Something wrong?" He was staring at my stomach.

"Nothing serious, Liam. Everything will be fine." I didn't believe it myself, and I went back to the toilet.

▪ ▪ ▪

The next morning, Rodriguez rushed to the university—it was his last year of studies—and I went to the hospital. I stomped into the doctor's office like a child, and when I was invited to come in, I was completely confused.

"Good morning, sweetie. What's the problem?" an African American woman addressed me in a soft voice.

"Good morning, Mrs. Sparks," I said. "I have a problem." I tried to find the right words. "I think I'm pregnant, but I don't think—or, rather, I know—that I can't raise that baby. I think it would be best if we removed the fetus." My heart sank.

She lowered her glasses and looked at me. "Well, let's go see if someone really lives there." She smiled.

The screen flashing various images, and the doctor said, "Do you see this bean? This is a child. You're about eleven weeks pregnant." She finished the examination and handed me a paper to wipe my belly.

I sat down and blinked. *I'm pregnant? Oh my God, a baby!*

"Now let's talk about the next part of the visit," the doctor said. "Do you want to do a removal?"

"Yes," I said. My voice was shaking.

"I will make an appointment for tomorrow morning at seven o'clock. Come without eating." The doctor looked at me again and added, "Dear, there is still time to change your mind."

I thanked the doctor and wandered the corridors of the hospital, trying to understand what was going on. *The baby ... mine and Iden's baby. I can't raise a baby alone. I can't. I'm not ready for that. I don't want to be a single mother who will be condemned by society. And my parents? My parents have already disowned me because of my brother's sins, and because of the baby, I will become completely dead to them. What shame and trouble have befallen me.*

I took a long walk around Old Town and tried to calm myself and my conscience. I kept thinking that I had to do the right thing—both for my own sake and for that of the unborn child. I sat on a park bench and watched the children playing. *If I don't remove it, my kid could be playing in this park next year. Life is hard for single moms. I wouldn't be able to work. What would I live on? I don't have a lot of savings. It would be enough for maybe half a year, but what's next? I couldn't go back to my parents. I wouldn't even want to. They wouldn't accept me with a child in my arms.* As much as I thought about my actions, I couldn't find a better solution than removal of the fetus.

I went back to Rodriguez's house and waited for him to get home. We met up with Elle and went to a fast-food restaurant for dinner. Elle insisted on going to the bar, but I lied and told her I was tired as hell. We headed home after dinner.

All night, I tossed and turned, sat on the edge of the bed, and looked out the window. At half past six, I got up and started walking from corner to corner: *I have to do this, I have to.* I kept repeating this in my mind. *I will have no chance to raise this child so that he will not lack anything as he grows up.* My head began to spin, and I sat down on the armchair in the living room. Rodriguez was sleeping peacefully on the couch. I couldn't tell my friends about the trouble that fell on my shoulders. *I don't want to confuse them with this joke; they don't deserve it.*

I arrived at the hospital early and waited restlessly in the corridor. I was finally called into the preparation room and followed the nurse on shaky legs. She handed me disposable clothes to change into before the procedure and left the ward. I changed my clothes slowly, sat down on the couch, and waited.

I looked out the window, and it was raining and thundering outside.

The nurse returned to the ward, told me to sign the documents, put me in a wheelchair, and took me to the operating room.

With trembling legs, I sat on the table and gasped for air. My heart was trembling.

A nice nurse inserted a catheter into my arm and explained how the anesthesia procedure would work.

After a few minutes, Dr. Sparks came in and explained the procedure in detail.

I listened to everyone and stopped panicking.

Dr. Sparks told the nurse that they could begin.

"No! Forgive me ... I can't ... I can't." I tried to pull the catheter out of my hand.

"It's OK, honey. It's OK." Dr. Sparks hugged me and. "You're not alone."

I rocked myself into her robe.

Dr. Sparks assured me that I was not the only one who changed her mind at the last minute and didn't regret it later. She told me that I was strong and could definitely handle raising a baby and working. I calmed down a bit and was glad that I had made up my mind in time.

I went home for lunch, and Rodriguez and Elle watching basketball in the living room. We chatted for a couple of hours, and then I left for the airport.

When I got back to Los Angeles, I texted Liza and told her that I had decided to give birth and raise the child alone.

She was waiting for me at the door of my apartment. "Lu, I don't understand." She hugged me and patted my cheek. "Really?"

"Yes, indeed," I answered calmly. "That child is innocent. I can't kill him. Liza, after all, this is my child. It's my flesh and blood."

Liza hugged me even tighter and said, "We will help him grow up."

NOVEMBER 27, 2019
LUKA

November in Los Angeles was like spring in Lithuanian. It was sixty degrees, and I put on a loose knee-length cotton dress and a long sweater. In my twenty-eighth week of pregnancy, my belly was clearly protruding, and walking was becoming more and more difficult. I had stopped wearing high heels a long time ago and switched to low heels or platform shoes. I still bleached my hair in strands, and it had already grown halfway down my back. I tied it into a loose knot on the top of my head.

I put on my sunglasses and walked toward the subway. It was the last day of work before the long Thanksgiving weekend. Everyone at work had stopped discussing my pregnancy a long time ago. Some had speculated about the father of the baby, and some people thought it was Nick. Nick really helped a lot during that difficult period. Sometimes I thought I would have been happier if I had met Nick before Iden.

I never heard from Iden again. He stopped all advertising orders with our office, and I breathed a sigh of relief. At work, the day passed like any other. Mrs. Maffin has been behaving like a mother to me lately. She was always spoiling me with delicacies and fresh fruit, but my real parents had no contact with me. Once a month, I called my sister. Fearing our parents' anger, she avoided telling me how they were. I didn't know anything about Arn either. I was still mad at him, but I wanted him to be healthy and happy.

Nick knocked on my office door and entered. "I wanted to remind you that we are invited to a charity party tonight. Liza and Karl are going. Will you join us?"

"Of course." I smiled with my puffy cheeks.

"I'll pick up you at half past seven."

I called Liza and asked what she was going to wear because I had never been to a party like that.

When I got home, I opened my closet and realized that I could only stuff my stomach and chest into a wide, long black dress and black silicone platforms. I twisted my hair and put it in a ponytail, leaving a few strands loose. I gently painted my eyelids with shadow and highlighted them with a pencil. After a few coats of mascara, I was ready. I'd been avoiding mascara lately because I was constantly scratching myself, and the mascara would run off in black streaks. Pregnancy also had its advantages. My chest increased by a couple of sizes, and my hips widened. I had never had such an expressive form in my life.

Nick picked me up at half past seven, and I grabbed my fur coat and went downstairs.

Liza and Karl were waiting for us at the venue. They both looked adorable. Liza wore a long navy blue guipure dress, and Karl wore a suit. We walked to our assigned table, and I was happy to see that there were tables with chairs. I'd been looking for an opportunity to sit down and rest my back. We were making friends with our clients, but I excused myself and scurried off to find the treats. The table was full of stuffed cakes and tarts. It took me five minutes to decide which one to taste first. I thought I was going to die of pleasure when I sunk my teeth into the fluffy cake—and then the baby started kicking my side. Placing my hand on my stomach, I smiled and said, "Iva, are you hungry too?" I don't know why, but I was absolutely convinced that a girl would be born. I had called her Iva since the very first days.

I licked my lips and fingers and chose the other delicacies that I would bring to the table. As I turned to walk toward the table, I practically bumped into Iden and Anna.

"Luka?" Anna asked in a surprised voice.

I smiled at her and tried not to look at Iden—he was staring at my bulging belly. I pretended he wasn't there and that I didn't even know him.

"Good evening, Anna." I hugged her. I had really missed her. "What are you doing here?"

"Probably the same as you." Anna laughed. "You look amazing, Lu. How long?" Anna pointed at my stomach.

"Twenty-eight weeks. Anna, excuse me, but I have to go back to my colleagues. They are probably missing me." I pointed toward the table. I needed to get away from Iden as soon as possible.

"Everything's all right?" Anna asked. "I hope we meet again."

"Yes, of course. Goodbye now." I hurried back to the table.

Liza was delighted with the treats.

I drank a full glass of water in one gulp and looked around to see if anyone was listening. "Liza, Iden's here," I whispered.

"What?" She choked on her cake.

Karl patted her on the back.

"Don't shout!" I said. "You will draw his attention—and don't look around! What the hell is he doing here?"

"How should I know?" She kept looking around.

I drank another glass of water and got up from the table. My bladder was being kicked by the naughty little girl, and I couldn't take it anymore. I went to the toilet. When I reached my goal, I was so happy with the relief that I almost cried.

After I washed my hands, I walked toward the door. It opened, and Iden blocked my way. I froze and automatically put my hands around my stomach.

"Are you pregnant?" Iden shamelessly stared at my bulging belly.

I felt like I was in an exam. "As you can see."

"Is it mine?"

"No." I felt my cheeks and neck turning red. I've never been good at lying, and if I did, I always blushed.

"Whose is it?"

"None of your business." I sighed.

The baby must have kicked me in the stomach because I felt like I was going to throw up. I ran to the toilet with my hand over my mouth and threw up all the delicious sweets I had eaten. It happened so often that I was used to constantly wasting food.

"Are you OK?" Iden asked.

"Get out of here. Leave me alone." I wiped my mouth, got up from the floor, and went over to the sink. I was exhausted, but I tried to pull myself together. I closed my eyes, counted to ten, took a few deep breaths, and felt better.

"Luka, is *that* child mine?" Iden asked.

My body was like a ball of hormones, and my mood changed every few moments. I laughed, I cried, I got angry, and I didn't know why. I was in a bad mood, and being angry at Iden was the perfect way to get rid of all my hormones. "That child, as you call her, has a name. And Iva is not yours. She is *my* daughter." I pointed at him. "So get out of the way. You're going to be mad—or I swear to God I'll throw up."

Iden listened calmly, took a step to the side, and let me pass.

I could finally breathe more freely. It was still hard to be around him. I returned to the table and spent the rest of the evening there. Nick went to the club with another company, and Karl took me home with Liza.

I trudged up the stairs to my apartment and was glad to take off my shoes. My legs swelled like bears, and it became more and more difficult to move.

I got to meet Liza's family for Thanksgiving and was very happy with the delicious home-cooked meals. After eating until I was full, I returned home and fell asleep on the couch in front of the TV. I don't know how long I slept, and I ignored a knock on the door. The sleep was sweeter.

I woke up, and the room was dark, but the TV was still on. After several unsuccessful attempts, I managed to sit down. I dragged my feet to the fridge, but there was nothing to eat. It was only eight at night, and I put on a sweater and went to the store.

Half an hour later, I trudged up the stairs again with a bag of groceries, cursing the house for not having an elevator. I unlocked the door and stepped inside, leaving the door to close by itself. I placed the bag on the table, leaned against it, and caressed my aching back. I felt footsteps behind me.

"Hello. The door was open … so I came in." Iden was standing by the kitchen wall. As always, he looked perfect in black jeans, a white sweater, and black boots.

"What are you doing here?" I crossed my arms.

"I think we should talk," he said calmly.

"About what?" I asked angrily.

"About this situation." He pointed to my stomach.

I sighed and started moving the shopping bag. I really wanted to eat, and I quickly made a sandwich with chicken, pickles, mayonnaise, and mustard.

Iden stared at me wide-eyed, waiting for me to say something.

"I told you before, and I'll say it again, there is no *situation* we should talk about," I said with my mouth full.

"Luka, I'm not stupid, and I can count." Iden sat down at the table.

"What do you want to hear, Iden?"

"Why didn't you contact me and tell me about your pregnancy?"

"Why would I have to contact you? I think you have already said everything you wanted to. I can't repay the debt unless you hand my brother over to the police."

"Luka, that money is not important to me."

I could see that Iden was uncomfortable because he didn't know where to look or what to say. For once in my life, I had an advantage over him. "As far as I remember, it was so important that you called me a liar and slapped me."

"I didn't control myself. Then I was overcome with rage."

"And what will you say now? Why didn't I remove the fetus?" I rolled my eyes. "Oh, I know what you're thinking. I wanted to give birth quietly and then sue you for custody of my daughter. After all, I'm a money-hungry bitch."

"Luka, it's not like that. I don't think so." Iden looked confused.

"You don't think so? Strange. As far as I remember, you didn't call it any other way—just a bitch." I sighed.

Iden looked at me, my stomach, and the stupid sandwich I was holding. "I wanted to hurt you because it was easier to hurt you." He squirmed in his chair.

"It doesn't make sense anymore," I said. "We can't turn back time and change the past, right?"

"I'm so sorry for all the hurtful words and behavior." Iden got up and walked over to me. "But I had a right to know you were expecting my child."

"And would you have believed me if I had told you when I first found out?" I looked into his eyes.

"I don't know." Iden looked puzzled.

"But I know." I paused. "You wouldn't be." A single tear rolled down my cheek.

"Do you hate me?"

I wanted to curl up in a ball and cry out all the pain that was flooding through me. "I hate it."

"Then why didn't you do a removal if you hate it?" Iden looked confused.

I looked up at him and gathered myself. "Because this child was conceived by two loving people." I took his hand and put it on my stomach to feel Iva moving. I burst into tears again, and the baby started squirming like crazy in my womb. She must have felt that the hand on my stomach was her father's.

Iden swallowed hard and smiled.

"And what happened later makes no sense anymore, Iden. It's beyond repair."

A tear rolled down Iden's cheek as well. He tilted his head—seeming to try to understand what I said—and quietly walked out the door.

My heart was bleeding again. This time, it was not from hatred; it was from the realization that love was not going anywhere. No matter how much I tried to convince myself and said that love was gone and had died, it was there. It was quietly waiting in the corner of my heart, and it had reappeared at the most unexpected time. I felt a deep heartache and guilt that I had taken away Iden's choice about whether he wanted to be a father or not. I had decided all by myself, but I had not had a choice.

Iden has hurt me too badly and done too much damage to our relationship to forgive him, but I think I should give him a chance to try being a father. I can't be completely selfish. He would have found out about our baby sooner or later. Now was the time to find out.

CHAPTER THIRTEEN

LUKA

I hadn't seen Iden for two weeks. It was hard not to think about him when his child was growing under my heart. Every free moment, I told Iva about her father, how handsome and strong he is, that Mommy loves him, but Daddy didn't want to be with us. I kept remembering all of Iden's actions: how he tried to hurt me, beat up Nick, canceled the order, and talked other clients out of doing business with our company. His lawyer made phone calls and sent letters about the money my brother had borrowed. In the end, I had offered to repay the debt by spending the night with him. After all, I only joined this game to punish him and myself.

After work today, I had to go to the hospital for an ultrasound. I was looking forward to it. I texted Iden this morning: "Hello. Will do an ultrasound today. The visit to the doctor is scheduled for seven o'clock this evening at the main LA hospital. You can join if you want."

I thought about sending that message for a long time, but I finally did. Of course, I didn't get an answer. The day passed slowly, and I kept glancing at my phone—maybe a little naively—hoping for a reply that he wouldn't come. His name didn't appear on my phone screen.

Before going to the hospital, I rushed to the shopping center to look for some new dresses because the ones I had were getting tight. I passed the children's section and bought some pink slippers. Buying small clothes was a real joy. I also found a couple of dresses for myself.

I walked the three blocks at a leisurely pace with satisfaction and got to the doctor's office at ten minutes to seven. I was reading a pamphlet about preparing for childbirth. Everything was described so beautifully, but it recommended participating in the course with a significant other. *What if there is no second half?*

"Miss Luka Ilgauskaitė?" asked the nurse.

"Yes," I replied with a smile.

"You can go to the office and get ready. Are you alone?"

"Yes, I am." I smiled.

In the office, I changed into my examination clothes and waited on the couch. I looked out the window at the twinkling city skyline and remembered my first visit to the doctor in Chicago. I patted my stomach and thought that I should thank God for the enlightened mind and the opportunity to become a mother. I'd probably be biting my nails about that decision right now.

The young doctor performed a general examination and took me to the ultrasound machine.

I really hoped that everything would be fine and that the baby was growing up healthy.

A nurse said, "Excuse me, Miss Ilgauskaitė's friend has arrived."

Iden came through the door.

I looked at him and smiled.

"Hello. Please join us." The doctor invited Iden to sit in the chair next to me.

Iden looked stunningly handsome in a black suit and dazzling white shirt. *He probably came straight from work.*

"Thank you," Iden said quietly. "Forgive me for being late."

"We were just about to do the ultrasound. Your girlfriend's

physical data is good, and now we will see how the resident is doing." The doctor smiled and turned on the machine.

We saw moving outlines on the screen.

The doctor turned on the sound, and we heard the heartbeat. It was very fast. Out of the corner of my eye, I could see Iden's smile.

The doctor looked at the screen for a long time and wrote something down. There was endless excitement, and I was hoping that everything would be fine—and the baby would be healthy. She turned around. "Want to know what you're waiting for?"

"Yes," Iden answered.

"OK, I can almost guarantee 100 percent that a girl will be born." The doctor smiled. "According to all indications, she is growing up healthy and happy. Everything's all right. Of course, the mother needs more rest and needs to take care of her health and to eat healthy."

I was so happy that Iva was growing up healthy. Iden helped me sit up, but I was confused when he touched me.

"By the way," the doctor said, "will you attend the preparatory courses? The new group will meet next week."

"Yes, I will," I answered. "I was just going to register this evening."

"It's very good that you decided to participate," the doctor said. "Will the father attend the birth?"

I turned to Iden and didn't know what to say.

Iden looked at me and said, "Of course, I will participate, and I will attend the courses too."

I went to the ward to change, and the doctor gave me a bunch of brochures about childbirth, the last months of pregnancy and the first months after giving birth.

Iden wasn't in the office anymore. *He must have gone home*, I thought. When I left the office, I was surprised to see him standing by the wall. "You're still here?"

"Yes, I'll take you home." He took the shopping bag from my hands.

"Thank you, but there's no need," I replied shortly. "I'll catch a cab." I smiled.

"I'm going that way anyway … it's really not difficult." He walked toward the elevator, and I followed him.

There was an awkward silence in the elevator. I stared at the toes of my shoes, and Iden was looking at me. The silence continued in the parking lot. I looked around for Iden's Lexus, but he stopped at a beautiful silver Audi sports car. Iden unlocked it and opened the passenger side door. "Can I help you sit down?"

"Thank you, I can do it myself."

I crawled inside and looked around.

Iden started the engine, which was running so quietly it was almost inaudible, and we joined the hustle and bustle of the street. Iden clenched his jaw and kept his hands on the steering wheel. His appearance reminded me of the day I left his house. He was tense and probably thinking about something serious.

"Luka, I'd like to do a DNA test," he said in a stern voice.

"I'm not asking you to take part in our life and raise Iva."

"If she is my daughter, I have exactly the same right to her as you!"

"Have the right? What is she to you, a thing?" I was starting to get angry. "Of course, I was a thing for you too, which you conveniently threw away!"

"Can you hear what you're saying?" Iden stopped looking at the road.

"I can hear—and you should look at the road." I crossed my arms. "In general, you can live peacefully. I promised to raise my daughter alone, and I'm not asking for your help or support."

"Luka, can you, for once in your life, not have a fever? I am her father, and I want her to have a mother *and* a father in her life."

"Is she your daughter now? And where is the DNA test?" I

said angrily, mimicking his manner of speaking—like Liam used to do.

"I know she's mine." He sighed.

"You see, now he already knows." I began my Lithuanian monologue. "He knows everything. He always knows everything. He knows when to speak, when to keep quiet, when to laugh, and when to cry."

Iden laughed. "Luka, I don't understand, but it sounds funny."

"Are you still laughing at me? Seriously?"

"You look like a little kid right now." He smiled again. "Maybe you're hungry?"

"Very much." I smiled too.

"Shall we go out to eat?" he asked. "I haven't eaten anything today."

"I agree."

We stopped at a snack bar on the way to my house and ordered steaks. I was so hungry that I finished it in a matter of moments. Iden pushed his plate over to me, and I ate half of his steak. I never thought pregnancy would change my eating habits.

Iden looked at me wide-eyed, amazed at my beastly appetite.

I shrugged. "I've been hungry lately."

"I see you're not complaining about your appetite." He smiled.

We talked about the weather and our acquaintances, drank tea, and headed for the car.

I fell asleep in the car.

Iden said, "Lu, get up. We arrived. Lu?"

I opened my eyes, and two dark eyes were staring at me. Iden's face was quite close to mine.

"I fell asleep?" I asked.

"Yes," Iden replied. "I tried to wake you, but you were sleeping like a bear in winter." He laughed.

"I've been so disconnected lately that I can't hear anything." It was dark outside. "How long have I been offline?"

"Three hours." Iden looked tired.

"I'm so sorry." I blushed. "You should have shaken me harder. I would have woken up."

"Everything is fine. Can I help you get out?"

"Thank you. My legs are numb." I couldn't lie.

He walked around the car and held out his hand to me.

I stood up and sighed. "Ow." The cramp had completely taken over my left leg.

Iden grabbed me and lifted me into his arms.

"What are you doing?" I squealed and held onto him, afraid of falling.

"Don't be afraid. I won't throw you out." He breathed heavily while climbing the stairs. "And you've gained weight," he said jokingly.

He stood me at the front door and let me unlock it. With his help, I slowly climbed to the third floor.

As he entered the apartment, Iden said, "This place is not suitable for living with a baby."

"I think there's enough room here for the two of us." I took off my shoes and leaned against the kitchen table.

"But the house doesn't have an elevator. You can barely move now. What will happen next?" Iden would not give up.

"I won't go anywhere later. I'll just be here."

"Move to the house in Santa Monica. You can live there. I will be calmer, and you will have more space."

"Iden, maybe you've forgotten that we're not a couple. You don't owe me anything. It's OK. I'll live my life, and you'll live yours. Thank you for tonight. You can go now."

He pounded at the door for a few more moments, but he finally left.

I locked the door and fell into bed. My clothes smelled of Iden, and I slept smelling him. It's stupid, I know, but my stupid hormones were taking their toll—and the awakening feelings completely messed with my mind.

IDEN

I sat in my car outside the hospital and tried to relax. I have become very sentimental these past few days.

Just knowing I am going to be a father brings tears to my eyes. Every time I look at Luka and that beautiful belly, I want to fall at her feet and beg for forgiveness. I long to be near her, to help her, and to treat her to the most delicious dishes.

How many times have you begged?

I realize it's not the first time I've said this, but I need one last chance. I've been in this relationship more times than I can count. I was a parasite. I treated Luka like some scumbag, and I even raised my hand in front of her. I wanted to cut my damn arm off. I still have a hard time dealing with the aggression that comes out. These are probably the effects of drugs I took as a kid.

What a piece of shit I am. I don't know how, but I have to get Luka back—at any cost.

I looked through the front window of the car at the hospital facade and saw her. She was walking like a duck with a wide grin, and her cheeks were red. A few loose strands fluttered across the face. She stroked her belly as she walked. *She's talking to her stomach again! God she is so sexy.* My penis immediately got hard. *Only Luka makes me feel this way. She looks really hot with that round belly and those rounded, ladylike features.*

Calm down, man.

No, today is the day I get my love back.

Luka, you will come back to me. You will come back—I promise.

LUKA

On Thursday I went to my first childbirth preparation lesson. I was wearing comfortable leggings and a half-length sweater, and my hair was in a knot. There were several couples in the hall, and I felt awkward coming alone. While we waited for the other participants, I opened a novel and started reading.

"Hello." Iden sat down next to me. He was wearing sports clothes and looked relaxed.

"Hello," I said. "I didn't think you would come."

"Why shouldn't I have come?"

"It doesn't matter. Since you have already come, you can stay."

Iden smiled.

The courses turned out to be quite interesting. It was necessary to learn to breathe and get to know the positions of your body in which it was comfortable to sit. Iden had to massage my back and hold me. I got so many touches and hugs from him that I was completely sexually aroused, but I couldn't do anything with myself. His touch, smell, and voice drove me crazy. Our bodies were touching during the exercises, and I felt my panties getting wet.

Iden seemed just as uncomfortable around me, and he kept moving and glancing at me.

After the course, Iden offered to give me a ride home. He got out of the car, helped me out, accompanied me to the apartment, and went inside to ask if anything was missing. His presence completely messed with my head. My whole body was on fire. I wanted to experience the relief I hadn't felt in so long. And then my mind went dark for good, and I pounced on Iden like a cat.

Iden stiffened and tensed, but he returned the kiss with a kiss.

"Oh my God," I said, realizing what I had done. I pulled back and covered my lips. "I'm very sorry. My hormones are messed up. I didn't want to do that. Or, rather, I really wanted to."

"Lu, don't apologize." He grabbed my cheeks and pulled me closer. "I'm at your service." He gave me a passionate kiss.

Iden led me to the bedroom.

I clung to his muscles, and I wanted to rip off all his clothes as soon as possible. I pushed him back, grabbed the hem of his jersey, and pulled it up.

Iden took off his shirt.

I kissed him again.

He gently placed me on the edge of the bed and removed my clothes.

In that moment, I cared about nothing but the physical closeness that had been so lacking in recent months. I pulled Iden closer and continued the journey of passion along the curves of his body.

Iden didn't stop kissing me or touching my thighs and chest. "They're huge." He moaned as he kissed my breasts.

I writhed like a snake. "Iden, please make it good." I purred into his ear.

He kept kissing my breasts, driving me even crazier, and he returned his kisses to my lips and my breasts. His hand slid to my sensitive spot, and his fingers slid in and out.

I couldn't stand it anymore, and a wave of pleasure ran through my body. I stretched out as much as my stomach would allow.

Iden smiled and continued what he had started.

Over and over again, I squirmed in satisfaction.

Finally, he entered me from behind, very gently and slowly, and he kissed my neck and caressed my breasts and stomach. Every touch raised a storm inside me, and his breath in my ear made my blood heat up.

I took the initiative, rubbing my hips into Iden faster, and he pressed closer to me, picking up the pace. The tension that had been building for a long time exploded inside me, and I began to squirm in relief.

Iden finished and wrapped his arms around me.

"Iden, I don't know how to explain this." I covered my face with my hands. I was so embarrassed.

"No need to explain." Iden turned my face toward him. "Those months apart drove me just as crazy."

"Really?" I asked.

"God, Luka." His gaze was so sensitive that I wanted to cry. "How many times have I sat in the car under the window of your apartment and watched you looking through it. At your office, I used to look at the window of your office in the same way." He sighed. "After a couple of months, Liam told me to go beg for your forgiveness or just move on. I was too ashamed to apologize, and I chose the second option."

"Iden, I don't know what to say. You're a maniac," I said.

"I just wanted things to be the way they were before." Iden ran his thumb around my belly button.

"It will never be the same," I said.

"Lu, please give me one more chance." Iden stroked my belly. "I want to be a part of your life ... part of *our* life." He kissed my belly.

"I don't know if I can trust you." I sighed. "And I don't know what will happen tomorrow. A part of me wants the same thing—to be with you—but the other part still thinks—still realizes—that nothing good will come of it." I wrapped my leg around Iden and snuggled against his chest. "We are constantly angry and constantly arguing."

"But isn't that what love looks like?" Iden looked at me. "I love you. I always have, and I will not stop loving you—no matter what happens."

"And I love you, but our love hurts us."

"I can't do it any other way, but I'm trying really hard." Iden sighed. "I have had problems with anger management since I was a teenager. I always act first and think later." He kissed the back of the head. "This only concerns my relationship with you, of course. You blew my mind. I can't even imagine that it could be someone else's happiness." Iden tilted my head toward him. "Lu, you are my happiness; can I be yours?"

I looked at Iden and didn't know what to say. I knew I loved him, and I knew he loved me, but I didn't know if our love would be enough to heal all the wounds we had inflicted upon each other. Our life was like a roller coaster; sometimes we fell, and sometimes we rose, but the desire to be with him always defeated my sanity. "I think Iva would like her mother to give her father one last chance," I said.

Iden laughed, and we were off to round two of our ring of passion.

▪ ▪ ▪

In the morning, Iden and I struggled to roll out of bed. This time, I didn't argue that my bed was too small for the two of us. While I showered, Iden made breakfast.

"I'll take you to work and fly to Chicago."

"OK," I answered. "When are you coming back?"

"Probably tomorrow ... the day after tomorrow at the latest. I will definitely be able to return before the next course." He smiled. "By the way, Liam will take you home after work."

At the office, Iden helped me get out of his sporty Audi, and he held my hand for a few moments. He kissed me on the lips a few times, said goodbye, and left .

When I entered the office, Liza was already standing at the door of my office with her arms crossed. She was stomping her foot. "You made up with Iden?"

"Yes," I answered.

"Luka, are you completely out of your mind?" Liza seemed angry. "After everything he put you through, you forgave him?"

"I just gave him one last chance." I shrugged. "Liza, sit down. I don't know if we'll make it, but I still love him. Our daughter is due in a few weeks, so I think I'm doing the right thing."

"Lu, I don't know," Liza said. "I saw how bad you were after your last breakup—and then the pregnancy. If you get your heart broken again, I don't think you'll ever recover."

"Yes, I know. I understand that I'm taking a risk, but at this moment, I'm listening to the voice of my heart." I smiled and hugged my friend.

Iden returned a couple of days later and went straight to the course. After that, we went home to Santa Monica. It was strange to go back there after so long.

"Didn't you sell the house?" I was surprised that nothing had changed. Everything was exactly as I remembered it: the same walls, the same furniture, and the same artwork.

"No. I used to live here," he answered calmly as he piled the boxes on the floor.

"You lived here?" I was surprised.

"Yes, I've been living here since you left. I'm rarely in Chicago." He came over and took my hand. "Come on. I want to show you something."

We went up to the second floor, and Iden opened the door next to the bedroom. When he turned on the light, I could not believe my eyes. The old room was gone! The walls were soft pink, the furniture was white, and there was a small cot with a canopy. One wall is painted with Disney castles and characters. The nursery had a lot of teddy bears, and a beautiful sign with Iva's name hung on the wall. The ceiling was painted with puffy clouds, hanging stars, and a glowing moon. It was the perfect little girl's room.

I turned to Iden and raised my eyebrows. "How?"

He shrugged. "Well, when you said you were going to have a girl, I was just so happy."

"What if my intuition had deceived me?" I laughed.

"There are more rooms in the house," he said with a smile.

We spent the whole evening tidying up the house. I took my things out of the boxes. I'd been doing that quite often in recent years.

Iden was very attentive. "Christmas is in a couple of weeks. Maybe it's time to decorate the house?" He wrapped his arms around me.

"OK." I clapped my hands. "Let's create a perfect Christmas this year."

"How about we get married?" Iden asked.

I turned to him and closed my eyes. "Are you kidding me?" I laughed.

"No. I am completely serious. I love you … be my wife."

"Maybe we should not rush that decision?"

"What decision?" Iden looked confused. "We are living together again, we love each other, and we will have a baby soon. After all, it's normal that I want to marry you."

"What if we fail?" I couldn't give in to Iden's pressure. "What if we get angry again and have to go our separate ways?"

"No matter what happens, I swear, you will not leave this house anymore. This is your home, do you hear? What's mine is yours, and vice versa. Please stop kicking—and let's get married."

"But how? When? I'm as fat as a watermelon."

"I don't care about banquets. I just want you." He shrugged. "If you want a banquet, we can organize one. We'll do whatever you want." Iden hugged me and kissed my hair. "During Christmas?"

"OK." I snuggled closer to Iden.

I called my mom the next day, but she didn't pick up. I texted her to tell her that Iden and I were getting married this Christmas and that I would really appreciate it if she and Dad, Grandma, and Agnes's family would fly to Los Angeles. I emphasized that we would take care of the trip. I wrote similar messages to Elle and Rodriguez because I was afraid to call them.

A few seconds later, I received a call from Elle.

"You what? Luka? Have you lost your brain? Seriously? Marriage?" Elle screamed.

I had to pull the phone away from my ear. I stood by the terrace window and showed Iden and Liam that the tree was crooked. Iden could hear her yelling into the phone, and he was smiling.

"Elle, calm down, please," I said.

"Don't calm me down. I'll pack my junk immediately and head to the airport. I'll make you mad." Elle was angry. I could only imagine how her face was contorting in anger.

"If you're going to fly, take Martin and Rodriguez with you. The wedding ceremony will take place on December 25."

"Luka, are you serious?" Elle asked. "After everything—after how much you have suffered—you still want to marry him?"

"Yes, I want to." I sighed. *I've been sighing a lot these few past years,* I thought. *After all, two people in love sometimes make mistakes.* "Elle, we want to try to be together."

"Oh, my friend," Elle said, "I don't know if I want to kill you or hug you, but I support you."

I talked to Elle for a few more moments, and then I texted Rodriguez and helped the boys decorate the tree.

A few hours later, as we were drinking hot chocolate with marshmallows, my phone rang.

"Mom's calling," I said.

Iden smiled and sat quietly next to me.

I braced myself for the interview, which I knew was not going to be easy, and pressed the green button. "Hello, Mom."

"Hello," she said calmly. "I got your message."

"Good. I called, but you didn't pick up," I said. "I wanted to report live, but I had to write a message."

I couldn't tell if she was happy or sad.

"Is that why you reconciled? And are you getting married?"

"Yes," I answered.

"This is your life. I hope you will be happy with him." My mother did not seem very happy about my marriage. "I don't think we will come to the wedding."

"I see." I looked at Iden. "If you change your mind, let me know. By the way, Mom, I'm pregnant."

"You're pregnant? Is that why you're getting married?"

"No," I answered. "That's not why. I just wanted you to know. We are having a daughter."

"I'm glad about that," Mom said. "How long are you?"

"It's already the thirty-first week," I said with a smile.

"And you're only now telling your parents about your pregnancy?" Mother raised her voice.

"You wouldn't talk to me," I said. "Mom, do you know anything about Arn?"

"No, I don't—and I don't want to know. I'll talk to your father, and maybe I'll be able to persuade him to come to you. I hope you will be happy. We will have another baby."

After saying goodbye to my mother, I snuggled up to Iden. I kept telling myself that everything would be fine. I sighed and looked at my future husband. "Well, everyone has been informed. What do we do now?"

"We will enjoy life now." He smiled and kissed me.

DECEMBER 25, 2019
IDEN

Christmas brought inner peace to my life. For the first time in years, I felt happy. I looked at Luka and smiled. When I am near her, I feel fullness and true, extremely deep love. Luka once said that love hurts us, but being apart is even more painful. And now, when she stands next to me in this white dress, her huge green eyes meekly looking directly into my soul, I thank fate that she appeared in my life.

"Iden Black, do you agree to marry Luka Ilgauskaitė, to love and respect her until death do you part?" asked the pastor.

Confused, I looked at Luka's bulging eyes. I smiled at her and said, "I do."

Luka returned my smile.

"Miss Luka Ilgauskaitė, do you agree to marry Mr. Iden Black, to love and respect him until death do you part?"

"Yes, I do." Luka smiled at me even wider.

"By the right given to me by God, I pronounce you husband and wife."

I couldn't stay calm. I wanted to kiss Luka so much.

"Iden, you can kiss your wife," the pastor said.

I grabbed Luka in my arms, and after removing the veil, I kissed her passionately.

Everyone clapped and whistled.

Luka caught her breath and began to blush. I've always been amazed at how often and vividly this girl blushes every time she feels embarrassed.

"I love you." I kissed her again.

"I love you too."

Luka looked so perfect today that I wanted to cry.

We decided to have a very modest wedding since Luka was constantly feeling tired. I didn't mind. Only our closest family members and friends gathered for the celebration. We flew Luka's family in from Lithuania. I could see that she was still sad about her brother, but she was very happy to see her family. My mother didn't like that we were getting married so modestly because she wouldn't have a chance to show off with an extravagant party, but she was happy about our marriage and the arrival of her granddaughter. After sitting down at the dinner table, I grabbed a glass of champagne and stood up.

"Thank you for coming to our modest celebration." I smiled and looked at Luka. "Today, I realized that I am lucky as hell because I have a wonderful wife who will soon give birth to our daughter." I struggled to find the right words because there were no words to describe this happiness. "I remember every moment since I first saw Luka and her green eyes. They enchanted me. I have already mentioned how I hardly realized the depth of the feeling that came over me, but when I could no longer breathe without her near me, I decided that I must do everything possible to have her. I have said it many times, and I will say it again—you are my happiness. Thank you." I bent down and kissed Luka on the lips. "Although we are mortal, I believe that this love is eternal. Bless you."

"Iden, honey, you make me blush," Luka whispered in my ear.

"I like it when you blush, especially when you're naked in bed with me," I whispered in her ear.

Luka squirmed in her chair. "Iden, someone is going to hear." She started blushing, which made me laugh.

That beautiful moment of the wedding celebration and the happy smile of Luka will remain in my memory for a long time. I didn't expect that in the most difficult moments, it would help me get through another new day—and it will happen again and again.

We rejoiced in love and in each other.

Eleven weeks later, after a long day of suffering, we got to meet our little Iva. We were so happy and crazy about our baby girl. She was a beautiful, big-eyed, brown-eyed girl. Every day, I would kiss her little toes and talk about how perfect she was. There was no free space left in my phone because I took photos of Iva and Luka dozens of times per day. I enjoyed watching her sleeping and playing. My life became real and wonderful. Luka was the most caring mother I had ever seen, and she never let go of Iva. She would our little angel in her arms, sit in a chair on the terrace, and sing Lithuanian lullabies. That memory that will live with me for as long as I breathe.

However, we enjoyed our idyll of happiness for only half a year—and then hell on earth began.

One summer day, we were going to visit my mother. Luka prepared for the trip, packed Iva's things, and took care of snacks. We were traveling by car, and we left early in the morning. After driving two hundred miles, Luka noticed that I hadn't remembered to bring the bag of baby supplies. She got very angry with me, and we started arguing. It was raining heavily. I was not paying attention and lost control of the car. I vaguely remember driving into the opposite lane and hitting a truck. Luka's panicked look was the last thing I saw before the crash and then blinding darkness.

I woke up in the hospital. I was thoroughly exhausted, but the first thing I thought about was how Luka and Iva were doing.

The doctor prescribed sedatives, and then he told me that Luka had been put into a medically induced coma due to a severe head injury—and our Iva was gone.

At that moment, the whole world slipped out from under my feet. I couldn't understand the doctor's words. I shook his hand and asked if he was joking.

Later, when some time had passed, I realized the painful truth: I had destroyed my property, my flesh and blood, and Luka could die without even knowing that our daughter was gone. However, that did not happen.

A couple of days later, she woke up—and everything changed. After endless days of grief, continuous crying, screaming, hitting everything, and blaming me, she just stopped paying attention to me. She became cold and indifferent. She no longer paid attention to me or my own pain. I experienced our tragedy just as strongly as she did, but I knew it was my fault. That feeling of guilt did not give me peace. It was hard to grasp reality, and that reality became so suffocating that I started thinking about the worst scenarios.

In the darkest moment of my life, Liam was my only pillar. He patiently dragged me out of the puddle, explained that I had to fight, told me that I couldn't give up. He ran the business while I drank for days and looked at pictures of my happy life on my phone. Luka stayed in Iva's room for days. Elle and Rodriguez often came to see her. They helped Luka, but it was not enough. I tried to approach her and reconcile, but she was unconvinced. She looked at me as her worst enemy.

And then the beautiful Nicole appeared in my life. I could relax with her. I started spending more time in Chicago than in Los

Angeles. Nicole became my haven of peace, and Luka remained a gray past that caused only pain. I loved her, and I did not want her to suffer.

When I came home one day, I couldn't find her. I realized that I had finally reached the end of the line. I couldn't blame her, but I was angry at her.

The moment I met Luka was the worst moment of my life.

Pictures of me with Nicole were scattered across the kitchen table. *She must have hired a private detective. Too bad.*

CHAPTER FOURTEEN

FOUR YEARS LATER
LUKA

An ordinary human life consists of four stages of existence. In the first stage, we are born and begin a long journey. The second is characterized by self-searching, and we try to go beyond all possible limits. In the third stage, we reach maturity and fulfillment, reflect on what special things we have done in the previous stages, and begin to realize with horror that the day of death is approaching. The fourth stage is death. From dust to dust. But my life turned into an existential black hole four years ago. My schedule has no time for self-pity, no time for joy, and no time for anything.

Every day begins with the same rhythm as the alarm clock rings at five in the morning. I open my eyes, sit up in bed, and stare blankly out of my bedroom window at the waking city of Vilnius. After morning coffee and a sandwich of toasted bread and avocado, I put on an impeccable suit and leave the still-sleeping Pilaitė district at exactly seven o'clock. I always leave at the same time; otherwise, I might hit the morning rush hour and be late. At exactly eight o'clock, I'm drinking my second cup of coffee in my office and flipping through today's press. I flip through the new issue of our weekly magazine and read the review I wrote for the fashion section. Even I find it hard to believe that my name is displayed in the most popular Lithuanian weekly newspaper. At eight forty-five, I make my way to the conference room. The editor in chief and several journalists are waiting for me with a pile of printed sheets. Looking at their angry faces, I understand that I have a long day ahead.

At five fifteen, I head down the central Vilnius street toward the hospice where I volunteer. It's a kind of self-torture, but at least I can be my true self there for a few hours. I cry with the dying, hear their life stories, try to be with them, and hold their hands as they go to heaven.

I can hardly remember the time when I wandered through the streets of Vilnius in a fit of rage. I had recently returned to Lithuania, and for some reason, I chose Vilnius to be as far away as possible from everyone I knew.

I wandered the streets and looked for something with wide eyes, but even then, I didn't quite understand when a little nun said, "Kid, are you lost?"

I fell down at her feet and went hysterical. My stop crying continued for several hours, and that good nun took me to a hospice building that was still under renovation. There were a few beds for sick people. She tucked me in and covered me with a blanket. Although it was warm, it was the end of summer, I was suffering from the cold. After the hysteria was over, I sat up in bed and looked in the mirror for the first time in a long time. My hair was tangled, my eyes were black, my skin was gray, my body was begging for a shower, and I smelled of sweat and dirt. I weighed maybe ninety-five pounds, which was tragically low for my height. I looked nothing like my former self, but that bony reflection reminded me that the former me was gone.

That evening, I had a long talk with the nun who took me home. Edith was an extremely warm person. She listened to my whole story, including all the yelling, gasping, and pain I went through. I told her the whole story—from when I went to study and work in the United States on the exchange program, the rape, my relationships, and the most painful experience, losing Iva. I also told her about Iden seeking solace in the arms of other women. Edith didn't interrupt me, and she didn't ask questions. She just listened as I poured everything out—like rain from a storm cloud.

"Maybe you want to help me work with sick people?" she asked.

"Of course," I answered without even thinking. I was glad to have an opportunity to do something meaningful.

I stayed there to volunteer. Even though I had a job with a decent salary, my own apartment, and a car, volunteering calms and comforts me. A part of me probably subconsciously believes that being close to death makes me closer to Iva.

I was standing at the front entrance of the hospice, and I smiled kindly at Ann. I washed my hands and changed into more comfortable clothes. The card on my chest says "Volunteer Luka." You are not wrong. This is the same Luka Ilgauskaitė who thought she had found her place under this sun, but, as I already mentioned, all life consists of four stages—and the stages of my life stopped when Iva was killed. I died with her that day.

2024, LITHUANIA
LUKA

July in Lithuania is as hot as ever this year. In the early morning, the heat is almost seventy-seven degrees—and even higher temperatures are expected this afternoon. I am very happy that I put on a thin linen dress this morning, and I feel comfortable enough in the office. I still am not used to my short hair, which falls intricately over my face, and I keep catching the unruly strands with my hand and tucking them behind my ear. With this heat, it is difficult to write about the upcoming autumn clothing trends.

After thinking for a long time, I picked up the phone and dialed Elle's number. She didn't have to wait long, and she answered just after the third ring.

"Hello." She talked a little too loudly.

I could hear the noise of the city in the background. "Good morning." I laughed. "Are you in a good mood?"

"Oh yes, I'm running to the bus stop." She was panting.

"Why didn't you drive?"

"Because I'm very smart, and I managed to lock my car keys inside the car."

Oh, yes, this is typical Elle. I laughed. "Everyone needs to clear their heads on public transportation sometimes."

"Make fun of me again, and I swear by all the saints that I will kick your seat when I return to Lithuania. I have to finish this interview. By the way, how are you?"

I feel like a fish in a net. "Everything is fine. I'm alive." I sighed. The editor in chief, Andrew, who was waving at me.

"Listen, I'm being called."

"OK, *chica.*" She laughed, reminding me of our good friend Rodriguez, whom I hadn't seen in a long time. *I don't want to think about him right now.* "I miss you—and send my best wishes to Martin."

I slowly got up from the chair and smoothed my dress with my hands. I still felt too skinny. I looked awkwardly at my bare legs and platform sandals. I really looked anorexic. I shouldn't complain though. Lately, I've been looking a lot more attractive than when I was staying in bed all day long. I had reached the bottom of my existence, which was extremely difficult to escape. I don't think any of my coworkers knew me when I walked around as a dirty, disheveled, smelly, and miserable twenty-six-year-old girl. I was drowning in grief, and I looked more like a middle-aged beggar than a self-confident lady.

I looked at my colleagues. The entire editorial staff was moving from corner to corner and catching the gusts of the air conditioner, which was humming like crazy. I wondered how long it would be before the fuse blew because all the lights in the building were flashing like Christmas garlands.

I opened the door to Andrew's office. "Did you need me?"

He was a handsome man—dark, tall, and masculine—but he had a very difficult manner. He reminded me a lot of the one whose name I try not to mention. Sometimes when he spoke, it seemed that *he* was speaking with his lips. I stared at them and heard nothing. Andrew was happily married, but all the girls in the office were secretly smiling at him or whispering to him. I was harsh. He reminded me of that dark shadow of the past that still haunted my dreams.

"Yes, come in and sit down."

I could tell from his tone that our conversation would not be pleasant.

"I have a few observations about your review yesterday."

"You mean because of the US Fashion Week events?" *Well, Mr. Cunt is now going to make a speech about high fashion.*

"Yes, because of them," Andrew explained. "You are really talented, but your article will not help us to maintain our good rankings."

I laughed. "It's as if the popularity of a weekly magazine depends on the fashion gossip section." Bite your tongue, Luka. Bite it.

Andrew looked at me and pressed his lips tighter. He really wasn't in a good mood, and my retorts didn't flatter him. Little by little, I started to stand on my feet again and express my position more firmly on work issues. I started resembling my old self.

"No, listen." He put his hands together and looked into my eyes. "Considering your previous work experience, I think—or rather, I know—that you are capable of much more. Luka, you are special."

"Thank you." I shifted uncomfortably in my chair. I felt uncomfortable about the compliments, but I blushed even more because of

Andrew's attentive gaze. *Sometimes he is like a wild cat lurking around the corner, but maybe it's just my imagination. As if someone is looking at you? Luka, come back to earth. He is a married man.*

"We received four invitations to go to weekend events in New York. Of course, I want you to go with Marius, Lina, and me."

"Me? To America? Together?" I shuddered at the thought. Shivers ran down my spine, and the hair on my arms stood on end. I felt like I was floating in a cold lake. My eyes were dark, and my head was ringing. No ... no ... no ... just not that. No way ... I don't want to.

"Of course, why are you surprised? You are a great worker. In addition, Marius and Lina want to make several reports about Lithuanians living in the USA. They are developing good businesses and creating jewelry. You could write a good article. Lu, are you OK? You look pale."

"I'm fine. It's just very stuffy here." I almost screamed in horror, but I couldn't show anyone my fears. In Vilnius, I was just a girl who was successfully climbing the career ladder. I was just Luka Ilgauskaitė. No one knew my past.

"Put on the best you have and be at the airport at five o'clock in the morning on Friday."

"OK." I nodded and walked unsteadily back to my office.

I opened the window and breathed in the stuffy air. Only now, a few moments later, did I realize the predicament I was in. Even though the ground wobbled under my feet, I tried to calm down and collect my thoughts. *What are the chances that I will meet someone from my former life in New York? Probably one in a million.* I shook my head and wrapped my arms around my waist. *I can't be weak. I can't give in to my emotions. I've already been through one stage of hell, and I can't go back to where it was so hard to escape from.*

Hours passed at my desk, and I was still wondering if I would run into the ghosts of my past during my stay in the United States. *I'm not going to Chicago. There is a long distance between Chicago and*

New York. Everything will be fine, and there is no need to worry. I began to bite my nails. Those numbers went round and round in my head, like a merry-go-round. *One in a million—or one in a billion? Luka, pull yourself together.* It was five o'clock. I couldn't believe I spent the whole day thinking about the past and life in the United States.

I parked in the hospice parking lot. After performing all the rituals of cleanliness, I went to visit a dear, seriously ill old man.

"Good evening, Michael." I received his warm smile. "Was it a good day?"

"Hello, my love. Now it is a perfect day."

Despite his age, Michael was a gallant gentleman. He was affectionate and sweet-tongued. He always made me his girlfriend when he got the chance, but that little game brightened up his dreary days.

"What would you like to do before bed? Maybe take a ride in the garden? Let's find some shade and stretch our legs on the grass."

"No, honey, I feel tired today. Could you read me the book of my beloved's memories?" Michael's wife, Sofia, had been a music teacher. She had dedicated her life to creativity and her beloved husband. Michael had been the chief botanist at the institute, and he taught at the university until his well-deserved retirement. God did not give them the blessing to become parents—no matter how hard they tried—but they loved each other until the end. Sofia died two years ago after suffering a stroke, reaching her eighty-ninth birthday. After Sofia's death, Michael's health worsened. Six months ago, he found out that his body was slowly being eaten away by a merciless cancer. However, this news did not upset Michael at all. He was happy to finally see his beloved.

I pulled out a small red book from the dresser. The title, *Reminiscences to Michael,* was etched in beautiful handwriting on the cover. I found the tab that Sofia must have taken, and I opened the page where I had finished reading last time. Michael knew the words of the book by heart, but the memories warmed his soul. I read all the stories over and over again.

"Today, we will read a crazy memoir." I smiled.

First impression. 1951

Dear Michael,

That summer, I was an unremarkable village girl, of average beauty or finesse. I didn't have fancy dresses or fancy jewelry, and even my shoes were two sizes too big because in those days we were happy to get anything to buy, even if it was Russian. I remember very well that I went to see my cousin Birute in Vilnius that summer. I was applying to a music institute, hoping to become a teacher. Aunt Antanina and Uncle John agreed to take me in until I get a dormitory, and Birutė didn't hold back because she would finally have a companion for the whole summer.

The first weeks in Vilnius passed slowly. I longed for the village and my family, I didn't want to go anywhere. I sat between the four walls and stared out the window at the Pobedas passing by on the street. On a Saturday evening, Birutė was stubborn like a goat and pushed me into a corner, clearly indicating that we would go to the May Day celebration. I was scared by Birutė's persistence. I even cried, but in the end, I agreed and went on this adventure. She diligently braided my tresses into a crown around my head and lent me her white polka-dot dress with puffed sleeves and little buttons down the front. She highlighted my lips with her mother's lipstick and darkened my eyes with charcoal. I looked strangely funny—at least that's what I decided after looking at myself in the mirror—but I didn't dare argue because, in Vilnius, fashion is different than in the province.

Until May Day, which took place in the forest, young people flocked together, joyfully chirping about summer, new cavaliers, crushes, beautiful fabrics from abroad, and other things that young people care about. I listened and admired their ease of communication. As we approached the forest, we could hear the sound of music mixed with the clamor of youth. The girls stood closer to the so-called stage, and the guys were farther away, with bottles in their hands. Daniel Dolski's piece I love, "Summer Cornflowers" was playing when I saw you standing under the maple tree. You were so young, so beautiful, and so blond. You held the pipe to your lips so carefully that I couldn't take my eyes off it, and you looked straight at me, smiled, and asked, "Miss, can we dance?" Do you remember that evening we danced more than one and not two, and after May Day, you accompanied me home. After saying goodbye, you promised to visit again, and that's how our souls found each other in 1951.

If you're reading these notes today, I'm sorry I left before you. I'm sorry I couldn't give us a baby, but our love beat all odds. I love you and until our next meeting.

Yours,
Sofia

As I read, tears rolled down my cheeks. It was hard to fathom that love could be so magical.

Michael gently caressed my hand, and I apologized for my exaggerated emotions. After all, I was there entertain him and listen to him, and I was babbling like a child. Michael was wise. His eyes reflected a million questions that had yet to be asked, and I knew he had a strong opinion about me.

"Oh, come on, Michael. I see you would like to ask me something."

"Angela, has there been a loss in your life? Have you lost a loved one?" He looked straight into my eyes.

Oh, how right you are. I lost everything—not only my lover, my love, but also myself. "It's a long story ... and it's rather confusing and painful." I sighed regretfully and began to nervously pick at my cuticles.

"After all, we have all the time in the world," Michael said.

"Oh, well." I could feel my hands getting wet as I prepared to talk about my life. "My story began in 2018. I went to study in the United States in a student exchange program. I was separated from my family, and I was finally able to live a little less restricted by those around me. My parents are real despots, believe me, and not everyone would be able to live and endure the constant pressure from my mother about marriage and building a family. I should have been the one who would never be ashamed. I met a guy in America. I fell in love with him, but he was lost and possessed by the devil." I didn't want to tell Michael my whole story. "I believed that we could be happy. He was rich, I was Cinderella, and everything was spinning like a whirlwind. We loved, we were angry, we scolded, we humiliated each other, we loved again, we broke up, we reconciled, and finally we got married. We had a daughter, Iva." My voice began to tremble.

Michael squeezed my hand tighter in his palm.

"When she was six months old, we went to visit Iden's mother.

At the time, we were living in Los Angeles, and his mother was in Chicago. We decided to go by car. We got into a fight on the road over nothing—I was just making a scene that Iden didn't pick up the baby bag—and he lost his attention and went into the oncoming lane and hit a truck. I don't know why we stayed alive, but Iva was no longer with us." Tears rolled down my cheeks again.

"Shh, shh." Michael stroked my hand sympathetically. It was reassuring, and his words lightened my burden.

"After everything, I thought I would go crazy. I shut myself in. I blamed myself. I blamed Iden. I blamed that tow truck driver. I blamed everyone. At first, Iden stayed patiently by my side, but I pushed him away. Later, he stopped being with me, and he spent more time at work. Eventually, we drifted so far that he cheated on me with someone else. My life became an open wound that throbbed and bled. I lost my sanity, and I lost my self-control. There were moments when I wanted to die. Everything was black and horrible. I was drowning in darkness. Being in the United States was becoming unbearable. I was suffocating. I didn't want to live in that nightmare anymore, and I packed my bags and returned to Lithuania. I filed for divorce in writing and haven't seen him since. Iden didn't mind the divorce; he just transferred a good amount of money into my bank account as compensation." I laughed.

Michael said, "Oh, my little flower, I feel so sorry for you. You're so young, and you've already suffered so much."

"Yes, my life has been interesting and joyful. Guilt and anger brought me here. That's my only solace. My relationship with my family, of course, completely fell apart. My brother has done a lot of harm and is hiding somewhere, and my sister is busy with her own family. She avoids calling me because I start to worry as soon as she starts talking about children. Mom and Dad don't understand why I'm sad and why I'm not looking for a new man here. I'm not trying again. I try to spend as little time as possible in their company—at least for now."

Michael seemed to have aged a few more years. His forehead was covered with deep wrinkles. He gently caressed my hand and kept sighing. Finally, I said goodbye to my beloved old man and went home. After taking a shower, having dinner, and drinking half a bottle of wine, I fell into a restless sleep. An ordinary night wouldn't be an ordinary night if I didn't dream about Iden.

In our dreams, the happy moments of our lives came back: the cozy sunsets when we sat on the shore and looked at the ocean, wrapped in a warm blanket. In my dreams, I sometimes smelled his aroma—masculine, wild, and woodsy—which matched his body odor. I used to hear his voice, and the hairs on my arms stood up. Most of the time, when I had those dreams, I would wake up with tears in my eyes, tighten my grip on the covers, curl up into a ball, and cry.

As often as I dreamed about Iden, I rarely saw our daughter in my dreams. During all the years, I only dreamed of her twice: the first time was when I was in the hospital after the accident, and the second time was when I returned to Lithuania. I don't dream about her anymore. I don't remember her smell, her voice, or anything else about her. I am afraid that I'm forgetting her features.

Those thoughts come to me only at night. During the day, I'm too busy with work. I don't have time for memories. *My life has become unbearably terrible. It's like a nightmare from which I can never wake up. Just thinking about the loneliness that awaits makes me shudder. What will happen next?*

CHICAGO, 2024
IDEN

Moving back to Chicago downtown was the smartest idea I could think of. Every morning, I was able to admire the views of Lake Michigan, and in the evening, I gazed at the glittering skyscrapers of Chicago. I was surrounded by life and bustle, and I could not bear the thought of being alone. Liam and his wife were happy with their extended family. Since I rarely got to spend an evening with him, I chose the friendship of all kinds of one-day girls. One more constant part of my life—the beautiful Nicole—has been patiently following my tail for more than four years. I know exactly what she wants, but I can't really give it to her. She doesn't lose hope—as if I care.

My mornings usually start with a hangover and heavy exercise. I spend at least two hours in the gym, letting out all my anger. And I don't lack anger. I'm angry at everything and at everyone. Liam says I've been left with a real headache in recent years, and I can't really argue with that. I can safely say that I managed to destroy my life from the ground up. I lost everything I had been looking for for so long. And most importantly, it's all Luka's fault. God, every time I say her name, the pressure rises. After the accident, Luka blamed me for being careless, for not taking that damn baby bag, for killing our daughter. How could she think that? And later, I really slipped. Nicole appeared in my life, and she was so young, fragile, innocent, beautiful, and obedient to all my wishes. One day, I did not find Luka at home. She had left. I was so angry that I packed up all the rest of her things in boxes, and when I got the divorce petition and found out her address in Lithuania, I sent all that junk to her.

Let her choke.

And now, all these years later, I can't forget those haunting green eyes, that silly temperamental manner, or those long bangs. It keeps sprouting like a weed in my heart, mind, and eyes, and no earthly method of relaxation can uproot it. This memory of her fuels my anger, and when I am angry, I become fierce and break all business standards. In recent years, I've been given the nickname "Iron Man," which I quite like.

And this morning is no different from any other. I'm punching a punching bag with a sore head, and my body is dripping with sweat, saturated with the toxins of yesterday's alcohol. Wet, slightly too long hair falls over my eyes with every blow, and my heart is beating like crazy. I take big gulps of air through my dilated nostrils and blow out steam like a bull. Each stroke gives emotional pleasure, and the physical exertion relaxes my body.

After my grueling workout, I take an ice-cold shower and stare into the mirror for a moment. Every time I look at myself, I see the same thing: the biggest fool in the world who believed his life could be full of love and happiness. I find a navy blue suit and a dazzling white shirt from my favorite designer in my huge walk-in closet, a luxury wristwatch, one-of-a-kind shoes, and niche perfumes.

I look almost tolerable.

When I got down to the garage, the first thing I saw was my bright red Tesla, which makes me smile every time. Next to it, Liam had a big smile on the phone screen. "Good morning, Liam. By your smile, I can tell it was a good night."

"Hey, bro." Liam grinned. "Oh, yes. Adelina has been up like a thousand times, and I'm sleep-deprived, but it's an amazing experience."

As soon as he said those words, my face contorted as if I had bitten into the sourest lemon. I slapped Liam on the shoulder. *He is innocent. His perfect world has a solid foundation, and happiness is pouring over the edges. I can't be a total asshole and not be happy for my best friend's happiness.* "You're the best father, Liam." I sat in the backs of the Tesla and went into my phone, pretending to read my mail, but in reality, I was rummaging through the remains of my long-ruined life.

It seems like only yesterday that I was cradling my perfectly beautiful daughter and enjoying her little fingers. I could smell her baby scent and kiss her chubby cheeks. Now I'm sitting in my embarrassingly luxurious car and trying not to be overwhelmed by my emotions.

My new office is in downtown Chicago. The perfect skyscraper has impressively mirrored windows. In recent years, I successfully developed my hotel business all over the world, and the new business direction has paid off financially.

Architecture has remained more of a hobby than a job, but all the hotels I manage are designed by me. I could easily stop working now and do whatever my heart desires, but that is not for me. I try to work as much as possible because too much free time haunts me with gray shadows from the past.

A few blocks from my office, I looked out the window at the smiling people walking down the street, thee happy couples leisurely going to work, and the trains rumbling overhead. It all seemed so simple. Everything around me is in constant motion. Life does not stand still, but in my life, there is only stagnation. Every day, I write on the same piece of paper—again and again—and I don't dare to open a new one. Liam has been saying for a long time that I have to let go of the past—that I have to let go of Iva, forget Luka, and move on—but that thought makes me sick and twists my stomach. I haven't seen Luka for four years. I haven't heard anything about her. She disappeared from my life like smoke. Was it just a dream? No, she was as real as could be.

I opened my phone and looked at Iva's photos. I scrolled through one photo after another, patting the screen with my finger and almost crying out in pain. Then I looked at Luka's photos. I couldn't delete them. They reminded me of how happy I once was. Moaning quietly, I tried to control the rising heartache. I bit my fist to keep myself from howling like a wolf.

Liam let out a loud sigh as he looked at me in the rearview mirror. *It happens every time I look at pictures of Iva or Luka. I feel so sorry for myself.* I wiped my damp eyes with my hand and put on my black sunglasses.

Liam was still staring at me.

"What?" I asked, *Liam, don't be self-righteous. Let me eat myself from the inside and die.*

"Nothing." He sighed again. "Iden, you're my friend, almost

a brother, but I can't keep quiet any longer. Please, get your hands on it and start behaving properly. How much longer will you suffer from your evening bar crawls and morning self-pity sessions? Find a normal woman and try to live. Do you think your problems will be solved by fools and one-night stands?"

"Don't play a priest. This is my messed-up life, Liam, mine."

"You're slowly killing yourself, and I can't watch it silently."

I sat with tight lips and clenched my fists. It's one thing when Liam stares and sighs and keeps his thoughts to himself, but it's quite another when he tells the whole painful truth, which I know too well. A vein in my neck began to throb, my tie began to tighten, and I began to squirm in my seat. I understood exactly what Liam was trying to tell me, but I wasn't ready to move on. I was totally enjoying the sweet agony. I had created my own personal prison of pain.

When he stopped at the office building, I thanked Liam and got out of the car. The summer heat stung my temples, and the girls walking down the street eyed my luxury car. *Yes, look, here comes the scoundrel who will devour and digest you. Iden Black, your life is hell—and you are the main devil stirring up that hell.*

CHAPTER
FIFTEEN

LUKA

New morning, new day, same routine. It's even hotter today than yesterday, and on my way to work, I climbed into the seat of my Fiat in a damp blouse. The street asphalt was just steaming, and people were hurrying to work. The air conditioner in the car was running at full capacity, but it didn't improve the situation one bit. There was an accident somewhere ahead, and the eastern streets of Vilnius were jammed with cars. I turned on the radio and the chords of "Shallow" filled the car. I sang, "Crash through the surface, where they can't hurt us," and I completely lost my cool when Iden's silhouette appeared in front of my eyes. He keeps visiting me like a curse at the most unexpected moments, reminding me that he was in my life. He gave me so much happiness, but he also gave me an immeasurable amount of pain.

This summer has been very difficult. All kinds of thoughts and memories about Iden and his past life come to mind. Although we were impulsive, we also experienced some good moments. I really loved him, unconditionally, but Iva's death and his subsequent infidelity destroyed all bridges. After returning to Lithuania, I hoped that he would knock on my door and loudly declare that I had no right to leave him, admit that he was wrong, and shake my sad world again. Instead, all I got was packed boxes with all my things and photos. He erased me from his life as if I didn't exist. I couldn't help but google his name sometimes. There were so many articles and photos about his fun life, night outs, and power around girls: "Black, Chicago's most sought-after billionaire, was on the lookout for a new bride." Reading those articles made me sad and angry. I saw that blonde Nicole in so many photos. She was always stuck to Iden's side. Remembering her face, I tightened my grip on the steering wheel and drooled painfully.

"I curse you. I hate you." My words were angrier than I intended them to be.

As always, there was no space in the parking lot near our office. I had to park the car three blocks away. I hurried to the editorial office, and I felt uncomfortable because my clothes just clung to my body.

Andrew reminded me three times that I had to show up at the airport on Friday morning at five o'clock . I thanked him several times, but the last time, I just nodded in agreement. That trip did not fascinate me at all; on the contrary, it terrified me.

My heart was pounding three times more than usual, and I felt a strange anxiety. The last time I felt this way was before my final school exams when a passing score was directly related to my bright future. I didn't realize then how treacherous life can be. My mother always hammered it into my head that I should get married as young as possible, have children, tie my husband to myself, and blindly obey him. She told me not object, be humble, and be good. When I told my mother that I was going to study—that I wanted to achieve something more in life than being a housewife—she looked displeased. Later, she was happy when I was the first in my family to graduate. My parents had high hopes for me. They expected me to be their honor, glory, and blessing, but I cannot boast of an amazing career or a luxurious life.

There are days when I start to blame myself for not staying in America, for returning to Lithuania, and for giving up. However, I am like that! All my life, I ran from difficulties, and if I have a problem, I melted. As a youth, I was shunned by everyone. If I hadn't left Iden, maybe things would have worked themselves out. Maybe we would have healed the wounds of the heart and had more children. Maybe we would have a daughter or a son, and I would be a happy mother and a wonderful wife. Thinking about it now is completely pointless. Iden is no longer in my life.

The first half of the day was a blur. For the first three hours, I wandered from corner to corner, trying to cool down and edit a decent article, but all my thoughts revolved around the upcoming weekend. I was going through my wardrobe in my mind. I didn't have anything fancy. After Iva's death, I took little care of my wardrobe or appearance. Those who knew me before would probably say that it's not me because I always knew how to combine clothes and dress up. The past and present me were as different as two drops of water, but I didn't want to look gray when I went to New York. When I got home, I would finally open the boxes that Iden had sent, which were stuffed in the garage. They contained all my dresses, which had been bought by Iden's personal stylist. I don't want to spend money on clothes I'll only wear once.

In the afternoon, I finally managed to concentrate and write a half-hearted article about the most famous Lithuanian designer and his latest collection, which will soon see the light of day. I was very nervous when I went to see him in Palanga for an interview, but when I met him, all my fears dissipated. He was a very simple and kind person, and his working facade did not reflect his real personality at all. I smiled several times as I remembered our long conversation over a glass of wine. At such moments, I could forget how unhappy and lonely I really am.

A few more sentences, and I will be finished—and then I can go to the hospice to see Michael. I flinched when the phone rang.

Breathe in. Breathe out. Breathe in. Don't forget to breathe—and don't break. You can be normal.

"Hello, Mom," I said.

"Hello, sweetheart. How are you? Are you at work?"

"Yes, and where else would I be? Everything's all right."

"Will you come to visit us this weekend?"

I could tell by the tone of her voice that she had a secret plan for me. Maybe a new courtship? Did something happen to my father? Was it Grandma? Agnes?

"This weekend? No, I can't come. Did something happen at home?"

"Why? Do you have plans? No, the family is are ... but your grandmother ..."

"I have to go to a work event with my colleagues." I told a half-truth, but I kept quiet about going to America.

"With colleagues? That's cool. Maybe you'll meet a handsome guy at the event."

"Mom, don't start. You know I'm not looking for anything at the moment."

"OK. Don't be angry. I am your mother, and I only want the best for my children."

"I know, Mom." I sighed. "How's Grandma? Was she discharged from the hospital?"

"Yeah," she whispered.

My father is probably nearby.

"That evil witch is bothering me. I can't wait for her to go to the sanatorium. It's bring it, give it, take it away. I feel like a maid."

"I understand, Mom, but she is old." I tried to soften the situation.

"I understand that she's old, but she drives me crazy—and she enjoys it!"

"Oh, Mom, I can't help you. My own life is not exactly a bed of roses." I immediately regretted comforting her. *She is so dramatic, and her surroundings are only black or white. In recent years, everything related to me and my personal life has been nothing but black. She always makes it clear and lets me know indirectly how undeveloped I am.*

"Luka, you can come back to live with us anytime."

"Mom, that's not what I'm talking about." I lamented bringing up a sensitive topic. "OK, Mom. I have to work. I'll call you later." *Not anytime soon.*

"And you say you don't want to talk? Bye, honey."

"Bye, Mom." I sighed and looked out the office window.

Light clouds floated across the blue sky. Through the open window, I could hear the murmurs of the day and smell the Lithuanian summer. I looked at the red roofs of old town and the castle of Gediminas on the hill, which lacked the greenery of the trees. In the past, these images charmed, attracted, and enticed, but nothing pleases me now. My soul is empty and broken. I wander through life like a lost child. I can't seem to find the right direction to go. I can't find my way home.

I wiped away a tear with my thumb and tried to collect my scattered thoughts. The upcoming trip was appropriately derailed. At this moment, more than ever, I wanted to share my thoughts with someone. I dialed Elle's number, but when I didn't get any response, I wrote her a message: "Hello. What are your plans for this weekend? It just so happens that I will fly to New York on Friday for the weekend. Will you get on a plane and come see me?"

After five minutes, my phone started bouncing on the table.

"Seriously?" Elle shouted into the phone.

"Hello to you too." I had not seen my friend for two years.

"You are coming to America—and only now thought of writing?"

"Oh, there's no need for drama, Elle. It just happened. My boss, without any objections, ordered me to go with the team to the Fashion Week events in New York." *Does Elle think I organized this trip? America does not evoke any pleasant feelings for me—only terrible pain, bitterness, and sadness. If I could, I would erase that continent from the globe.*

"Oh good," Elle said. "I work on Saturday. Can you come to Chicago? Rodriguez was just here. Shall we all meet up like in the good old days?"

"I don't know if that's a very good idea, Elle."

"Well, stop it. Pull yourself together. Maybe it's time to stop being sad and start living! I miss that old sarcastic Luka."

"Ha, ha, very funny."

"Come on. I'm serious. I already sent a message to Rodriguez. Are you attending the event on Friday?"

"Yes." I sighed. "And there is a conference on Saturday morning. After that, I will have free time until Monday."

"Very nice. I'm already looking at tickets from New York to Chicago. It's just an afternoon flight. You'd be in Chicago by six o'clock."

"Hold your horses, Elle. I haven't agreed yet."

"Oops, it's too late. I just booked the tickets for you." My energetic friend laughed.

"Oh!" I hissed angrily into the phone. "Why are you so impulsive, ungrateful, and completely callous?"

"It's great. We'll have so much fun. I can already imagine a perfect evening in the company of wonderful friends." She sighed. "Enough drooling, I have to get ready for work. Goodbye, honey. Oh, before I forget, bring a nice dress. Let's go to the coolest club in town and have a good time."

"Oh, Elle. Bye, honey. I miss you."

I sat there with a stupid expression on my face. *Elle has always been impulsive, but now she resembles an atomic bomb. Why am I surprised? She is such a supernova.*

IDEN

My head split in two. The bright light made me nervous, and I tried to hide under the blanket. I opened one eye and looked at the clock on the bedside table. It was nine o'clock in the morning. I groaned loudly and rolled onto my side. My mouth felt like in the Sahara

Desert, and my eyes seem to be filled with sand. I blinked hard and took another look at my watch.

Shit, I overslept.

I tried to sit down, but everything around me was wobbly. I felt a little nauseous, and my memory was failing. After a while, I managed to remember yesterday with Larry Crof, an old friend from college. We had pounded a few glasses at the bar and then moved to a strip club. The whiskey flowed freely, and coke replaced the powdered sugar that we licked so deliciously off the girls' breasts. I shook myself again. I could not understand the depths I was in at that moment. A pile of messages and voicemails flashed on my phone.

And what's up with you, you old bastard?

I took unsteady steps toward the bathroom, and the contents of my stomach jumped out before I could reach the toilet. I slipped on the contents of my own stomach and injured my left wrist when I fell.

"Shit." I forced myself to stand up after a few moments.

After propping myself up with my good arm, I got into the shower and stood under the icy water. The pain in my arm didn't go away. My wrist started to turn blue, and I cursed loudly. After the shower, my general well-being improved a little, but the pain in my hand only got worse. Gritting my teeth, I got into my suit and called Liam.

He wasn't too happy about my fun last night, and when I told him we'd have to go to the hospital, he let out a loud sigh and didn't say another word. A surgeon I knew, Charlie, worked at Central Hospital in Chicago. Of course, being chatty, he didn't miss an opportunity to tease. An x-ray revealed that my bone was intact, but my wrist was badly bruised. He bandaged my hand and gave me a bottle of painkillers.

Liam ignored me as we drove to the office.

"Liam, can we stop by the pier?" I asked.

Liam didn't say a word.

The car rolled smoothly into the dock, and I adjusted my sunglasses and got out of the car.

Liam stayed inside. I looked at him again, walked to the quay, and sat down.

Liam joined me fifteen minutes later. "Mate, you gotta stop." His husky voice broke the long silence.

"I know." I sighed and stared blankly at a ship on the horizon.

"If you know, why are you behaving like such an idiot? How much longer will you keep destroying yourself? How long will you drown yourself in alcohol and drugs? Yesterday, you looked like you lived on the street and not in high society."

"Liam, there's no need. I understand very well that I am behaving inexcusably, but my life is a complete ass. It's the only way to relax and not put a bullet in my head."

Liam shook his head. "You scare me."

"I am afraid of myself too. Every morning starts the same way: my head is split in half after the party, and I taste the alcohol in my mouth. I try to go back to the previous evening in my mind and remember what and where I drank and which girl I dipped my head into. When I remember all the adventures of the evening, I usually throw up because I am disgusted by my actions." I sighed. "After an intensive workout, I try to pass the day in some magical way. By the end of the evening, anger toward Luka fills my head—and all the shadows of the past return. To stop thinking about her, I get dizzy again." I took off my sunglasses and looked him straight in the eyes. "That's my life, Liam. That's how messed up I am."

Liam stared at me for a long time. "Why didn't you try to get her back?" That question had never been asked before.

"You think I didn't want to?" I laughed. "Liam, she blamed me for Iva's death. You have no idea how she looked at me that night in the hospital. When she woke up after the accident, the doctor gave her the terrible news. I shudder when I remember that horror in

Luka's eyes. After that evening, she wouldn't look at me anymore. She shut herself up and lived in her own world. She spent days in Iva's room, curled up on the couch, crying, and hugging her clothes. Can you imagine how painful that was?"

"No, I can't." Liam shook his head. "I fully understand what kind of hell the two of you had to go through, but it does not justify your infidelity to Luka."

"Liam, don't judge—and you won't be judged." *My conscience reminds me of this every day.*

"Don't be angry ... but someone has to tell the truth."

"Yes, and that someone must be you." I smiled and patted his shoulder with my healthy hand.

We sat on the dock and looked at Lake Michigan. The water was glassy, and the seagulls searched for prey. An image from the past came to mind. I saw Luka walking along the shore of Lake Michigan. She always walked there when she was angry. She would shout at me, shed tears, and not speak to me. If she did speak, it was only in Lithuanian. However, she always forgave me.

When she left me for the first time and went to live in Los Angeles, I was angry. I said that I would not be a fool and run after her skirt, but my heart thought otherwise. I tried for a long time, and I got her back. I was the happiest man in the world again, but our paths diverged. This time, I didn't try. I lowered my hands, and now I'm sitting on the embankment and trying not to break. I'm afraid to admit that Luka is the meaning of my life.

LUKA

On Thursday evening, Vilnius was washed away by rain. Michael and I sat in his small room and read old collections of poems. Michael was not happy to hear that I could not visit him for the next few days, but he understood that I had to leave. Michael was the grandfather I never had because my mother's father died when my mother was expecting me, and my father lost his father when I was five. I enjoyed Michael's friendship every day, and he liked my presence. He even called me his daughter. After the poems, Michael asked me to read a short letter: "I Have Learned to Forgive." chosen by.

Year 1965.
I Have Learned to Forgive

Those years were very difficult for us. So many years of unsuccessful attempts to have children left a mark on our hearts. I saw you wanting to be a father, and I felt so drained, but my womb couldn't give us a baby. I was very sad when you started avoiding me, and I finally realized that your coworker Mari had caught your attention. How many tears have been shed, how many sleepless nights, when I found a letter she wrote to you, in which she cannot forget the night you spent together. My heart was broken, but I suffered in silence and continued to make breakfast in the mornings, leave for work, and wait for you to return to a steaming dinner on the table. Finally, after a few weeks, you asked me to sit down. You said you wanted to talk. I already knew what we were going to talk about, and I calmly sat down on the corner of the flowery armchair and looked into your eyes. You looked confused, but I guess you realized that I knew everything. You just said sorry. We sat in silence for a few moments, and then you left and didn't come back for a week. I tried to move on. Every day, I felt like I was in agony. I was going through a real loss. One morning, you appeared at the door with broken eyes. I was powerless to drive you away. I loved you despite the betrayal.

In that moment, I realized that love is the ability to forgive. I forgave you, and you forgive me for not being able to give birth to the children you so wanted.

With love,
Sofia

I read that letter for the first time today. I knew it was very dear and sentimental to Michael, but I understood why he asked me to read it today.

"My Sofia was a wise woman. She was able to forgive me—even at times in my life when I had completely lost my way. Maybe you should also forgive your husband—"

"My ex-husband," I said. "And I already forgave him."

"Really, honey? If you had forgiven him, you wouldn't be spending time with an old bum like me."

"Dear Michael, why are you so perceptive?" I laughed and shook his hand. We both knew that his time on earth was running out.

After returning from hospice, I made up my mind and opened the boxes. Iden's staff had put a lot of effort into packing my things. Everything was sorted down to the last detail, and it didn't take much effort to find the right clothes. I had completely forgotten what wonderful clothes and shoes I had. I also found all the beautiful jewelry Iden had given me. I was really surprised that he had delivered it all to me.

I packed my suitcase and tossed and turned in bed anxiously. I finally fell asleep, but before I could fall into a deep sleep, the alarm went off. I had to get up.

Rodriguez had left a message on my phone: "Hello. I'm waiting for you very much. I miss you, chica. "I smiled at my phone.

I took a shower, got dressed, and headed to the airport. After leaving the car in the parking lot, I hurried to the front door. Andrew and his team were waiting for me. He praised my appearance and suggested that we go to a cafe after checking in for our flight. After a good cup of coffee and Belgian waffles, I felt much better.

The beginning of the flight was great. I calmly looked out at the puffy clouds and admired the sun rising over the horizon. Although my heart trembled, that sight released all my fears.

After landing in Finland, we had three hours before our next flight. I decided to walk around the entertainment area of the airport and buy some trinkets. I wandered lazily from store to store, and then I saw a face I knew on a poster in one of the windows: Nicole was looking at me in a bikini that perfectly emphasized her figure. I thought I was going to throw up. My body was covered in sweat, and my head was spinning. I grabbed the back of the nearest bench so I wouldn't fall.

"Are you OK?" Andrew ran over, grabbed my elbow, and helped me sit on a bench.

"Yes, yes, thank you." I licked my dry lips and looked around. "Just dizzy."

"Maybe you need medical help? Let's go to the medical office."

"No, everything is fine. I felt dizzy, but now I feel good." I smiled.

"We can certainly find help," Andrew said.

"No, I really feel good. There's nothing to worry about." I stretched myself to my full height and looked at Andrew. "I was about to go to the gate."

"OK, we can go together."

I managed to sleep and read a book during the flight. I also had a lot of time to reflect on my life, my relationship with my family. My brother treated me so mercilessly, took advantage of my kindness, and had completely dropped me from his life. I wondered if he ever loved me with true brotherly love—or if I was just always his fifth leg and his scapegoat. Iden was a good person for not turning in Arn to the police when I was kidnapped or when he robbed him in Los Angeles. Arn just took a chance and ran away. I still don't understand why he did that and didn't even try to apologize. The men who kidnapped me could have killed me, but Arn didn't care at all.

There are many things I should be thankful to Iden for, but even remembering his name makes my heart shrink to the size of a raisin. I have too many feelings bubbling up in my body.

My life was gray until Iden and then Iva appeared in it. However, as sad as it is, I will not turn back time. I will not change fate. I have to accept all the painful blows and move forward.

I looked out the window at the New York City skyline and smiled. *This time will be different.*

CHAPTER SIXTEEN

IDEN

Yesterday's conversation with Liam got me thinking, but the more I thought about it, the more uncertain my future seemed. I've gotten into fights more than once, but I'm sure something good has to happen in life—even for assholes like me. Have I already wasted everything?

With my good hand, I rattled the pen on my desk and stared at the Chicago skyline. Today, everyone in the office was working quietly; they must have been afraid of me because of my mood. Nicole's name flashed obsessively on my phone. She's probably back from the fashion show and wants to meet up. She is nothing to me until she threatens to speak her mind, but her company is the last I want at this moment.

My secretary had left a bunch of messages from my mom about attending New York Fashion Week this weekend, but I definitely am not going with her. I sighed again, leaned back in my chair, and covered my eyes with my hand. *I am so tired of my life.*

The door slammed, and my mother walked in.

"Hello, Rose."

"Son, why are you ignoring me?"

Mom looked great as always. She wore a flawless black dress, pointed high heels, and short, bleached hair. She looked like she had just left the beauty salon. She certainly didn't resemble those middle-aged ladies; she was more like a modern-day diva who makes men go crazy.

"I'm not ignoring you, Mom. I just don't feel like talking." I straightened up in my chair and looked at her. *Don't you understand that your company is like dog's fifth leg at this moment?*

"Oh my God, what's wrong with your hand? Did you get into a fight? What? Tell me." She grabbed my hand and examined it with her neatly arranged fingers.

I groaned in pain. "Nothing, Mom, I just slipped." God, she is annoying.

Mom pouted and sneered at me. She paced anxiously around the office, and I waited for the end of her visit.

"Honey, you know I love you, but I can't watch you destroy yourself anymore. All that fun, all those girls." She rolled her eyes.

As if she knows how many girls I spend time with.

"All the tabloids are writing about your sins. They are just washing our family's laundry in public. Don't you care at all?"

"No." I tried to remember how many photos of me with girls had been published in recent years. *Yes, a lot.* I smiled.

"Iden, please get a hold of yourself."

I stared at her without lowering my eyes, and I batted my eyelashes. *Why does everyone suddenly care about my well-being and my behavior? Did they see that I live in a twisted hell just now? They've all been blind and deaf for four years while I've been doing all kinds of shit, fighting in bars, making out, fucking all kinds of girls, and taking drugs? They were all silently watching what would happen next, waiting for me to hit rock bottom, and now they all care about my well-being. Are they more concerned with their own interests? When I became overly strict and brutal in business, everyone clapped their hands and called me Iron Man. I feel like a beaten loser because everyone thinks they know how I should live.* "Why now?" I asked.

"What?"

Mother, it seems, did not expect such a question—or maybe she did not understand what I was asking. "Why did you decide to express your opinion now?"

Mom sat down next to my desk and folded her hands in her lap. A fingernail scratched at her pearl bracelet. She looked me in the eyes, took a breath, and puffed out her chest like an ostrich before a fight.

I prepared for the longest sermon of my life.

"Why now? Iden, I've been silent for too long. We have all been silent for too long. We've been watching your struggles, hoping that you'll finally get your act together, but year after year, the confusion doesn't end. After Luka left, you completely broke down, and now you're at own rock bottom. You have to let go of the past and start moving forward. Everyone says that you should have found Luka and begged for her forgiveness. I wasn't inclined to agree with them, but now … maybe you really should try to reconcile with Luka." Her eyes were moist.

"Rose, don't mention Luka's name ever again," I said slowly and clearly.

My mother changed from a combative ostrich to a fearful mouse. Her chest sagged, her shoulders slumped, and the fire of victory in her eyes died.

"I'm an adult, and I can manage my life properly. If I want to, I'll kiss. If I want to, I'll go bang every girl from here to the East Coast. But for God's sake, don't you ever mention her name or anything related to her again!" I gripped the tabletop. My eyes felt like they were going to pop out.

My mother seemed stunned, but she sat with her hand on her chest and watched me in horror. She looked like she didn't understand what was happening. She looked she was about to cry. Rose would never reveal her true feelings, and her face quickly regained that businesslike expression. Mom always knew how to be a cold bitch who gets her way at any cost. "OK," she said coldly. "You are right. You can live as you want. Did you get my messages about the New York event?"

"I got it, but I won't go."

Mom closed her eyes and squeezed the bridge of her nose. *She is so predictable that I can predict her next five moves. Now the hand will caress the neck. Now the hair. Dramatic sigh.*

"I see." She stood up. "I hope you have a fun weekend. I'm going to the airport."

"Have a good flight," I said.

Mother said goodbye and quietly closed the office door. I listened to her Jimmy Choos stomping down the hallway.

I thought about my distorted vision of the future, which had become a complete mess after our conversation. I wondered what I would do over the weekend. Maybe that's why I still have to answer Nicole's calls? She's like a stick in my seat. Four years after we met, I really don't understand what I saw in her. Because of her, my marriage to Luka collapsed—and Luka left me. When I look at her now, I see an empty girl who will do anything for my fat wallet. I let out a loud sigh. *What the hell? She'll be fine for this weekend too. One blonde less or more in my life.*

I picked up the phone and found twenty-five missed calls from Nicole and several messages. I rolled my eyes. *What am I doing again?* I dialed Nicole's number, and I didn't even have time to catch my breath before she happily mumbled hello.

LUKA

The plane landed at Kennedy International Airport in New York at exactly 4:00 p.m. It was as sweltering outside as it was in Lithuania, and I was glad to be wearing thin cotton shorts and a country-style blouse. Andrew hailed a cab, and the whole company left Queens for the Upper West Side.

I admired the views of New York from the cab window and tried to memorize the silhouettes of all the buildings. I had never been to New York City before, but I easily recognized Central Park, the Trump Hotel, and some streets from the movies. The summer sun shimmered playfully in the trees, and New York was boiling.

The car stopped at the corner of Ninety-Fourth Street. Our hotel was small, and it was not of the highest class. It was unlikely that any famous people were staying in it, but it looked cute. Fortunately, Central Park was not far away, and I looked forward to strolling through it whenever I had free time.

Andrew told us to go to our rooms and get ready for the evening's event. It would take place on the Upper East Side, and we had a couple of hours to wash off the fatigue of the trip.

I shared a room with Lina, and it was beautiful, neat, and tasteful. Everything smelled clean. The beds were sparkling and in perfect order, and the bedspreads were neat and straight. I was impressed with such thoroughness.

I ran to the window and looked down at the street. I had forgotten how lively America can be, and while Lina was taking a shower, I ran down to the street and immersed myself in the crowd. People flowed past me in different directions—with different stories, moods, and jobs. I watched the people and admired the skyscrapers. I took a few pictures with my phone and hurried back to the room to get ready for the evening.

Lina wore a velvet evening dress, and I chose a black floor-length dress that was decorated with small scales. The slit of gracefully exposed my leg up to my groin. I had never worn it before, and I didn't think I would ever see it again, but I was happy to find it in the box. I put on light evening makeup, lightly tousled my hair, and put on my favorite French perfume, which covered my shoulders like a veil.

Lina even watched my transformation from Cinderella to a swan in awe.

"What?" I asked nervously.

She shamelessly stared at me. "Nothing ... you look very beautiful. If I didn't know it was you, I wouldn't recognize you."

"Thank you." I smiled. Lina was a sweet girl, but I didn't communicate much with her because she was more reserved than me.

We went down to the lobby, and our colleagues were waiting for us. The men looked at my appearance with appreciation, and Andrew blushed. It was nice to get such a reaction. I felt like a woman again. *Maybe this trip won't be as unpleasant as I imagined.*

We took a limousine to the venue. Lina seemed enthralled by the luxury and grandeur of the city, and my heart sank. It was unlikely that I would meet any acquaintances from the past in New York, much less Iden, but my heart still fluttered. In Lithuania, we were separated by thousands of kilometers, but in New York, those thousands of kilometers changed to tiny miles. I could almost physically feel his presence next to me. I was probably exaggerating, but I kept reassuring myself.

As expected, the event was spectacular and chic. The country club housed a ballroom, a catwalk for the fashion shows, and a space for dancing with a live orchestra.

Lina stared with bulging eyes and gasped as she saw each person. She kept pulling my hand and pointing at the faces of the fashion world. It was funny to see her so fired up and excited, but five years ago, I had been like that too. I had been full of hopes and dreams.

Andrew greeted a few men and pushed me forward with his hand on my waist. "These two gentlemen are interested in investment opportunities in Lithuania. I would like you to show all your charm and tell us about our editorial office and how we can be useful to them."

"Me? But you're the boss here ... I shouldn't—"

"Shh." Andrew put his finger on my lips, which was completely unexpected. I flinched, but Andrew was in no hurry to withdraw his finger. He looked into my eyes. "You'll be fine. They have a construction company in Lithuania, and if we get the opportunity to become their partners, we will accumulate a good amount of capital from advertising."

"OK." I turned to the gentlemen, smiled kindly, and told about our editorial office, how much better our team is than others in Lithuania, and how special and wonderful our magazine is.

They were interested in preparing a series of video reports that would tell the stories of the rich of Manhattan and be shown in Lithuania and all over the world. Rich people could conquer the Lithuanian market and become heroes. I couldn't stop talking, and I was very happy to dive into my heartwarming job in advertising.

After our conversation, I interviewed some famous faces for my report on Fashion Week. After gathering my material, I returned to my colleagues and raised my first glass of champagne of the night.

"Oh my God, I can't believe it, my *preciosa*."

When I heard that sweet familiar voice, I froze. Alvaro Rivera was standing in front of me in a bright yellow suit and blue moccasins.

"Alvaro!"

He grabbed me in his arms and kissed my lips.

"My beautiful Luka Black! I thought I would never see you again. You look so beautiful." He circled me again and pulled me closer.

"Thank you." I looked at my colleagues. "Guys, this is an old friend, Mr. Alvaro Rivera. Alvaro, here are my colleagues from Lithuania."

"Ah, that's very nice, but I'm mad at you, *preciosa*. Four years of silence? I understand you're mad at Black, but why are you mad at me?" He dramatically wiped the corner of his eye with his thumb.

"Everything is not as you say, Alvaro, but this is not the place to talk. Can we meet on Monday for an early lunch?"

"How could I refuse?" He kissed my cheeks, put his business card in my hand, and went on his way after apologizing to everyone.

When I finally lost sight of his yellow suit, I breathed a sigh of relief. He was the first shadow from the past. Everything was going smoothly, and I started to calm down.

"Who was that?" asked Andrew.

I smiled. "A friend from the past."

"Is he a designer?"

"Yes, he is." I sighed.

I remembered my first meeting with Alvaro and how Iden had joined us. That afternoon changed my life. All the memories were still alive; it was as if everything had happened yesterday. I was young, stupid, and gullible. I will never forget the look in his eyes, the tone of his voice, manner of speech, and his radiant self-confidence. That afternoon, Iden Black invaded my little world and turned it upside down. I shook as I remembered the pouring rain as I sat on the bench and cried myself to death.

"Why did he call you Luka Black?" Andrew asked.

"Andrew, please, not now." I finished my champagne.

The following evening passed without any major events. We had a good time, and I danced with a few times guys. I was glad I remembered the dance steps.

We returned to the hotel at one o'clock in the morning, and Andrew offered to bring us to the hotel restaurant. Our fun evening continued.

After a few cocktails, Marius and Lina went upstairs.—I suspected that an office romance was brewing between them—and I stayed with Andrew. I sipped my martini slowly and stared blankly into my glass, wondering if Alvaro was still in contact with Iden.

Andrew smiled. "Will you tell me your story now, Luka Black?"

"My story is not as interesting as you might imagine. Is it worth wasting time bringing old hurts to the surface?"

"No, not at all." Andrew shook his head and looked into my eyes. He was a really handsome man, but he was married. I couldn't allow myself to fantasize about his touches or stolen glances; it would be indecent to say the least.

"You are mysterious, intelligent, unpredictable, and full of beauty. I would like to get to know you better."

My heart began to beat faster. "What do you mean?"

"Luka, you are not a little girl. You should have realized long ago that you caught my eye."

"Do you want *physical intimacy?*"

"Intimacy, of course. I like you," he said. "Luka, from the moment you walked through the door to my office, I knew that you would be mine—sooner or later."

"You're so self-confident." A string of femininity began to coil between my thighs. *God, you're a scumbag.*

Andrew leaned closer. "How is it, Luka?"

"You are married, and you have a child. For me, family always comes first. Unconditionally." I folded my arms.

Andrew scratched his barely gray beard and looked at me again. "I will divorce my wife."

I couldn't believe my ears.

Andrew looked confused as he waited for my answer.

"Andrew, are you kidding me?" I was hoping it was a joke. "Do you have any idea what nonsense you just said?"

"I am completely serious. I don't love Monica. More precisely, maybe I should say I don't love her anymore. Our marriage was impulsive and thoughtless. When I realized that I had made a mistake, she announced that she was pregnant—and then Beata was born. My life is the real suffering. Every night, I look at her and want to scream."

Andrew only sees things from his own perspective. Do all men think alike? Are all men like that? I really don't think Monica begged him to marry her, and I don't think she started the baby on her own. He acts like he is a victim—a mouse caught in a trap. "So, are you the victim of your family?"

"I don't know if I can describe my current state of mind or my life like that, but it may appear that way from the outside."

"I don't want to take part in all this." I pushed my chair back and stood up. "I really hope that—sooner or later—all your problems are solved!"

I left Andrew at the table, and I headed toward the elevator. Out of the corner of my eye, I saw Andrew shaking off the napkin with his hand and holding his head theatrically.

IDEN

The morning light was annoyingly creeping under my eyelids, and I turned over to my other side. I was unpleasantly surprised when my hand touched the warm body that was lying next to me.

What the hell? I cursed in my mind and opened my eyes. I thought Nicole was lying in my bed, but the sight I saw made me flinch. Luka was sleeping peacefully next to me. Her long hair was on the pillow, and her light blue bedclothes highlighted her lightly tanned skin. Her plump lips would come in handy a bit. I was afraid to move. I didn't want to wake her, but I breathed in her breath with all my lungs and almost cried with relief. My lungs had finally filled with air after all these years, and I could breathe more freely. Emboldened, I gently touched her face with my hand. It was pleasantly smooth. She was beautiful as ever. My eyes had forgotten that sight in the mornings. I missed watching her sleep, and I enjoyed the spectacle without restriction. I leaned in for a kiss, and her green eyes opened. She looked at me and said, "It's just a dream, Iden."

I jumped up, sweating and gasping for air. I began to suffocate, and my heart was squeezed by a pain I had never experienced. It felt like my chest was being torn in opposite directions with pliers. For the first time in four years, I couldn't hold back my tears. I started to cry, and I held my head in my hands. Tears rolled down my cheeks, and the pain poured out of my chest. I wanted to scream and shout. I felt the same terrible feeling as when I found out that Iva had died in the accident. This time, I had lost the hope that had so deceptively seduced me.

Exhausted, I collapsed onto the bed and stared at the empty place next to me. I touched the pillow and tried to remember Luka's face, smell, and voice. The memories were so vivid, and it felt like everything had happened yesterday. I really needed help. I needed to get out of that damn vicious circle. I needed to start moving forward, but I couldn't figure out where to start. One part of me longed to see Luka by my side, but the other part wanted to destroy her. The two conflicting feelings tore at me from the inside. I could not breathe for a moment. Could I create a new life with another woman?

I had been infatuated with Nicole, and she seemed like the most suitable option for turning over a new leaf. Luka did not pay any attention to me when I wanted to end everything, but last night had finally worn out my patience with Nicole. I decided that I would have nothing more to do with her. When I took her home and said good night, I let her know that it was all over. She looked offended, but she realized that there was no point in resisting.

Returning home early, I spent the evening alone. Had loneliness finally knocked me off my tracks? Since the day she left, I had never dreamed Luka, but apparently my psyche was completely crippled. Why was my subconscious pulling such pranks? I was going to spend the evening alone, but then I changed my mind. I decided to take advantage of my friend's offer and go to the club to have some fun. Will this evening be the one when a new star of happiness begins to shine in my life?

I stayed in bed for a long time and stared blankly out the window. I wonder how Luka lives. Does she think about me? Is she happy? What does she do? Should I look for her? Does she need my help? No, she would probably be very angry and offended.

After a long workout and an even longer shower, I decided to work on the drawings for a project that had been on my desk for a long time. I was creating a project for a children's oncology hospital.

I wanted to do something useful for society, and I was hoping to atone for my wrongs. Liam was happy that I was interested in this project, but I wasn't completely happy. I had no one to share that happiness with. Luka would probably be extremely happy with my decision. She would be crying tears of happiness and planning volunteer activities at the hospital, but she is not here. I am alone with my thoughts. My efforts to be better are completely pointless. Why bother? I live alone, and I am not responsible for anyone. Why should I prove anything to anyone? I am doing this because, deep in my heart, I believe Luka will notice my good deeds, and when she realizes that I have changed, she will finally forgive me—and maybe even come back to me. Of course, I didn't tell anyone about my thoughts, but I foolishly believed all of them.

You need to start talking to flowers and officially declare yourself mentally ill.

I looked out the window and sighed like a little girl. I came to the conclusion that alcohol my lifestyle had completely softened my brain. I was a complete loser—the typical hero of novels who is unable to deal with the fragments of his previous life and becomes a recluse. Eventually, everyone will forget about my existence. I will die alone and lonely. It will take time for anyone to miss me, and when they do, my body will turn into a mummy. Liam once said the same thing to me, but I called him a fool. I now see my future clearly, and it's really not happy.

Iden, when did you become such a dumbass? I don't know the answer.

CHAPTER SEVENTEEN

LUKA

In the early morning in the hotel room, I remembered fragments of my previous life, when I could afford to have everything, but most importantly, I could have Iden by my side. He was everything I needed. I was addicted to him—breathing him, wanting to touch and possess every part of his body—but I didn't understand how temporary and fragile everything is.

When I woke up, I stared out the window at the blue sky and secretly wished I could turn back time and go back to the summer when I first came to the United States, the moment Iden, and I crossed paths. I wouldn't change a thing. I'd leave it the way it was, but I'd probably never leave it. It's too late to long for what is already lost. He erased me from his life. I chose this path myself, and there is no one to blame.

I finally got up and packed my suitcase for my trip to Chicago. I felt strange; everything seemed so familiar and familiar. It was as if I had found my way home after years of wandering in the fog.

We had breakfast in the hotel restaurant with Lina and Marius, but Andrew did not join us. I was still mildly shocked by his proposal. I never would have thought I had caught his eye. He had always treated me with gallantry and restraint, and the thoughts he expressed yesterday did not fit at all with the image of a boss he had created. I asked Lina to warn Andrew about my trip and said I would return to New York on Sunday evening.

I left for Kennedy Airport, and my heart was restless. I missed my friends, and I missed Chicago. I rubbed my hands on my knees and smiled; everything was so close. The cab slowly moved along the Hudson River, and the sun's rays pleasantly warmed the face. I looked out the window and saw the Brooklyn Bridge in the distance. *There is so much I haven't seen here yet.* Three months after Iva's death, Iden suggested a vacation to the Hamptons and Times Square, but I was so broken that I didn't even want to think about fun. Iden got angry and left alone. He probably met Nicole on that trip.

It's your fault, Luka. You wanted it yourself.

I hated the voice of my conscience reminding me about my mistakes and bad choices. That thin voice was always unexpected. I have only myself to blame for all the drama in my life. I needed to go to New York then. I needed to admit the painful truth that Iden was not to blame for the accident—he was not to blame for Iva's death—but I couldn't.

I sighed and looked out at the motorboats on the Hudson River. I touched the glass that separated me from the outside world and thought how glass can be a solid barrier when we want it to be, but it can also be fragile. Life can be as fragile as glass or as strong as steel if we protect it.

At the airport, I quickly went through all the security checks and found the right gate. Several travelers were already waiting. After a few hours, I was walking through O'Hare Airport. As always, it was full of travelers. Friends, relatives, and loved ones were impatiently waiting with balloons and flowers. Others saw off their departing ones with tears in their eyes. I looked longingly at the young couples who rushed to each other, hugged each other, and turned around in joy that they were together again. *Maybe I will experience that feeling of fulfillment and happiness again someday.*

At the other end of the waiting room, I saw a red-haired couple hurrying toward me. Elle, as always, was late. Her long, luscious hair was disheveled, large sunglasses covered almost half of her face, and bright freckles dotted her face and bare shoulders. She looked healthy, beautiful, and happy.

"Luka." She smiled when she saw me. "Oh my God—you've changed. New haircut?" I was examined from my feet to the ends of my hair, and then I was grabbed in a strong hug. "I missed you so much!"

"I love you, Elle." I squeezed my friend tighter.

"I can't believe it. Where is your long hair?"

"I just decided to change it up." I shrugged and smiled.

"You look so grown up."

"Yes, I'm old and lonely. I need to buy a dozen more cats, and then I will be a real dream of the old boys." I laughed.

"Enough standing around, let's go home and prepare for a wonderful evening with friends. Hungry?"

"I'd eat a sandwich." My stomach reminded me that it was time to eat.

Elle grabbed my arm and dragged me toward the parking lot. I was not at all surprised by her talkativeness. She's probably the only person on earth who can tell a book-length story about her life in ten minutes in the week since we have spoken.

I could hardly believe that I was back in Chicago. Everything looked as if I had been there yesterday: the same roads, the same people, the same buildings, the same colorful shop windows attracting the eyes of passersby with trinkets for sale.

While driving, Elle talked about her relationship with Martin, and I tried not to let my mind wander to the memories that flooded me like an avalanche. On the way home, we stopped at a fast-food restaurant and chowed down on a huge portion of macaroni and cheese. Elle laughed at my dismay at the portion sizes, but I was so hungry that I ate everything without even thinking.

Finally, we arrived at Elle's house. Her one-story cottage was cozy and bright. Inside, there was a lot of misplaced stuff, which was very typical of Elle.

"And where is Martin?" I asked while looking at the photos on the walls.

"He left for a business trip in Minnesota, and he won't be back until Friday." Elle pursed her lips.

"I understand. I was hoping to see him," I said.

"It's sad enough—now it's time to party." She pulled out a bottle of red wine from the fridge, and I couldn't help but start laughing.

After a couple of hours of talking and tears—and emptying the bottle of wine—we started getting ready for the fun. It would be my first entertainment since the fatal accident.

I opened my heart to Elle and poured out all the accumulated bile, hurts, lost hopes, and joys of life. Elle, like a real sister, cried and got angry with me. I really needed it, and I felt much better. I felt more like myself than ever before.

When my face returned to its normal color, Elle straightened her long hair and was satisfied with the image she saw in the mirror. I started to get ready for the evening. I decorated my hair with light curls, and Elle added bright evening makeup. I put on a white jumpsuit with wide straps, a matching handbag, and black pointed shoes. Elle chose a turquoise dress that circled around her hips and brown ankle boots. We stood in front of the mirror and took pictures; it was just like the good old days.

"Rodriguez will be waiting for us at the club in an hour. We have to go to the city," Elle announced.

We chatted happily in the cab. I admired the evening and the city lights. The cab was very nice, and the driver cranked up the radio. Elle and I rocked out to Kygo's "Younger." It was fun to remember our carefree youth and enjoy the moment.

There was a queue at the entrance to the luxurious club, and Rodriguez was standing by the guards. One of them must have been his friend because they were both having a good time while the other guard was letting people in. When Rodriguez saw me, he grinned from ear to ear and opened his arms wide for a hug. I rushed into his huge and warm embrace.

"Rodriguez, my friend, how I've missed you!"

"*Chica*, you are so beautiful," Rodriguez said. "If you hadn't shown up, I was planning a trip to Lithuania to visit you."

"It would be great if you came." I smiled. "I would show Vilnius and its surroundings. You would really like the old town and its architecture. You would find some great shots."

"Don't tempt me, *chica*." He laughed. "Hello, Elle." He patted her cheek. "Well, let's go crazy!"

"Oh, yes," Elle said. Rodriguez put his arm around our shoulders and led us inside.

The impressive club featured a modern design, flashing lights, and pounding music.

Rodriguez had reserved table with soft chairs. "So, girls, champagne?"

It was like old times again, and the three of us had a good time. Rodriguez talked about his photo studio, incoming orders, and exhibitions. He was a promising photographer. Many famous people had hired him to capture important family moments or purchased his artwork. I was happy for Rodriguez's success. He had a girl who was very important to him, but he didn't want to introduce her to us yet. He said, "It's too early to be happy."

My phone screen lit up with a message from Andrew: "Hello, Luka. Sorry about last night. I was too direct. I really didn't mean to scare you. I really like you a lot, and everything I said yesterday was really sincere. Just say the word, and everything will change."

I read the message three times, and my cheeks turned red. *Is Andrew's mind completely twisted? Does he not care about his wife or daughter?*

I wrote a text to him: "Andrew, I was serious yesterday. I

certainly would never want to be the woman who destroys a family. If everything had been under different circumstances, maybe we would have come to an agreement. Please don't complicate our relationship."

I sent the message and put my phone on the table, but it came back to life.

> Andrew: Maybe we can talk live? Tell me where are you, and I'll come.
> Luka: I'm not in New York. I asked Lina to warn you. I will be back on Sunday evening.
> Andrew: I can come to Chicago. Where are you?

I rolled my eyes and read the message again. *Andrew can come to Chicago? What the hell?*

> Luka: I really don't want to spoil the mood for myself or for you tonight. I'll see you later.

When Andrew didn't write back, I breathed a sigh of relief. It seemed that one drama in my life was over, and I could finally breathe easier. Out of nowhere, my handsome boss was determined to give up his family for me. I took a sip of champagne and told my friends that I was going to the bar to order something stronger. I wanted to get drunk and forget everything.

The club was packed, and we had to push through the crowd to get to the bar. When I reached the bar, I sat down in an empty chair, stared at my hands, and thought about Andrew's decision to leave his wife and how it would change all their lives.

"Luka?"

That voice shook my subconscious and my heart as it ran through my body like an electric current. I couldn't move for a few moments, but I finally got up the courage to turn my head to the person who had just called my name. Dark fashionable shoes, black pants that emphasized every leg muscle, loose white shirt, sleeves rolled up to the elbows, and Rolex on his wrist. At last my eyes came upon his face. He had stubble on his chin, deep, dark eyes, and a stern jaw, and his hair was a little longer and grayer than before. Iden stood next to me; one bandaged hand was leaning on the bar, and the other tightly was gripping the back of the chair.

I opened it easily and forgot about it when I lost it. I forgot how to speak and how to breathe. He was so familiar, yet so strange at the same time. He was waiting for me to speak, but I couldn't. I was frozen, and I looked at him, unable to believe he was there. Or was it a mirage?

Iden stood there for a few more moments, probably losing hope that I would answer, and then he turned, took a step away, and said, "Good luck to you."

IDEN

My friend from the gym and I decided to visit several clubs, but we ended up going back to the first one we started our trip at around midnight.

My hand hurt a little less today than yesterday, but I couldn't say that I was completely healthy. I finally made a deal with myself not to cross the line, but Ted kept fueling the fire. I couldn't give up. There was no shortage of girls in our company. Ted invited a dozen of them to our table, but my face was decorated with an artificial smile. I didn't order the champagne; it just evaporated. A dark-haired girl with expressive curves kept looking at me through her eyelashes, but my thoughts wandered elsewhere.

It was hard to think about anything but Luka. That dream haunted me like a nightmare all day long. It was stuck in my brain. At one point, I wanted to call a private detective and ask for Luka's number. I wanted to find her and ask her if everything was OK. I had a strange feeling that she needed me. I felt like something was wrong.

"The earth is calling, Iden," Ted said.

"What?" I asked as I turned around.

"Could you go to the bar and order some more champagne?"

"Yes, I can." I smiled at the girls and got up to go.

The club was packed, and I pressed my injured hand to my stomach and made my way through the crowd. I placed my order and was about to head back to the table when my eyes stopped at a girl sitting a few chairs away from me. She was wearing a white jumpsuit and had short bleached hair. Light curls covered her face like a veil. Her hands were folded on the bar. With a graceful movement, she tucked a strand of hair behind her ear, revealing her face. I was shocked. I wouldn't confuse that profile with any other. Luka was sitting at the bar. It looked like an illusion, and I had to hold on to keep my balance.

Luka. I repeated her name a thousand times in my mind.

She sat at the bar and looked at her clenched fingers. She seemed to be thinking about something. For a few moments, I could not move. I concentrated and moved closer, but she did not notice me. In the past, we both felt each other. We didn't even have to see each other; we knew we were there. And now, it seems, that fragile chemistry was no longer working.

"Luka?"

She froze—her face was covered with pink spots—but she didn't turn to me. I leaned back again because my legs were bent. Finally, as the tension reached its peak, Luka turned to look at me. She was as beautiful as the first time I saw her, but she didn't say anything. She just looked at me silently. Her green eyes were so pure and so gentle, and I couldn't look away. She looked confused. I was probably the last person on earth she wanted to see. After receiving no response, I wished her luck, turned and walked into the crowd.

In that moment, the solid foundation I had been standing on became fragile. Disappointment gathered in her eyes, and her heart was gripped by anguish. I was halfway to the table when someone grabbed my arm. Intuitively, I wanted to pull her out of that warm lap. I thought it was the dark-haired girl who had been clinging to me for so long, but before sending her to hell, I look back. Luka was standing next to me. She looked at me with such a pitiful look that it was hard to hold back my tears. I couldn't hold back anymore, and a tear rolled down my cheek.

"I'm sorry," Luka said, and she hugged my torso.

I was in shock. I didn't know what to do, but my hands knew what to do. I gently hugged Luka and pulled her tighter. Everyone was dancing to the pounding music, but we stood still. Bright lasers played on Luka's face as I stared at her and asked myself what had just happened. She didn't say anything; she just stood there with her arms around me tightly.

"I'm sorry too," I said. "I'm sorry for everything."

Luka looked up as if she had been waiting for this all her life. In that moment, the shackles of guilt that had tormented us since Iva's death were broken. We had become free, open, and more mature. We weren't the same anymore. I saw the same goodness in Luka's eyes as before.

"Do you want to get out of here?" Luka asked.

Without answering, I grabbed her hand and led her toward the exit. I turned to look at Luka to see if everything was OK, and she was still smiling.

We left the club and stopped on the sidewalk.

"What now?" I asked.

"Let's just go where we can see each other?" Luka said.

I laughed.

"Hang on. I'll write to Elle so she doesn't have to wait for me."

"Are you here with Elle?" I asked.

"Yes … and with Rodriguez. I return to New York tomorrow,

and then I go back to Lithuania." Luka talked as simply as if we had just broken up yesterday.

"Understood." I was a bit disappointed, but I didn't want to waste any time. I texted Ted to let him know that I had to leave immediately.

Luka gently grabbed my hand, and I flinched. As we walked down the street, there was no need to talk. It was just good to be together.

"How are you?" Luka asked.

"Me? I don't know. To be honest, I seem to have been a bit lost lately." I smiled at her. "And how are you doing?"

"I have also been wandering around in a fog for a long time."

We both laughed. That teenage charm had taken over our mature bodies again.

"There's a cab." Luka motioned for the driver to stop.

"Where are we going?" I asked.

"The night is short, and there's a lot to see." She told the driver to go to the center of town.

The driver turned on the radio, and the voice of Ellie Goulding filled the car. She was singing about love.

Luka was calmly looking out the window, and when she saw that I was staring at her, she turned and smiled. "What?" She laughed.

"You cut your hair," I said. It was the first thought that popped into my head. I touched her short curls.

"Yes, don't you like it?"

"No, no, I really like it. It suits you." *Iden, you're totally screwed. There is a woman sitting next to you who hasn't given you peace for so many years, and you can only give her a compliment like that?*

"Thank you." She turned back to the window and the bright lights of Chicago.

I found her hand with my fingers and continued watching her and thinking how lucky I was that she was there and that she was talking to me, smiling at me, and letting me hold her hand. *I don't know what tomorrow will bring, but I will certainly not waste a single minute of this night.* I squeezed Luka's hand even tighter, put my chin on her shoulder, and breathed in her smell—so close and familiar—with my lungs. With my free hand, I touched the strand of hair falling on her face. It was as soft as silk. I traveled down the curve of her face with my fingers, and without holding back, I kissed her bare shoulder.

Luka shuddered, but she did not push me away.

My heart began to beat at an indescribable speed. I felt bliss, relief, joy, and faith that everything would be fine. It was hard to believe that the one I had lost so suddenly was back in my life, and she was right there by my side.

Luka touched my knee, and it caused an unearthly storm of satisfaction in me. I felt starved for love. I was longing for warmth and the physical closeness we once had. I think Luka felt the same way. She was confused like me. We didn't know what tomorrow would bring, but we would enjoy the moment and each other's company.

LUKA

I didn't hesitate when I saw Iden walking away, and now I could feel him next to me in the cab. He clung to me like a cat waiting for a tastier bite. Every touch of his caused an uncontrollable storm, and the air around me seemed electric. I could feel it. His innocent look, greedy eyes, and lips drove me crazy.

When the cab stopped at Millennium Park, we got out of the car—but neither of us let go of the other's hand.

"And what should we do?" Iden asked with a smile.

"We'll go to Cloud Gate." I smiled. I felt a stupid euphoria that we were together, and I wanted to fix everything that we couldn't do together back then.

"Cloud Gate?" Iden seemed surprised.

"Yes. Why not? After all, we haven't been there before."

Iden said nothing. He shook his head as we walked along. Although it was after midnight, the park was full. Young people were having fun by the lighted fountains, ignoring the fact that their clothes were soaked through. Other people sat on benches and chatted. The Chicago Bean reflected the lights of the city. I admired the view and took out my phone. It flashed a dozen messages from Elle and Rodriguez:

> Elle: I don't understand!
> Elle: Where are you, Luka? Not funny at all!
> Elle: Luka, answer me.
> Rodriguez: Luka, where did you go?
> Elle: Luka!
> Elle: I swear to God, if you come home alive, I will kill you with my own hands.

There were many other messages with similar content. I texted Elle to tell her that I was fine and would explain everything when I got home.

Iden watched me silently.

I turned and beckoned him over. I took some pictures with the Bean in the background. For the next shot, I pecked him on the cheek.

Iden turned his face, and our lips met. I didn't have the strength to fight myself or use common sense. I surrendered to the moment and sank into the sweetest kiss possible. I wrapped my arms around his neck, and Iden wrapped his arms around my waist. I was very happy to be able to spend at least one night together. I knew the spell would be broken in the morning, and we would have to go back to our lives, but I wanted to break all the rules today.

Iden pulled away and whispered, "I missed you so much."

"I missed you too, Iden." I kissed him again.

It was good and calm, and all the bad words and feelings melted away. Iden was the one I had fallen in love with. No shadow of the past remained between us; there was only the deafening present. Iden's hands tightened on my torso, seemingly wanting to leave a mark on my body. I was melting with each of his movements. I finally ran out of air, tore my lips away from his hot kiss, rested my head against his chest, and listened to his anxious heartbeat.

His heartbeats echoed through my body like a love lost in the past. I wanted to cry, but it was not because I felt unhappy. By no means. I had found what I had been searching for for so long: inner peace.

I said, "Should we find a restaurant? I'm hungry."

"Of course."

We headed downtown.

As we walked, we discussed the buildings we saw and the bright lights of Chicago. Iden explained what he had been up to for the past four years. I loved how passionate he was about his work. He told about Liam and his growing family. I was happy for Liam's success. No matter how hard we tried, we couldn't discuss family or children. When we found a cafe that was still open, we ordered a hamburger and hot coffee.

"What happened to your hand?" I pointed at the bandage.

Iden frowned, but after a while, he relaxed and scratched the back of his neck. He took a sip of coffee.

It's probably a very uncomfortable subject.

"Well, let's just say that I've gone back to my old habits in recent years, which sometimes gets me into fights or accidents." He gave me a pitiful look.

"Have you started drinking again?"

"Luka, can we not talk about this?"

"No, Iden, we can't. Why are you destroying yourself? Are you going to let go of everything you fought so hard for?" I felt myself starting to preach.

"Luka, this is my life—from which you left of your own free will."

That was the end of our beautiful and understanding evening. Iden put his unreadable mask back on.

I was upset that I hadn't kept my mouth shut. *Why can't I keep quiet?*

Iden pushed away his half-eaten hamburger and glared at me. "Luka, why did you come back?"

I stared at him, but I didn't know what to say. He probably expected some kind of guaranteed answer from me, but I was confused. All I knew was that I would fly home on Tuesday and never come back here. "I came to New York for work. I wanted to meet Elle and Rodriguez, but they couldn't come. Instead, I came here."

"If it wasn't for them, you wouldn't have come here?"

"I don't think so," I said, looking away from him. "I wasn't ready to meet you, and I couldn't even imagine that we would be walking around Chicago or eating at four o'clock in the morning and talking to each other like best friends."

"Do you consider me a friend?" Iden's mood seemed to be falling. He went from being a loving and romantic man to being the same angry jerk he often was when I did something wrong.

"Yes and no," I answered. "You were the great love of my life, Iden."

"And now?" He was pushing me into a corner.

"Iden, stop." I showed the waiter that I needed the bill. "Let's leave the past where it is destined to be. We must move forward and not look back."

Iden was silent, and he looked out at the street. I could see tears welling up in his eyes, but he quickly wiped them away and regained his composure. My heart was bleeding, but I had to let him go—just like he had let me go. We were both too different to be together. We had too painful a past, and we really could not build a common future. The shadow of dead Iva would follow us for the rest of our lives, and we could not silence that guilt, further damaging our wounded souls. The night had become a farewell night.

Luka, are you doing the right thing?

A small voice in my head screamed that I was doing the wrong thing, but I couldn't get over myself and turn over a new leaf. *Where would Iden's name be written again?*

CHAPTER EIGHTEEN

IDEN

Luka had made it clear what she thought of me. She only considers me a friend. It hurt and angered me a lot. I sat there with my fists clenched. I wanted to split the stupid cafe table that separated us like a wall. I had started to believe that everything was resolved, that Luka was not there for nothing, and that she had come to me with the hope that we could be together, but she just wanted to express everything that she had not said four years ago. I felt like an idiot, a hapless psychopath, and a cursed patient who had finally recovered from her touch—only to be reinjured by the same woman.

She looked so pure and beautiful, but in her green eyes, I no longer saw the love for me that I used to see. She seemed like a completely different woman. I wanted to open up and say that the past four years of my life had been the blackest, that I couldn't live without her, and that I couldn't breathe, but would that change anything? Her gentle gaze was sympathetic, but it was like a sister sympathizing with her brother. I was seething with anger, fear, and anxiety and felt a damned desire to be with her.

Am I going to lose her again? Four years ago, I was the last fool to be seduced by a short skirt in that dark moment when I should have been by Luka's side. I tried to lick the wounds of loss. It was my mistake—my disastrous mistake—that ruined our lives forever. Can't I do anything?

"Luka, one more thing," I said in a raspy voice. "I'm so sorry that when we were hurting, I took the easy way out and just turned away from you. Forgive me for being so selfish," I said a little too coldly.

"I'll repeat it again. Let's leave the past in the past. I forgive you," she said calmly.

"Are we friends?" I almost fainted as I said those words.

"Friends," she said in an unhappy voice.

A waiter brought the bill, and before Luka could pull out her wallet, I handed him my credit card. Luka objected, but I told her she would pay next time.

By the time we left the cafe, she was much quieter and less bubbling with enthusiasm than she had been at the beginning of the evening. She still gave me her hand. We walked down the street in silence, but I didn't know how to change anything. I had made enough mistakes in the past to make our life unbearable. Luka is a particularly strong character, and I am overly bossy, but I think we met for a reason today. Fate brought us together and gave us one last chance to start all over, but we need to do everything right this time.

I said, "Do you want to go home or sit on the old pier and admire Lake Michigan and the sunrise?"

"Of course we can. I don't want to sleep at all." She smiled.

We headed for the waterfront, and I relaxed a bit. We sat on a bench and waited for the rising sun. I put my arm around her, and she rested her head on my shoulder. I was glad that it was warm outside.

The sun rose slowly, and the sky turned bright orange. Birds were flying in the distance, and seagulls were flying all around us.

"How beautiful," Luka said.

"Very beautiful." I looked at Luka's face. She looked so young. She was looking at the horizon, and I was looking at her. I tried to remember every moment. She was a perfect woman—still *my* woman—and I would definitely try to get her to come back to me.

"Tell me what you're doing in Lithuania."

A wrinkle appeared on her forehead. "I work in the editorial office of a magazine. I have my own fashion section, and I write what I like."

"You completely changed the nature of your work?"

"Yes, I wanted a change. I also volunteer at a hospice. I've met a lot of good people there."

"Sounds interesting." I was surprised. "And how is your family?"

Luka tensed, but after a while, she relaxed her shoulders. "My family is like they were. Nothing has changed." She turned her eyes back to the horizon.

We listened to the waves crashing and the city waking up. After an hour, I realized Luka had fallen asleep. I hugged her even tighter and enjoyed the moment.

Time stopped and began to turn back. I went through our entire life together in my mind: the arguments, anger, fears, misunderstandings, angry words, laughter, joy, tears, kisses, love, hopes, and pain. We had been through everything and suffered everything, but at some, we just stopped believing in each other. For so many years, I blamed Luka for my cooling off, for our broken marriage, but now I realized that we were both to blame. I turned away from her when she needed my support the most, but how could I blame myself? I was tired of fighting for us. Luka was tired of suffering and grieving. We were both vulnerable and fragile.

I gently caressed her smooth skin and admired the peace that emanated from her. She was the same sweet, sincere, and good-hearted Luka I had once loved—and had never stopped loving. My heart finally revived and started beating again. *Luka is the meaning, the essence, and the destiny of my life. I have to fight for her. I have to fix everything we've broken. I just don't know how yet.* I wanted to caressed her face, lips, and eyebrows. The rising sun was kissing every patch of her skin with its rays, and I longed to be that ray of sunshine. I longed to kiss and touch her body freely like I used to.

Luka opened her green eyes and looked at me. For a moment, I thought I saw surprise in her eyes, but after a few moments, her gaze became as friendly as before. "Hello. I must have fallen asleep. What time is it?" She started rummaging in her bag.

I looked at the clock and tried to move my numb hand. "It's almost eight o'clock."

"Wow. We sat here all night. I think it's time for me to go back to see Elle; otherwise, I'll have big problems."

My high spirits evaporated, and the beautiful morning—promising an even better day—melted like spring snow. *I can't change anything. I can see that she is uncomfortable, and yesterday's enchantment has dissipated, leaving only sweet memories.* I felt the anger again.

Luka tensed up. "It was nice to see you, but it's time for me to go." Luka straightened the folds of her overalls and looked around.

"Me too." I clenched my teeth. "Are you flying to New York today?"

"Yes. This evening. I need to go see Elle and Rodriguez."

"Of course." I gritted my teeth, and my fists were shaking with tension. I wanted to be angry. I wanted to shout and give Luka a good shake so that she would finally open her eyes and understand that we were meant for each other. *It's not worth wasting our time anymore.*

Luka slung her handbag over her shoulder and hugged me gently. I felt like I was made of glass.

She whispered, "Iden, thank you for this wonderful evening and for the conversation. I really needed this to move forward." Her breath tickled my neck, and her words tore my heart to pieces.

"Luka, I still love you." I grabbed the last straw.

She froze, and she did not answer. Finally, she pulled back and said goodbye. Luka had left my life again—as she had come—and I was left standing there alone. I could not move. I no longer had the strength to resist the feeling that fell on my shoulders like an avalanche. I loved her, and that was the only truth I needed to know.

You'll be mine again—no matter the cost. I promise.

LUKA

At the airport, I hugged Elle and Rodriguez for a long time. Elle was as angry as a hundred devils, but she did not want to part like that. When I got back to Elle's house in the morning, she put on an Oscar-worthy scene, but she didn't get any information out of me. There was no way I could say I was with Iden; she wouldn't have forgiven me. I wanted to keep this important moment to myself; it was better leave my friends in the dark.

Elle was convinced that I had met some nice guy at the club and spent a stormy night with him. I didn't try to challenge her, and I let her think it was true.

After returning to New York, I went to the hotel. Lina was not in the room. I took a shower, went down to the restaurant, and found them sitting at the table. They looked like they were having fun.

"Good evening." I sat down in the free seat.

"Hello," Lina said happily. "How was the meeting with your friends? Did you have a good time?"

"Yes, it was so much fun." I smiled and tried to ignore Andrew's angry look.

Lina and Marius kept asking me what I did, where I went, and what I saw.

I tried to explain everything as vividly as possible so they would feel as if they had visited Chicago too. I told them about the club, the strange interior, the noise, and the music. I told them about Chicago at night and how we walked the streets and admired the spectacle. I didn't mention the part about meeting my ex-husband, but I did tell them the rest.

They listened in amazement, and Andrew drank a second glass of whiskey and remained silent. I could feel the warmth of his leg near me and I felt strangely irritated. I ordered a vodka cocktail with cherry syrup and drank it in almost one gulp.

Andrew leaned closer to me and whispered, "When can we talk?"

A shiver ran down my spine. *Does he still expect me to accept his offer to be his lover?*

"Later," I answered calmly and smiled at my colleagues.

"Luka, this is important." Andrew was making it clear that he would not leave this matter unfinished.

I turned and glared at him. *I guess he doesn't understand that I won't be his whore.*

Andrew smiled crookedly.

A waiter came to our table with a chilled bottle of Cristal champagne and four glasses.

With bulging eyes, I looked at Andrew and my colleagues, but they also looked confused.

"Are we celebrating something?" I asked.

"I don't know." Lina looked at the waiter. "Excuse me, but we didn't order champagne."

Andrew almost killed the waiter with his look.

"The gentleman at the bar ordered it to be brought to your table. The champagne is for Miss Luka."

I already knew who had ordered the champagne.

My skin shuddered, and the air around me became static again—just like it always did when I felt Iden's presence near me. I turned to the bar and saw his dark jeans, black chunky boots, white shirt with the sleeves rolled up to the elbows, tousled dark hair, and his piercing gaze. Iden was standing at the bar, and his teeth were dazzlingly white. He was the most dangerous beast in this city. He was a predator. He was on the hunt again. I understood what he was after, and I instantly understood the rules of his game. I knew him better than I knew myself, and I was sure that the situation would not lead to anything good. My heart skipped a beat. *He's here for me.*

Alvaro Rivera stood next to Iden.

Bastards.

The waiter filled the glasses, and I grabbed one and raised it to them to say thanks.

Iden smiled again.

"Who is that?" Lina asked.

I couldn't take my eyes off of Iden's gaze. He paralyzed me. "He …" I started, but I couldn't think of a name for Iden. *Should I say he's my ex or an acquaintance? Should I introduce him as a friend?* "He is my friend."

"What a handsome man! If I were you, I would jump into his arms immediately. Look at the way he's looking at you. It looks like he's about to eat you." Lina laughed.

Marius and Andrew were not pleased. Marius was probably not impressed by Lina's praise, and Andrew was jealous.

Iden was not one to give up easily. He and Alvaro approached our table as if nothing had happened. Alvaro, as always, stood out from the crowd in his luxurious suit.

"Hello, Alvaro." I got up from the table and patted his cheeks. "What are you doing here? We agreed to meet tomorrow."

"Hello, my love. I'm sorry, *preciosa*, but I couldn't help it. When Iden said he was coming to New York, I had to meet him for another glass of bourbon. I really didn't know you were staying in this hotel."

So Iden planned it all again? He's started playing the game of cat and mouse again.

"It's OK. It's nice to see you," I replied.

Alvaro relaxed when he realized I wasn't mad at him.

"And you won't say hello to me?" Iden held out both arms, inviting me into his embrace.

I laughed at his dramatic behavior and quickly let myself be embraced by Iden's strong arms. He held me possessively to his firm chest and kissed the back of my head. I breathed in his scent, that eerily familiar and intoxicatingly pleasant smell.

Alvaro looked surprised.

I almost burst out laughing. "Iden, Alvaro, this is my boss, Andrew, and here are my colleagues Lina and Marius."

Iden greeted Andrew quite matter-of-factly—and Lina and Marius a little more warmly.

Andrew looked incredulously at the intruders. "Will you join us?"

"Sure," Iden said. "Why not?"

We all sat down. At the beginning, the atmosphere was heated. Andrew was staring at me with a red face. I was staring above Lina's head. Iden was staring at Andrew and me and tapping his fingers on the table. Alvaro was staring at all three of us and chewing his nails. Lina and Marius didn't seem to understand what was happening.

"So?" Alvaro broke the awkward silence. "What are you up to now, *preciosa*?"

"I work in the editorial office of a magazine," I answered. "I have my own fashion section."

"Oh, how sweet. Are you no longer working in advertising?"

"No, I've changed the nature of my work a little." I smiled at Alvaro and tried not to faint from the strange tension that emanated from the men sitting across from each other.

Andrew was not much different from Iden in height or muscles. They both had strange lights in their eyes. They are not males; they are behaving like goats in heat.

"I'm sorry to hear that. You were the best in the world of advertising." His hand patted my palm.

Andrew made himself a little more comfortable and put his hand over the back of my chair.

Iden's body tensed up, and a shadow of pain crossed his face.

"And what do you do, Iden? That seems to be your name." Andrew asked smugly.

I closed my eyes.

"I am in the hotel business," Iden replied with a smile.

Oh, how modest you are!

"What is your last name? I wonder if have heard of the hotels you manage. Business in America?" Andrew continued pouting.

"In America," Iden said with a smile.

"And how do you know Luka?"

Well, that is the essential question.

Iden remained calm. "She did an internship at a company in which I had shares." He answered. A stone fell from my shoulders.

"And how could I have forgotten ... we were married."

Lina gasped, and Andrew almost choked on his drink. Alvaro seemed pleased with Iden's slyness, and I didn't know where to turn. Everyone was staring at me. I felt the strange assessment of those around me. Iden was pulsating with strength and energy, and I was a little gray mouse. We were two completely different people who were completely unsuitable for each other.

"You were married?" Andrew asked me in Lithuanian.

"Yes," I replied.

Iden looked pleased.

And what did you come up with, you twisted bastard?

Andrew said, "Is that why you were called Luka Black? His last name is Black? As in Black Industries?"

Lina and Marius were straining to hear our conversation.

"I'm sorry." I sighed and stood up. "I need to go get some fresh air. Will you go with me?" I pointed at Iden.

He seemed to be waiting for an invitation. "I'd be happy to keep you company."

I walked in silence, and Iden followed me. I didn't turn to him until we had crossed the street and entered Central Park. I turned so suddenly that Iden almost bumped into me. "What the hell?"

Iden kissed my lips without saying anything, and all my anger evaporated. "Oh my God ..."

"You can call me by my name." He laughed.

"What are you doing?" I asked between kisses.

"I am kissing the most wonderful woman in the whole world."

"Iden, we broke up."

"So what?" Iden asked.

I was melting. It didn't matter that the people around us were clapping and whistling. It didn't matter that they shouted words of encouragement. I surrendered to the magic and the pleasure of that moment. My lips were thirsty for kisses and love like honey. It took time for us to pull ourselves together and back off.

Iden ran his fingers over his lips, and I blushed in embarrassment. Everyone on the street was staring at us.

Alvaro Rivera was standing across the street with a big smile. He had always enjoyed the drama of our love affair. I think he was addicted to it. He could have written a great novel about our love story.

I pushed Iden away and headed into Central Park by myself.

"What I have done wrong now?" asked Iden.

"Are you still asking? Why all the drama? Why? Iden, we broke up. Our lives have gone our separate ways. I live far from you, and you are far from me. *Pabaiga. The end. Finito. Kaput. Basta. Kaniec.*" I frantically waved my hands and tried to describe the end of our relationship in all the languages I could remember.

"You mean last night meant nothing?" Iden asked with raised eyebrows.

"Last night was a moment of weakness. Feelings, memories, and sentiments flooded in." I defended myself as much as I could. "You looked so handsome, and I couldn't stop. I wanted to say goodbye properly."

"Handsome, you say?" Iden grinned.

My cheeks turned crimson. *Luka, keep your mouth shut. Your brain is not functioning properly.*

"I'm short of air." I fanned my face with my hands and stomped my feet. "I think it's time for me to go to the hotel—and for you to go wherever you're staying. I need to pack my suitcase."

"Luka, are you running away from me again?" asked Iden.

"Iden, please don't behave like nothing hurtful or bad happened in the past." I had finally managed to say what I was thinking. "I loved you. I loved Iva." My voice broke as I said her name. "But she is gone. We are gone. Don't try to get back what's already lost."

After many years of silence, tears rolled down his cheeks. Iden looked as confused and as sad as I was. I had reopened his long-closed wound with my words. He scratched his neck with his good hand and cupped the corners of his eyes. He was in pain.

One moment, I was relieved and happy that Iden was finally feeling something that I felt—only a million times stronger—and the next, I wanted to hug him and apologize for hurting him.

Finally, Iden removed his hands from his face, said goodbye, and walked out of the park .

I wanted to stop him, but I lacked the strength and the will. *Do I really want Iden out of my life? Am I just trying to convince myself that I do?* I was left standing alone with my thoughts.

EPILOGUE

IDEN

It's early morning in Chicago. In my luxurious living room, I'm wondering what the point of my life is without Luka. I thought about the last year, how hard and lonely it had been, and I really didn't want it to go on. Luka was open, and she said everything that she had kept in her heart for so long, but her body language said something completely different. We didn't need human language to understand each other; our bodies spoke the same language.

I now understand why all the famous poets, artists, sculptors exalted love so much. Love is the driving force of the world; it is the main element that fuels the engine of life. Because of love, the biggest wars, quarrels, and angers have arisen. Love has separated the closest friends, families, and siblings. Love has worked wonders. Fools like me turn love into a tool of destruction.

After this weekend, I realized that the love between Luka and me is eternal. I could see that little glimmer of hope in her eyes—the faint and silent promise that everything might be OK—but I have no plan to get her back. Her lips said I must forget her, but my heart cried out. I was powerless to resist the call of my heart, and I was powerless to resist fate.

I stared at the Chicago skyline and realized how I could start all over again. *Luka and I deserve to be happy. We deserve to live better.*

I dialed my secretary's number; it didn't matter that it was five o'clock in the morning. "Good morning. Arrange a meeting with the young doctors as early as possible. *Today.*"

My secretary probably jumped out of bed and freaked out, but it didn't matter to me. The most perfect plan was already simmering in my mind. *The history of Luka and I will finally be rewritten, and we will finally open a new sheet of life and move forward. We will not be on different paths; we will be together. She will smile again just for me. She will snuggle against my side again, and I will be able to listen to how peacefully she breathes. She will be my happiness and my peace again, and I will be her protector and her biggest supporter.*

Yes, it is a new day. This is my return to normal life. I twisted the wedding ring on my finger and wondered how long I would have to struggle before Luka would finally agree to try again. I wondered how long I would have to wait for Luka to miss me and for my plan to work 100 percent.

Luka, my beautiful Luka, I once promised to love you until death does us part. No one did—and no one will. I looked out at the outlines of the ships and the soothing blue sky. *Someday, my life will be the same again, and Luka and I will look in the same direction and plan our lives. I just have to hope that my idea will succeed.*

To be continued ...

Translated by Nerijus Šarauskas
Published in Lithuania by Obuolys Publishing House

ACKNOWLEDGMENTS

When I wrote this book, I didn't know if it would ever see the light of day, but I was happy that I could write and create it.

I want to thank my soul mates and my sister for encouraging me when the going got tough. You weren't afraid to say a stronger word or even hit my back. I probably wouldn't be me without you. To my beloved mother, you believe in me even when I lose faith in myself. To my husband, you bless my every whim—even my strangest wish. To my guardian angel, Dad, I'm so sorry you didn't get to hold this book in your hands. I hope you're looking down on us from heaven. I miss you so much.

Thanks to the readers who accompanied Luka and Iden on their difficult road to happiness. I promise that this is not the end.

Printed in the United States
by Baker & Taylor Publisher Services